The Secret of La Danta

By Alex Zabala

"I think I can safely say that nobody understands quantum mechanics."

Quantum Physicist Richard Feynman (1918–1988)

ARCANI ARTS
A multi-media publishing company

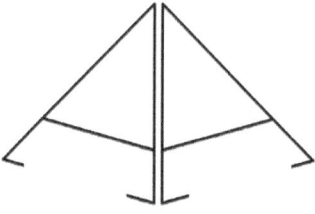

ISBN: 978-0-9885471-7-9

ACKNOWLEDGMENTS

This book would never have existed if not for the following awesome people. I am eternally grateful for their talent and patience.

Anita Zabala: Editor
Dyego Alehandro: Story editing / authoring
K.C. Riva: Story engineering and consultant
Timothy Rivadeneyra: Book cover art

Chapter One

"Get out of there!" a voice yelled in his ear.

He kept his hands steady. "No, we're almost in."

"The guards changed their course, Troy, we have to abort," a second voice chimed in.

Troy Rollock gritted his teeth. "I'm fine, quit chattering." He tried to concentrate on the schematics in front of him. First left, second right was the plan originally. If the guard pattern changed, that meant...

"First left, first left," an older voice cut in. "Stay there for thirty seconds."

His grimace turned to a grin. "Thanks, Erick. Sub mode." He sprinted to the first door on the left, slipped into the new hallway, and then ran for the next door on the left. It was a private office, but fortunately it wasn't locked. He clicked the timer on his watch and hid behind the desk. Sure enough, ten seconds later the two guards walked by outside, chatting loudly about their bets for who would make it to the Super Bowl. At the thirty second mark he exited the office slowly, checking to make sure the guards were indeed gone.

"Good catch," he said quietly into the comm. "Back to regular plan."

Breaking into a museum was a new experience for Troy. Breaking the *law* was a new experience. The arguments made by his team members, both for and against the operation, were still in his mind. In the end, it was the money that had convinced everyone, as well as the fact that they were only doing this for the right reasons. He double-checked the schematics, making one-hundred-percent sure that he was going where he was supposed to.

"I've identified the new pattern," a fourth voice said. "The guards are increasing their surveillance every two-point-five minutes so they will be able to watch the last quarter of tonight's game without interruption."

Troy rolled his eyes. "Monday Night Football. Of course. Thanks, Nolan." He pulled out his phone and tapped a few times before slipping it back into his pocket.

"What does that do to *our* schedule?" Erick asked.

"I'll keep him covered, okay?" Nolan flippantly replied. "Just keep going, Troy."

Troy was already going. The next door had an old-school lock, super-simple to pick. The long hallway on the other side had alcoves and display cases scattered 'artistically' about. He'd never liked the layout of this museum, truth be told, but the haphazard displays would play to his advantage tonight. His target door was the fourth on the right at the end.

His phone vibrated just as Nolan announced the next patrol, and darn if he wasn't right. He hid behind a display about Bronze Age relics, quietly fuming as the guards did their next round. These guards were responsible for keeping history safe and they were doing their job poorly for a *sport*.

At least it made his job easier tonight. He ducked in and around the displays for the next seven minutes, barely needing to hide from the incompetents. He made it to the target door and pulled out his multitool. Torx screws, as he'd expected. Nothing too difficult. He unscrewed the bottom part of the keypad and plugged in the receiver that would give Nolan access.

"I'll give them marks for this," Nolan said. "Having the door locks separate from the outside security. Not half-bad."

"You're still able to crack it, right?"

A snort was the only answer he got. It was really the only answer he expected. Nolan was very good at his job, he liked to remind everyone constantly. Fifteen seconds later, a full minute before the next guard patrol, and the door was unlocked. Troy replaced the keypad cover and slipped into the room beyond. Two more keyed locks later and he was in the secure storage room.

"Alright, gang, what's the number of Bollinger's lock box?"

"Seventy-two. It's your show now, Troy."

Troy grinned and made a beeline straight to seventy-two, which was one of the extra-large, floor-level safes. His entire crew could fit in there, probably, although David Nix would have a panic attack if they ever tried it. He sat down cross-legged with his left side against the safe and pulled out his stethoscope. He slowly turned the dial, listening intently to the inner workings of the device. Being kidnapped and carted off to Mexico had changed his life in more ways than he could count, and one of those ways was his determination to learn everything he could about safecracking. His parents had objected at first, but he'd insisted. His vow was that he would never again be in a position where he was locked away somewhere, relying purely on blind luck to get out. He'd gotten very good at it in the last few years. Cracking a safe was different from picking a normal handle lock. It was more intimate. He had to listen with his entire being, envisioning the gears and levers and springs as they moved and clacked in his ears, anticipating where each number would land. Hearing that final click was a magical moment that always made him grin, as it did now. He pulled the handle and the door pressed up against him. He put his stethoscope away, stood up, and pulled the door the rest of the way open.

The locker was empty.

"Uh, guys? We've got a problem. The locker's empty."

The exclamations of his team were cut out by the loud sirens of the alarm. "We've *really* got a problem! Nolan, silence the alarms."

"Working on it."

"Troy, get out."

"But where are the artifacts? We need those artifacts, Erick, or we've defaulted on the job."

"If you get arrested then it will be worse. Get *out*, Troy, and listen to us this time."

He swore up and down and then found himself amused despite the situation. If his parents knew he used language like that! "Fine, what's my escape route? And Nolan, can you please turn off that sound?"

"The security system has reverted to some obscure protocol," Nolan said. His voice, what Troy could hear of it anyway, sounded strained. "Working on it."

"You need to get out of the room first, Troy," Ashni answered. She'd kept quiet since she'd told him he had to abort and he'd ignored her. "You left behind a ringer?"

Troy nodded, his mind clearing. He ran to the door and opened it, grabbing the thin plastic piece that kept the door from locking completely. The ringer, as he named it. "Good call, Ashni. Where are the patrols?"

"Halt!"

Well, that was his answer. Troy bolted to the right as more voices called out after him, telling him to stop. He pictured the layout of the museum, gauging where he was and where he needed to be. If the patrols had kept to their increased activity from earlier, then the second group would be ahead and to the right. They'd almost certainly converge on him--

"Stop right there!"

He turned at the junction without slowing down, slamming into the wall and still running. He didn't have time to think about how much his shoulder now hurt. All he could think about was contingencies, backup plans, the museum layout and guard patrol patterns. His mind zipped through all of the information and gave him the only possible solution. There was one way out of here now, and only one. He oriented himself in the right direction and kept running.

"Pack and ship, north end," he ordered. "Book it."

"Troy, we aren't--"

"Pack and ship! North!" he shouted. He pulled out his phone as he ran and shut it off. The ear piece he crushed in his fist, the keypad decrypter he jumped on several times and then flung into a trash can. He had precious few moments left as he navigated the museum, running as fast as he could to the north. If he gauged this right, the rest of the guards would be there in exactly ten seconds.

Three seconds early he turned a corner and a burst of electricity burned through his body. He spasmed and fell to the floor, everything going black.

8

The sharp pain in his shoulder brought him gasping back to reality. He looked around in a panic, unable to see anything through his blurry vision

"Lie back down, Troy, or you might vomit."

His panic disappeared, to be swiftly followed by nausea. Erick was right, as he usually was. He valiantly fought the rising of his stomach, his eyes and teeth clenched tight. The nausea subsided in time, but the pain in his shoulder did not. He opened his eyes slowly and looked around.

He was on the back bench seat of their van. Erick and David were in the middle seats, both turned around to look at him. That meant Nolan and Ashni were at the front, Ashni probably driving.

"How'd it go?" he finally managed to ask.

"Neither good nor bad," Ashni answered loudly from the front of the van.

"At least I got the cops to go to a different location," Nolan said. "That's good."

"Yes, but it was not as flawless as we might have hoped," Erick said.

"How are you feeling?" David asked.

Troy closed his eyes again, nausea once again threatening him. The barrage of conversation was attacking his ears like a war zone might. "Everyone please be quiet for a second," he said through his clenched teeth.

"You're the one who started the conversation," Nolan, predictably, objected.

"Just please, quiet."

He'd never been tasered before. He wouldn't recommend it. Everything tasted coppery, for starters, and that was one of the main reasons his stomach was trying to empty itself all over the back of the van. The swaying of a vehicle in motion wasn't helping. Neither was the weird burning feeling he had all over his skin.

Eventually everything settled into a dull throbbing pain that he could deal with. He opened his eyes again, let them focus, and waited to see if he was going to puke.

"So, how'd it go?" he asked again.

Erick laughed."You are here and not in custody. Is that good enough?"

"What happened to the antiquities?" Ashni asked.

Troy started to sit up, thought better of it. "No idea. The entire locker was empty."

"Was there any sign of other forced entry?"

Troy focused on David. Focusing his attention seemed to help the nausea. "Not that I noticed. Nolan? Did the system look odd?"

"Not an ion. Everything was squeaky clean: no reports, no red flags, no signs of digital entry. You think Bollinger cleared out his own collection?"

Troy turned and stared at the cabin light above him. It would be just like Bollinger to clean out his antiquities and claim the insurance money. To everyone else, Gerald Bollinger was an upstanding citizen, generously donating time, money, and antiquities to local and global causes. But Troy knew the truth. Gerald was a grave robber, a tomb raider, and a black marketeer. This was their second time butting heads with the man. The first time had ended poorly, with them unable to prove anything conclusive about Bollinger's real activities. Not only that, but they'd alerted him to the fact that someone was after him. They were going to pull back and let things cool off, but the latest job offer had convinced them to try again sooner than expected.

He heard somebody's phone buzzing and he turned his face toward the front of the van. Speaking of the job offer…

"It is for you, Troy," Erick said. His face was grim as he held out the cell phone.

Troy took a deep breath as he took the device. "Troy here."

"What happened tonight, Troy?" the voice asked him. It was, as usual, electronically masked and impossible to tell who was talking. "You were not supposed to get caught."

"What are you talking about?"

"It is all over the news, Troy. Several private collections have been stolen from the museum. You were only supposed to get one item from one collection. Do I need to take my business elsewhere?"

Troy mentally cataloged every swear word in every language he knew. None of them were quite strong enough for this situation. "Absolutely not. Bollinger's collection was already gone by the time we got there."

The silence on the other end of the line was getting uncomfortable by the time the client finally spoke."Do you believe he stole the other antiquities?"

"Wouldn't put it past him. Look, we'll get you the item you need. I made a guarantee and I stand by that. All of Bollinger's collection is stolen, so we have no qualms stealing it back for you. I told you that."

"But now you do not know where the item is, do you?"

Troy rolled his tongue around in his mouth, thinking fast. "We have a few ideas. Would you give us some time to figure it out and get back to you? We are committed to this job."

There was more silence, but not nearly as long this time. "You have twenty-four hours to give me a solid explanation of where the item is now. If you cannot do so in the time allotted, then our business is over and your reputation is ruined. Do you understand?"

He swallowed. "Perfectly. We won't let you down, I promise."

The line went dead and Troy finally whispered one of the words he'd thought of just a moment prior. He handed the phone back to Erick and closed his eyes again. "We've got twenty-four hours to figure out where Bollinger has stashed his ''stolen' collection. Otherwise the deal is off."

Erick, as always, refused to panic. "We had best get to work, then, hmm?"

*　*　*

They took a shortcut back to their headquarters, Ashni driving through the New York City streets like an expert. Slightly more than an hour after being tasered, Troy was showered and ready to tackle the newest kink in their plans. It was something he was good at, and something he was used to. Somehow, there was *always* a kink in their plans.

"Bollinger obviously stole his own collection. That much we're all agreed on. The chances are good that the other stolen collections are also his work, to cover his tracks. Anyone object so far?"

None of his crew objected, so he pressed on. "Bollinger has a massive ego. He's going to milk this stolen collection thing for a bit, using his ''oh I'm so hurt' routine that he's used before. He's going to be questioned by the police and the insurance companies, both his own and the museum's. We need to figure out two things. First: where is he most likely to stash his stolen goods. Second: what's our way in to steal some of it back. We are on a deadline, but we need to think this through properly. This is our last chance, and we absolutely cannot screw this up again."

He looked at his team as they considered his words, a touch of pride swelling in him. Erick Hausen had approached him about starting the next generation of the Secret Society of Savants Association, and at first he wasn't sure what he was going to do. Going off on random Mind Games across the world, like the previous generation of SSOSA had done, did not really interest him. He loved the idea of being the one selected, instead of his father, true. During his last year of college he'd finally come up with an idea that piqued his interest: savants for hire. There were all sorts of jobs to be done across the world that required specialists in antiquities. He'd run the idea past Erick, who'd approved, and he'd started the Secret Society of Savant Archaeologists. They were for hire to help recover anything of antiquity. He'd started with what was most familiar to him, the Mayans, but had branched out quickly.

He'd also, just like the SSOSA of old, picked his partners carefully. David Nix, 25, was antisocial, which was fine for an archaeologist, but he was also claustrophobic. Not so good for the often-tight situations of the ancient world. He was, however, the best mechanical engineer Troy had ever seen. He was constantly inventing robotic devices and drones to go into the tight spaces that he was personally terrified to enter. He was also the first to answer. "He wouldn't fly them out," he said, obviously calling upon his own experience as a pilot. "Too many variables and watchful eyes, even at private airports."

"Flying is also too dangerous for the delicate items of his collection," Ashni said. Ashni Sengupta, 28, was a brilliant electrical engineer with a degree from the Indian Institute of Technology. Troy had met her during an outreach program at his New York university. She'd caught on to his little SSOSA recruiting games faster than anyone else and had demanded to know what he was up to. "So land transportation is obvious. He probably used a moving truck."

"A moving truck is too obvious," Nolan said, shaking his head. Nolan Smith, also 25, was occasionally cantankerous, often prideful, but always a wizard at computers and networking. Their resident hacker, as all good teams needed nowadays. "I'd wager he used several vans like this one, staggered in their arrivals so as to avoid suspicion."

"That is the most likely scenario. So we know how he probably removed the antiquities. Now we need to figure out where he took them." Erick Hausen, 77, was the last surviving member of the old SSOSA. He'd stressed the importance of passing the baton on to the next generation, but he'd refused Troy's suggestion of actively joining. He'd finally relented to being a consultant, and Troy could tell that the old man still liked being involved in adventures, even if he wouldn't admit it.

Troy looked out the window at the overly bright lights of New York City. "We need to analyze Bollinger like we would any other job; a problem to be solved. Bollinger is infinitely prideful. He loves the attention, but he also likes to *possess* things. It's probably why he started stealing in the first place."

"You are not suggesting--"

"I am, Ashni. I think he took his stolen antiquities right back to his private collection at his so-called chateau."

"He wouldn't be that dumb, would he?" David asked.

"Think about it. His collection was stolen, not from his house, but from a museum. The last place the police would look would be his home. They wouldn't even be suspecting him, I think, because of the other stolen collections. Last place the authorities would look, check. A very secure location, check. Most importantly, though, it's a place where he can look at it and feel like it's in his possession still. Check."

They all looked at each other. "Worth checking out, I guess," Nolan said.

Troy pulled out his personal phone, not the one he took on missions, and dialed in the number of their client.

"That was fast," the disguised voice answered after the first ring.

"We're good, and we have an idea."

"Just an idea, or proof?"

"At the moment it's just an idea, but we've all agreed to it. We'll need a little more time to prove it."

Silence, as he expected, for a few heartbeats. "How much time do you need?"

Troy looked at SSOSA, *his* SSOSA. "How much time do we need to break into the chateau and get what we need?"

The others held a whispered conversation. "Four days minimum."

"Your deadline has been extended by four days. Do not fail."

Troy slipped the phone into his pocket and clapped his hands. "We have seventy-one hours, SSOSA, to break into Gerald Bollinger's chateau and steal a rare item of antiquity. Let's get started."

Chapter Two

"Well, it's no military institution, but it's not going to be easy to infiltrate."

Troy blinked several times before having to rub his eyes. He'd been staring at the schematics for Bollinger's chateau for the last two hours, and he had to agree with David. "Okay, let's run this through again."

He ignored the collective groan that erupted from his group. "Bollinger keeps his antique collection in his second level basement, which was added in the last few years. It runs on its own generator, which is enclosed in the same level."

"Yes, and the basement itself is at least three-feet-thick concrete, and has integrity sensors that were designed to identify potential flooding, but will just as easily detect any attempt to dig into the basement. We've been over this a dozen times, Troy."

Troy stopped rubbing his eyes and peered at Nolan. "And we're going to go over it again and again until we come up with a plan. There's one elevator in and out of his collection, which is not connected to the elevator that goes to his basement."

"What is occupying his basement level one?" Ashni asked.

"Servers, an office, and storage."

"What about water pipes?"

Troy looked at the schematics again. He'd thought by now that he'd have it memorized. "No water to basement."

"Air?"

"Obviously there are air ducts, but they are far too small for any of us to fit."

David stood up and began to pace the room. "How small? Would one of my drones fit?"

"The only two air ducts that go to the collection are about the size of a football."

"American armored rugby football, or actual football?"

Troy snorted at Ashni. "The American kind."

"One of my drones will fit through," David said excitedly. "That's our way in."

"Only one problem with that," Troy said, shaking his head. "The censer won't fit. It's too wide."

"I didn't mean we take the artifact out with the drone," David said with obviously strained patience. "We send the drone down to activate the elevators for us."

"And the armed guards? How do we deal with them?" Nolan asked.

Sudden inspiration struck Troy. "Wait a minute. Erick, that new-fangled tech of yours--"

Erick held up a hand to stop Troy, a knowing smile on his face. "It is already on its way."

All of the others turned to stare at Erick. "Wait, you already knew what we were going to need?" David asked.

"I made an educated guess on the way back from the museum."

"And you just let us sit here spinning our wheels, going in useless circles?"

"You were exercising your minds, David, and that is never a waste of time. I was also not entirely sure that my technology would be the answer."

"Doesn't matter," Troy interrupted. "It's on its way you say. How long until it gets here?"

Erick consulted his watch. "It has been just over three hours since the museum, so the package should be here in another hour."

"All the way from Germany?" Nolan asked.

Erick smiled that same superior smile of his. "It has been tremendously useful having the world's first supersonic business jet."

Troy couldn't help but grin broadly. "Alright, we have an hour to plan how this is going to go down."

*   *   *

The operation was going great when the warning came. "Red Alfa Romeo approaching," a voice whispered in his ear. "Bollinger inbound."

Troy swore under his breath. He looked up from his tablet through sheer force of habit, as if he could see through the solid Victorian brick structure and watch the car. "ETA?" he whispered back.

"Three minutes. Recommend scramble now."

"I haven't tagged it all!" he hissed back, thinking furiously. His grin broadened. "Keep the feed live."

"But-"

"Just do it!" he ordered, moving more quickly through the room. He'd only categorized half of the stuff in here and still hadn't decided which object was worth the most.

He'd finally found the skull censer he'd been looking for, but his victory was short-lived. He spun around to hide in a corner just as the elevator car descended into place.

"Who the devil are you? And how did you get past my security?" the man exiting the elevator demanded.

Troy paused to look over his target. Gerald Bollinger was entering his 40s and middle-age was catching up to him. He'd clearly been quite fit at one time but was now getting pudgy around the middle. The receding hairline neither added nor detracted from any semblance of attractiveness. Gerald was plain-looking and would pass almost anywhere in the world without any giving him a second glance. It was precisely that quality which he'd used to further his illicit relic smuggling trade.

"I'm Troy Rollock, Mr. Bollinger," the intruder finally answered, "and I'm impressed. By the collection, I mean, not by your so-called security."

Bollinger tilted his head ever-so-slightly to the side, the anger and surprise on his face fading quickly. "You've been after me for a long time now, Troy. Your previous attempts all failed, so you come to my house personally? That was a grave mistake. You find my security lacking? Well, considering where you are, I can agree with that part of your assessment. Tell me, how did you get past my guards and dogs? And past the biometric security of the elevator?"

"You've spent several hundred thousand dollars on your security, and you expect me to tell you how I broke it for free? I'm a businessman, Mr. Bollinger. Nothing is free."

Gerald sent the elevator back up, then walked between the relic display pillars and over to a desk in the corner of the basement. "I suppose not. You should stop following in your father's footsteps. Chauncy Rollock is quite well known. The last time you were famous, however, was when you were kidnapped in Mexico. Are you trying to become famous again like daddy? I don't think being arrested for breaking and entering will be quite the fame you, or he, is looking for."

Troy worked his jaw back and forth for a few seconds, trying to keep his blood pressure in check. He decided to ignore Bollinger's threat and just press on. "There are many very rich people who are willing to pay very good money to get back their stolen antiquities."

Gerald flushed red. "Just what are you intimating?"

"I'm not intimating anything. I'm stating facts. Take this relic, for instance." Troy stepped to one of the pillars and pointed to the object resting on a velvet cushion. "This golden insect was made by the *Quimbaya* culture from the *Antioquia* province. Colombia, circa 1500 AD. And this skull censer from northern Guatemala, Mayan. Innocent blood was spilled to add this to your collection, and the original owner wants it back."

Gerald was still as a stone for several long heartbeats. He finally broke out laughing. "I believed you to be clever but not clever enough since I've stopped your investigations this past year. Now I see that you aren't clever at all. It is a pity that you haven't inherited Chauncy's brains. Yes, blood was spilled to get that artifact. More blood will spill to keep it here. Dublin will be taking you somewhere quiet to dispose of you and your tablet."

Troy looked over his shoulder as the elevator reached the bottom. A positively huge man with a handgun came stalking out of the lift. His beefy hands reached for the tablet and passed right through. Dublin's momentum caused him to fall flat on the ground, but he was on his feet in an instant. "It's a ghost!" he exclaimed.

Troy couldn't keep a smirk from his face. "I guess that's my cue. *Adios*, Mr. Bollinger."

*   *   *

The room swirled in and out of focus, the purple Victorian wallpaper slowly replaced by stark contemporary steel walls. Troy began to unbuckle the SURVR headset and accessories. The Suche-Und-Rettung-Virtual-Reality system was two-part: the part in Gerald's basement was about the size of a grenade, able to be delivered through the air ducts. The part Troy was interacting with was about the size and shape of a standard Virtual Reality Headset. It could be used all on its own, but it worked best when it was wirelessly connected to the server apparatus that currently hummed quietly in the corner.

"Did we get it all?" Troy asked.

Ashni stepped forward to help Troy out of the contraption. "Yes, we got it all," she answered. "Why did you antagonize him? We had all we needed without your magic disappearing trick."

Troy chuckled as he tried to extract himself from the backpack and failed.

"The digital recording of the room and stolen artifacts is good, yes, but even better is a confession of guilt." He clapped his hands and rubbed them together. "We did better than I expected. We finally got Bollinger!"

There were cheers from the people in the room with him, which he hushed with a motion of his hand. "We've been after Gerald for over a year now. He defeated our three previous attempts. Today, we finally proved that SSOSA is better…and I couldn't have done it without all of you."

"What about wiretapping laws?" Ashni asked. "I did not think recordings were admissible."

"Oh, calm down Ashni," a short, wiry man chided. "New York is a one-party recording state. Troy was one party of the conversation that was recorded, and he consented, so it should pass just fine."

Troy pointed to the man who'd spoken and then spoke up himself. "See? Nolan knows his wiretapping laws. Gerald will be locked away for a very long time and his relics will be returned to their rightful owners. Tomorrow the police crew will look through all of the artifacts, and that is when we'll nab the skull censer. We'll get a nice paycheck from our client and you can take a vacation to the Caribbean. Or wherever."

"I still do not think you should have shown your hand there at the end, taunting him like that," Ashni continued earnestly. "It is too…"

"Cocky? Hubris-filled? Awesome?"

A smile tried to plant itself on her face. "Yes, all of those things."

Troy walked over and gripped Ashni's shoulder. "I had to let him know we'd finally bested him. It felt good to rub his face in it. Besides, we did the job and we're going to get a huge paycheck. The details don't matter right now."

"The details always matter, young Troy," a gravelly voice stated. "But you are correct in that the job is done. Congratulations."

Troy spun around and smiled broadly. "On behalf of the new SSOSA I would like to thank you for lending us your technology, Erick. We couldn't have done it without your help."

Tonight Erick looked every single day of his seventy-seven years, but the smile on his face seemed to take a decade off. There was also a spark to his eyes, a vividness, that belied his fierce and active intelligence. It was obvious, due to his arthritic knee, he was having difficulty standing as he commenced talking. Everyone was aware of the arthritis that was plaguing him. "It was my pleasure. It was unfair that we were defeated at the museum by Gerald's own duplicity. He is a horrible man who deserves everything coming to him and I am glad that I was instrumental in finally capturing him with you. In case you were wondering, however, the rental fee does not include me taking it all apart."

"Yeah, yeah. No, David, put that down. We've got two days left on this room rental, we can pack it all up later. Tonight we're going to party at Dudley's Bar. I'm buying."

David put the VR goggles back down. "Now you're talking! What about the rest of the paycheck, though? I've got bills up to my eyeballs."

"You know the drill: payment upon receipt of the artifact. We'll take care of that detail tomorrow."

"We need a faster-paying job," Ashni said. "Do you have any work coming?"

"We can talk about work after we're drunk. Come on, shoo! I don't want to have to drive you all to Dudley's."

His crew filtered out of the room and he found himself alone. The adrenaline rush from the completed job was fading quickly so he went out onto the balcony. The Manhattan lights were crystal clear and the air had a chill to it. He shivered violently for a moment, closed his eyes and gripped the railing tightly. Images of a pretty redhead named Sheila flickered through his mind and he gritted his teeth. He'd deleted the pictures from his phone but he could never delete them from his memory.

He opened his eyes and let his breath out slowly. He knew why he'd taunted Gerald. He knew why he'd stayed in the virtual space of the man's basement long past the point of detection. Erick had designed the entire SURVR setup for search-and-rescue operations in extremely dangerous situations. The two-way visual system allowed rescuers to be seen by victims, and it allowed the rescuers to record and tag potential approaches to safety. Troy heard about the system and immediately knew he could use it to explore caves or buried tombs, but it was Erick's idea to bring one over for invading Bollinger's basement. Troy knew that Gerald would be able to see his holographic projection snooping around and he'd chosen to stay, chosen to taunt the man.

It was the adrenaline. He was addicted to it right now. The thrill of the chase and the bantering with victims provided a great high…a high that came crashing down when he was back in the real world, forced to deal with real things like breakups and ex-girlfriends.

His inability to keep a girlfriend had nothing to do with his looks. He'd had it on good authority from friends of both genders that he was handsome and attractive. He got his blond hair from

21

his mother Anita, and his so-called sparkling blue eyes from his father Chauncy.

"Am I interrupting?"

He spun around, his heart jackhammering for a few seconds. "I thought you went to the bar with the others."

Erick smiled and stepped closer. "I do not drink as much anymore, I am afraid. Maybe I should, to numb the pain from my arthritis."

"I'm sorry."

Erick waved a hand in a dismissive gesture. "Would you prefer I left?"

"No, I'm glad you're here." And he meant it, Troy realized. Erick might be only a consultant for SSOSA, but he was still incredibly intelligent. It was that intelligence that made them excellent friends, plus the fact that Erick treated him like an adult of his own making, not like the son of the famous archaeologist.

"Girlfriend troubles again?" Erick asked quietly.

"I just can't find a keeper, one who's interested in intellect and commitment," Troy said, sighing again.

"Most men your age like to play the field, don't they? Twenty-four is much too young for commitment these days, it seems."

Troy looked back out over the city. "I'm not like most men."

"And so you look for a woman who is not like most women, then, I take it?"

"You ever get married, Erick? Or even date?"

"I was married. My wife died of cancer."

"I'm sorry," Troy said with a grimace. "I forgot."

"It is okay, I have accepted the twists of life. All SSOSA members were married, but our wives were never truly involved in the Mind Games. It was not what I was looking for. Rene, especially, wanted his wife to have nothing to do with the Mind Games, and she was just fine with that."

"Rene Sova," Troy said, a smile finally coming to his face. "I remember Dad's stories about him. Was he really as pompous as Dad says?"

Erick barked out a laugh. "We were all pompous fools! Too smart for our own good and too dumb to realize it. As the last of

22

the old SSOSA, I can look back and see the mistakes we made. That is why I am glad to hand the baton over to the next generation. As the last surviving member, I had to make sure the baton was passed, just as it was passed to us so many, many years ago."

"It started at university, didn't it?"

"Precisely. It is odd, now, to think that it all started with a note left on Rene's bed. 'Are you smart enough to play?' it goaded us. Rene, especially, was not one to let that kind of challenge go unanswered. I am glad that the tradition lives on, and will continue to do so once I am gone."

Troy turned his back on the city lights and rested his elbows on the balcony railing. He looked directly at Erick. "Even though we've completely changed the game?"

"You mean by turning it into a profit-making venture?"

"Exactly. That's not how it was in the beginning."

Erick shrugged. "Intelligence must adapt and advance to accept new information, so there is no reason why SSOSA should stay stagnant. It would actually be the opposite of its original goal, which was to expand our minds. If making money playing a more dangerous game, retrieving stolen and long-lost artifacts, is expanding your mind, then so be it. I am not in charge, nor would I want to be."

"How do you think I'm doing? Honestly."

"Your crew is still new to this, and you are all young, so you have taken a few missteps. That is to be expected. But I would say that you are doing a fine job. And no, before you ask, I will not tell you what steps you need to take to do better. That is up to you to figure out, if you are up to the challenge."

Troy felt a smile come to his lips. "And so we've deftly changed the subject from women. Nice."

Erick mirrored the smile. "I thought so."

"But still on the subject of women, please don't ever tell my mom what I really do for a living."

"She still believes that you evaluate archaeological relics and only play harmless Mind Games?" Erick inquired.

"Exactly. She had enough of a fit when you first wanted to train me in the SSOSA ways, but if she knew what I'd done with the idea..."

"Rest assured, my friend, that she will not hear about your new venture from me."

Anything Troy was planning to say was interrupted by the buzzing of his phone. He sighed and pulled it out of his pocket. The number was unfamiliar to him, but apparently they'd been trying to contact him ever since he was using the SURVR. He handed the phone to Erick. "Could you answer this? It might be work and I'm not up to talking to anyone."

Erick shrugged and took the phone. "This is Troy Rollock's phone, Erick Hausen speaking. How may I help you? No, if you have something to say to Troy you can say it to me. As you wish. Here, Troy, you better take this. She sounds frantic."

"She who? Sheila? If it's Sheila, tell her to go pound sand."

"It is not Sheila. Here, just take the phone."

Troy sighed, took the phone, and tapped the speakerphone button. "Yeah?"

"Troy Rollock, have you acquired the skull censer?" a Latin-sounding voice asked.

He sighed. It *was* work. This was something new, though. He'd never heard his client's real voice. He had no idea that he was working for a woman."Your voice isn't masked. What's going on?"

"Do you have the skull censer or not?"

"Everything is in place to acquire it tomorrow. Gerald Bollinger was arrested and we're going to slip the artifact away during the inventory that will be taking place in the morning."

"Excellent. I have another high-paying job for you and your SSOSA crew, Mr. Rollock. I cannot explain the details over the phone, but I need to meet you in person. Please destroy your phones and meet me at the nearest gas station."

He tried to suppress his laugh and failed. "Listen, lady, I'm in no mood for jokes. We will have completed the job for you tomorrow, well within our 72-hour deadline. What more could you possibly want?"

"The Department of Homeland Security is going to arrest you, Troy Rollock, for the simple fact that you've spoken with me. You have no choice. Meet me at the nearest gas station and I'll explain everything."

The line went dead. Troy lowered the phone slowly, his brows knitted. "What was that all about?" Troy asked, before explaining the call to Erick.

Erick didn't get a chance to offer an opinion. He tapped Troy's shoulder fervently and pointed to the street. Troy turned around just in time to see three black SUVs come to a screeching halt. Men in serious-looking black suits with serious-looking sidearms spilled out of the truck like water from a broken glass.

"It appears that our caller was not exaggerating," Erick said solemnly. "We are three floors up with no way out."

Chapter Three

Troy's brain screeched to a halt for a frozen second in time. He'd been threatened, intimidated, and insulted quite a few times since starting the new SSOSA. There was something completely different about the sight of armed government agents storming in.

"Time to use that SSOSA brain of yours, Troy."

He blinked and a feral grin spread across his features. "Thanks, Erick. Now give me your phone and follow me!"

He grabbed Erick's phone and sprinted to the elevator, slapping the up button before he even stopped. He called Erick's phone with his and answered it. Once the doors opened he stepped inside, pressed the button to the lower floor, and dropped the phones on the floor.

He looked at Erick as the older man finally caught up with him. "They're tracking our phones. They'll think we're on the elevator going down, C'mon!"

"Where are we going?" Erick asked. "That trick will only buy us a few minutes at most."

"I've got an idea," he answered, closing his eyes and trying to think. They'd rented office 354, but they'd originally wanted..."This way."

Two hallways down and they were there. "We wanted to rent 312, because it's a bigger office with more electrical power to it. But they were replacing the carpet. Remember?"

The smile on Erick's face abruptly disappeared once Troy opened the door. "Wait. You are planning to go down the *garbage chute*?"

Troy stepped into the room, his gamble having paid off. Sure enough, the window to the office had been replaced by a large, yellow garbage chute leading straight to the outside world and freedom. "That's the plan."

He could hear Erick swallowing. "I do not have vertigo, but suddenly I feel queasy."

"We've got two choices, Erick. We can stay here and get arrested and/or shot for something we didn't do, or we can run and see what this lady wants from us. If this is really the DHS, they probably have the front and service entrances covered. The only way to get out of here without being in custody is probably this."

Erick took a deep breath. "After you."

Troy climbed into the chute and held onto the top, sudden doubt swirling through him. Three stories up was not a trivial distance to fall. If the garbage in the dumpster at the bottom was anything other than the carpet he expected, this might be a short trip to a painful injury. Well, only one way to find out. He let go.

The trip was short, all right, but thankfully the pain was very little. An entire collection of carpet and floor foam buffered the sudden stop quite well. He called up, very quietly, for Erick to follow. It was probably difficult for the older man to maneuver into the chute, but it was only a few seconds before he came hurtling down. Troy did his best to help break the fall.

"That was…interesting," Erick whispered. "Now what?"

"I checked the closest gas station before dumping our phones on the elevator. Apparently, we've got to cross the Manhattan Bridge and go to Brooklyn."

"Is that the nearest gas station?"

"It was the closest one to show up on the maps. There might be convenience stores or something closer, but I didn't have time to check. It's not like we have cars this deep in the city."

"Lead on, then."

They snuck through the alley, keeping a careful eye out for ambushes. They made it to the Manhattan Bridge without incident and started over. Every siren in the distance, every police car that passed, all of them caused a spike in blood pressure for Troy. It was half adrenaline, half pure terror, and wholly awesome. He never once thought about lying ex-girlfriends or other troubles.

Once they reached the gas station he realized that he had no way to identify his caller. That problem was quickly solved when a red van pulled over to them. The heavily-tinted window rolled down to show an olive-skinned woman about the same age as Troy.

"Where is the rest of your crew?" she asked, and it was the same voice from the phone call.

"They're getting a drink," Troy answered. "What does it matter?"

She made a noise of exasperation. "We will have to meet them later at another location. Get in."

With very few other options presented, Troy thought it best to at least see this through. He opened the rear door for Erick and then climbed in the other side. He wasn't even belted in when the van shot into traffic with near-reckless abandon.

"Forgive my impertinence, but we do not even know who you are," Erick said, his voice carrying that quality of strained-civility that he did so well. "Why are we here?"

"My name is Rio Jordan, and I have a five-million-dollar job offer for you."

Troy felt his eyebrows try to escape his forehead and consciously forced them back down again. "That's quite a bit more than you were going to pay for the skull censer. But money is of little importance if we don't live to spend it. Why are we on the run from the DHS?"

"Did you destroy your phones as I requested?"

"Let's just say we got rid of them. Answer my question. Why are we on the run from the DHS?"

Rio cut across several lanes of traffic and abruptly they were traveling in a new direction. Troy's knowledge of Brooklyn was a little hazy, and he couldn't read any of the street signs, but he thought they might now be traveling northeast on the 278. Traffic was amazingly lighter than usual, so they made good progress.

"Why are we-"

"My associate told me to hire you," Rio interrupted. "Please be quiet, I need to make sure we aren't being followed."

Troy very much wanted to *not* be quiet, but he decided to sit on his simmering temper and practice a calming technique he'd learned shortly after his stint as a kidnapped kid in Mexico. The situations were remarkably similar: the Latin accent, the inability to go anywhere, and the ever-looming threat of people pointing guns at him.

His calming technique managed to bring him down from the realm of melodrama. This situation was nothing like getting kidnapped at gunpoint by crazed cultists. He'd rather voluntarily jumped into this one. Oh well.

"My associate is Javan Benson. He has a problem that he believes can only be solved by SSOSA. I am disinclined to agree with that, but I have agreed to acquire your assistance. That was why I hired you to get the skull censer, to see if you were a capable crew."

"Javan Benson? Doctor Benson?" Erick asked, perking up at the name. "I have read some of his work on quantum physics. He is in prison, is he not? Is that why the DHS is after us?"

"Oh great, just what we need," Troy said, trying to keep his eyeballs from rolling too violently. "We usually get people put *in* prison, now somebody already there wants us to break him *out*? Sorry, lady, but we aren't interested."

"You are not interested, even for five million dollars?"

"Not for five billion dollars. We do have standards, after all."

"That is excellent news, because Javan does not need your help escaping from prison. He instead wants you to finish his project and prove his theory correct."

Troy cleared his throat. "Are you aware of what SSOSA stands for?"

"Of course, Javan told me. The Secret Society of Savant Archaeologists."

"That funny little word there at the end? Yeah, archaeologists. What exactly will we be able to do about a quantum physics theory?"

"This may sound crazy, but the machine that we need to build is based on designs found in Mayan temples. Correct me if I am wrong, but Mayan temples fall under the category of archaeology, do they not?"

Troy snorted. "True. I'm still not sure about all of this."

"Then let me use the rest of this trip to persuade you. I am sure that we can come to some form of agreement."

Troy looked over at Erick, who merely shrugged. "Fine," he said after letting out a sigh. "Might as well talk, since we have nowhere else to go. But this had better be good."

Chapter Four

The door splintered with a satisfying *crack* and the team moved in. Weapons at the ready, they scoured the office room in less time than most seasoned professionals. Each location got a distinct "Clear!" from one or another of the operatives before the final 'All clear' was sounded.

"What *is* all this?" Rick Cannon demanded of his men.

Kenneth Sims, his second-in-command, looked very uncomfortable, which was rather easy for him to do. His appearance was that of a bookish scholar who would be more comfortable in a library or a cubicle, not out in the field. It was an appearance that had fooled many people over the years. "We don't know. It appears to be some sort of virtual reality setup."

Rick shook his head and stepped over the thick cables that ran across the room. Rio Jordan had called a man named Troy Rollock, and that man had been in this building less than ten minutes ago. Now, neither Rio nor Troy was anywhere to be found. He swore silently, trying to keep his frustration from his face. It had taken months for the Secretary of the Department of Homeland Security to listen to Rick's warnings about Doctor Javan Benson's work. As usual, the government moved glacially slow on things that weren't headline-grabbing. Once the Secretary had finally listened, it had taken far too long to find and arrest Doctor Benson. By that time it was too late.

Rick himself was only Executive Secretary, but as he walked through the office he vowed once again that he would never work this slow when he finally climbed to the top of the ladder. Even today, right now, he was doing more than was usual for his position. The Secretaries, Deputy Secretaries, and Executive Secretaries never went out into the field. They always left that dirty business to their agents and operatives. It was lazy and irresponsible, a typical short-sighted stance from entrenched bureaucrats. Staying in their offices and only dealing with 'executive' matters had softened them to the real threats and to the real action that was needed down at the street level. They missed out on the little details that could make the difference between success and failure, between stopping a terrorist attack and losing thousands of lives.

Plus, they missed out on the sheer invigorating effect their presence would give to the agents. Nothing made a subordinate work harder and better than having the biggest brass watching them directly.

He came back to reality. "Repeat your last statement, Sims," he said softly. Years of talking on headsets had morphed his speech patterns, but he didn't even notice anymore.

Kenneth may have noticed, both that his boss had drifted and that he was talking like the old days, but he would never mention it in front of subordinates. "The words and logos are all in German. We're sending the info to our translators and should have an answer quickly."

German. Were terrorist cells connected to Doctor Benson working in that country, too? This just got worse with every twist.

He crouched down to get a closer look at the machine. It wasn't unlike a normal computer server, but there were quite a few peripherals attached that he didn't recognize. It all looked state-of-the-art, and probably had something to do with the VR headset that some of the techs were fiddling with. The technology present was rather unlike anything he'd ever seen outside of a sci-fi movie...or the lab he'd worked at with Doctor Benson. Putting the pieces together and figuring out what was really going on was his trade, and he was very good at his job. He traced the wires and circuits with his eyes while his mind went through all of the possibilities. "This isn't just virtual reality," he said slowly as he moved over to another piece of technology. "This is a compact, high-bandwidth antenna that looks like it's not part of the original device."

Kenneth crouched next to him, eyed the machine for a moment, and nodded. "The design and even coloring are different, and that cable right there was spliced in recently. The original device has a receiver over there, so it was originally designed to receive information. This added-on antenna--"

"Means that they were receiving *and* sending at a high speed," Rick finished for him. "Exactly. Problem Number One: were they using this to communicate with Rio, somehow?"

"Doesn't track," Kenneth said. "Why would she call them with something as primitive as a cell phone?"

"Good point. So they were using this setup for something else when Rio called them. Okay, Problem Number Two: we need to know who else was here, because this setup cannot be run solo. Problem Three: who were they communicating with? Rio interrupted whatever they were doing, so we need to find out *what* they were doing."

He paused to inhale. "We know one of them is Troy Rollock. We need to find out any and all of his relatives and associates, and we need to get a message to them fast. Has Troy been kidnapped? Or has he been duped? We need to warn him before he does anything rash."

"You're assuming Troy is innocent?"

Rick felt his face twisting in surprise as he looked at his assistant. "That's how the American justice system works, doesn't it? Doctor Benson and Rio Jordan have been proven guilty and are the most dangerous terrorists living in this country. That remains to be seen of Troy Rollock, and we need to find out his position as soon as possible. If Operation Pakal becomes fully operational...well, none of us want to see the kind of destruction that it might unleash."

Kenneth immediately pulled out his cell phone and started dialing numbers.

Rick smiled and turned back to analyze the room. That was one of the many things he liked about Kenneth: how quickly he got to work and how few questions he asked. It was one of the reasons he'd first recruited Kenneth to his narcotics squad, so many years ago in Los Angeles. Those were the good days. Back before he'd lost everyone else on his squad to a botched mission, betrayed by a fat-cat senator with too many fingers in too many drug pies.

He felt the seething rage try to engulf him. He closed his eyes and accepted the emotion, acknowledged it, and put it back on hold. He did not believe in suppressing emotions, including anger. But neither did he believe in being ruled by them. He had lost extremely good men and women, people he'd worked with for years, and had nearly lost Kenneth, all because of the greed of an entrenched bureaucrat. Anger was an honest, appropriate, and acceptable reaction to such a betrayal. But instead of being controlled by that rage and doing rash, unthinking things, he'd simply channeled the power into his goals. It had taken him seven years to track down all of the evidence he needed, but he'd finally proven the senator's involvement in the drug trade, as well as all of the senator's cronies. It was one of the biggest scandals the country had ever seen, and a very public humiliation for the senator. Rick still relished that day, and the subsequent promotions and transfers to the DHS, but he knew even then that his work was not done. He had found one snake in the grass, but he knew that corruption and back-alley deals were rampant in every level of government. His goal was to root out and expose as many of the other snakes and their schemes as was humanly possible.

The scheme that currently engulfed him was the oil and coal companies. He had proof of six mayors, three governors, and at least five senators who were illegally profiteering from the 'dirty energy' industry. He knew there were others, but he didn't have the proof yet. That was one of the reasons he'd been so excited about Operation Pakal. An endless, clean energy source would not only be a huge boon to America and the world in general, but it would cut the legs out from under the scheming politicians still trading the earth's ecological future for cold cash now.

But then, of course, Javan had stolen all of the blueprints and gone rogue. Yet another disappointment in a lifetime of them, but he wasn't going to be bogged down by that. He let his anger fuel his determination and kept it firmly in check. He would need all of his wits about him to capture Javan's surreptitious assistant.

"We have a few names, Mr. Cannon," a voice called to him from across the room, cutting into his thoughts.

He immediately ran over to the woman who'd called him."Who are they?"

"They call themselves the Secret Society of Savant Archaeologists, they use the acronym SSOSA."

"What kind of name is *that*?" someone else in the room demanded. Laughter erupted, but Rick quieted it immediately.

"Who are they?"

The woman handed him the tablet, which showed biographies of several people. "This is an excellent start. Keep digging, ladies and gentlemen! We have a terrorist to capture, a weapon of mass destruction to stop, and the world to save."

SSOSA. Now he had a name of the group helping Rio. It was indeed an excellent start. Time to get to work.

Chapter Five

Nolan Smith lifted his shot of tequila and downed it in one gulp. He immediately coughed and sputtered, his face turning red.

David Nix started sputtering as well, only in his case it was out of laughter. He knew this was exactly what was going to happen the minute he saw the shots. "See? I said you couldn't handle it!"

Dudley's was crowded, loud, and nobody cared that the SSOSA members were making fools of themselves. Everyone in the bar was doing the same thing.

Everyone except Ashni Sengupta. She kept looking between her watch and the bar's door. She finally turned to her two male friends and interrupted their drinking game. "Has Troy texted either of you?"

They shook their heads. "I wonder what's keeping him and Erick," she continued. "They should be here by now."

"Troy's probably off sobbing about his breakup with Sheila," Nolan said around his coughs. "He should get over her already."

"That is easy for you to say," Ashni said. "It is not easy to endure the end of a relationship."

Nolan stopped coughing long enough to look at her, his eyes watering. "If you're so worried about dear Troy, you need to call him or something."

"I'll text him," David cut in quickly as Ashni looked coolly at Nolan, her lips pressed into a thin line. He didn't want to see yet another passive-aggressive jab by Nolan degenerate into an argument. "He's supposed to be paying for our drinks anyway, and there's no way Nolan's footing the bill."

Nolan's face darkened for a second but he turned back and ordered another shot of tequila. David pulled out his phone and dialed for Troy, idly counting down the seconds until the voicemail prompt came up. Undeterred, he called Erick next.

"Okay, now *I'm* worried. Erick didn't answer either. Troy may be nursing his wounds, but Erick never not answers. Should we go back to the office?"

Nolan shrugged and downed another shot of tequila, still trying valiantly to avoid coughing and still failing. Ashni looked uncomfortable, but shook her head. Apparently, they were going to wait a little longer. It didn't sit very well with David, but he agreed. They'd been here for less than thirty minutes, after all. Surely that wasn't enough time for anything seriously bad to happen.

The text that followed proved him very wrong. His phone buzzed, he picked it up, and he instantly felt the blood drain from his face. It was from an unknown number, but the message could only have come from Troy:

Red October-Burn Notice.

He looked at Ashni and Nolan, both of whom were staring at their phones. They'd gotten the same message and it was sobering Nolan up fast. They looked at him and were as pale as he felt. *Red October* was their Code Red signal, and Burn Notice meant it was time to ghost. They'd get one more coded message with instructions, and then they were to lose their phones and get moving without drawing attention to themselves. Something very serious had happened in less than half an hour, something so serious that they were in possible mortal danger.

Nolan went back to his tequila, but he was no longer drinking it. He spilled it on his shirt, swore loudly, and got up. He nodded surreptitiously at David before disappearing into the bathroom. David took a deep breath and held it in as long as he could, trying to steady the sudden hammering of his heart. All of SSOSA had discussed these plans once, what seemed like an eternity ago, but they'd done so in a joking manner. They knew that their work was occasionally dangerous, but to go all Ghost Protocol didn't happen in real life. David wasn't ready.

Ashni and Nolan were already taking this better than he. Ashni called the bartender over and paid for their tab, also insisting that the bartender not let Nolan consume any more alcohol. She was cool, calm, and supremely confident, the color in her face already returned along with a steely determination. David wished he could be like her.

His phone buzzed again and he almost dreaded to look. His hands were shaking as he keyed in his passcode. *Feces: Why New Yorkers are depressed.* He had the clue "feces," aka Number Two, which meant that Nolan and Ashni would have whatever other clues were needed to decipher their instructions. By giving each member a different clue with a weird name it meant that it would be harder for anyone to intercept and decode the instructions. He burned the clue into his memory and looked up.

Ashni was already gone.

His pulse skipped several beats before he forced reason into his emotions. *She's the only one with a car. She's going to be out there waiting for us in her car, probably around the back of the bar. Why am I rhyming?*

Thankfully, Nolan stumbled out of the bathroom, his movements far more erratic than they should have been. This was going to be Nolan's excuse to get out of the bar, as well as David's. He stepped over to his 'drunken' friend, supported him on his shoulder, and escorted him slowly out of the bar while saying soothing nonsense that people usually said to drunks. On the way out, David dropped his phone on the sidewalk and crushed it with a powerful stomp.

They kept up the charade until they reached the side of the bar, out of view of the patrons. Nolan straightened up and pointed. "Ashni's car. Let's go."

Even Nolan seemed to be taking this in stride. Was David the only one terrified? He trotted over to the nondescript 90s era sedan and climbed into the front passenger seat. Once in, he twisted so that he could see both Ashni and Nolan.

"Who got clue Riker and Feces? I got Bad Luck," Nolan said once David was settled.

Bad Luck always comes in threes David thought to himself. That meant Nolan had clue Number Three.

"I received Riker and Tetragrammaton," Ashni said. "That means David has Feces."

Commander William Riker of *Star Trek: The Next Generation* was always being called 'Number One' by Captain Picard, and the Tetragrammaton was the four letters of God's personal name. That meant that Ashni had clues number one and four.

"The Riker clue is as follows," Ashni continued. "*He was the 16th President.*"

"Great, we're in grade school again," Nolan grumbled. "How are we supposed to look that up with Burn Notice on? My phone's gone and I've got no WiFi for my laptop."

"Wait, you still have your laptop?" David demanded. "I thought Burn Notice meant get rid of *all* electronics!"

Nolan glared at him as he patted his netbook. "I'm not getting rid of this. It's powered off and in airplane mode, there should be no way to trace it. Now, how are we supposed to remember who the sixteenth president was?"

"Those of us who became citizens by naturalization truly know more about this country than those born here," Ashni said with disdain. "The sixteenth president was Abraham Lincoln."

"So our first clue is Abraham Lincoln," David said, once again stepping in before a fight could break out. "My clue was: *Why New Yorkers are depressed.*"

Nolan worked his jaw for a moment, clearly still upset by Ashni's remark. "Mine was: *Horace Greeley's advice to the Dutch village, land of the smoking pipe.*"

"And the last was: *Quadrilateral carrot, 504,100.*"

"Quadrilateral carrot? Has Troy lost his marbles?"

"Let's take them one at a time and see what we come up with," David said. "Our first clue is Abraham Lincoln. Wait! I know the answer. We need to get to the Lincoln Tunnel."

"Why do you say that?" Ashni asked.

"Because *my* clue is an old joke. Why are New Yorkers depressed? Because the light at the end of the tunnel is New Jersey."

Nolan chuckled. "True. That does coincide with my clue. Horace Greeley is quoted for saying 'Go west, young man.' So we have to go west through the Lincoln Tunnel to get to New Jersey. But why would my clue be a double? We already know we're going west."

"What was that bit about the Dutch village and the land of the smoking pipe, then?" David asked.

Nolan stared out the window. "Ashni, get us to the Lincoln Tunnel, after that we need to go south."

"But your clue says to go west, doesn't it?"

Nolan smirked. "Hoboken is Dutch for 'land of the smoking pipe.' *West* Hoboken is a hotel in Hoboken, which is south of the 495."

"That would coincide with the final clue," Ashni said as she eased into traffic. "We are to look for room 710 when we arrive."

David stared at Ashni. "How on earth do you know that?"

"The Tetragrammaton clue. A quadrilateral carrot and 504,100."

"Still lost."

Ashni's smile lit up her whole face. "A carrot is a *root* vegetable. A quadrilateral is a *square*. Square root of 504,100 is 710."

"Holy moley, that's amazing," Nolan said quietly from the back. He was rare with his compliments, especially to Ashni, but when he said them he meant it. "How did you figure out a square root that big without your phone?" he asked.

"I have a bachelor's degree in electrical engineering and I have always been inclined toward mathematics. It is not difficult once you know the methods used. Now we just need to make it to our destination. It would be quicker to get to Hoboken another way, so there must be a reason Troy wants us to take the Tunnel."

They weren't entirely certain what to expect when they knocked on the door to Room 710 nearly two hours later. There was no light on under the door and no sounds could be heard from within. David, for one, certainly wasn't expecting to hear a voice from behind him.

"Glad you guys could make it," Troy said from the room across the hall. "David, you need to work on that yelp. You sound like a girl."

"That's sexist," David said once his feet returned to the ground and his heart had stopped fibrillating.

"Probably. My bad. Get inside, all of you. You weren't followed and got rid of your phones, right?"

"That is what Burn Notice code means, is it not?" Ashni answered as she entered the room. "What is this all about, Troy? And is Erick with you?"

"I'll answer all of your questions in the bedroom. Let me close the door and give you your new burner phones."

They filed, one by one, into the bedroom, Troy handing each of them a new phone as they entered. Erick was waiting in the room, sitting on the bed, and there was one other occupant: a Latin-looking woman, tall, gorgeous, and with a worried expression on her face.

"Rio Jordan, this is the rest of SSOSA. Ashni, Nolan, and David, this is Rio Jordan. She's going to give us a job that pays five million dollars."

David felt his eyes trying to bug out of their sockets. His mouth opened, obviously trying to ask how, why, what, when and where…but all that came out was a gurgling sound.

Ashni, of course, had much better control. "That amount of payment would imply dangerous or illegal work, and you have already initiated Burn Notice. Which one is it, Troy?"

Troy's face almost, but not quite, hid a grimace. "A little of both. If we take this job, we will get paid a lot, yes, but we'll have to do it with the Department of Homeland Security after us. And they aren't going to go easy on us if they catch us."

David glanced between Ashni and Nolan. They'd worked on dangerous assignments before, but never *truly* illegal ones. Skirting the law was one thing, being hunted by the DHS was another. Was five million dollars enough of a carrot to push them into a new, criminal element? David wasn't sure one way or the other.

"I think you had better lay out the terms for us, Troy," Ashni said, once again fully composed.

"Alright, let me finish with the introductions. Rio, Ashni Sengupta is our Project Manager, electrical engineer, and resident babysitter."

"Babysitter?" Rio asked, her accent as gorgeous as her features.

"These men act like toddlers," Ashni answered, "and need tending to. Perhaps you know how the male ego works."

Rio nodded without saying anything, so Troy continued. "David Nix is our mechanical engineer. He and Ashni together can build practically anything. Nolan Smith is our programmer and IT guy."

"IT Master," Nolan corrected.

"I see what you mean about male egos, Ashni," Rio laughed. "I am delighted to meet all of you. I am Rio Jordan, a nuclear physicist. I work with Doctor Javan Benson, a quantum physicist, and we-"

"Hold on a minute," Nolan interrupted. "Nuclear and quantum physics aren't our scope of expertise. What do you guys need with *us*?"

"If you would remain patient, I will answer that," Rio said, her demeanor still calm. "Doctor Benson needs SSOSA to prove his theory correct and exonerate him. You are going to do that by assisting me in finishing a re-creation of a specific Mayan temple."

David cleared his throat. "A Mayan temple? What do Mayan temples have to do with quantum mechanics?"

"More than you would imagine, Mr. Nix. I can explain the exact situation in more detail later. Right now you all need to decide whether or not to take this job."

"I am a naturalized citizen," Ashni said. "If I am to take a job that runs afoul of the Department of Homeland Security, they may decide to revoke that status. I need to know why they are after you, Rio Jordan."

Rio glanced at Troy, her face finally showing a troubled emotion. "Doctor Benson figured out various secrets of Zero Point energy. Before he could prove his point to the world, the government took over the research and jailed him under false pretenses. Javan wanted to use the technology for good, but the government...well...they want to turn it into a weapon."

Chapter Six

"A weapon? Really?" Nolan asked, his sarcasm hitting new highs. "What is this, the Cold War? The United States of America is not involved in clandestine, oh-so-secret conspiracies to build weapons of mass destruction."

"Your naïvety knows no bounds, Nolan," Erick said, stiffly standing up and facing the group. "The US spends billions of dollars every year on the so-called 'defense' budget, money that could be spent on healthcare, education, or infrastructure improvements. The money spent on this country's military is three times that of all other NATO countries *combined*. If you think they are not still building and researching new weapons, you are unworthy to be SSOSA."

"Cool it, Erick," Nolan shot back. "You may be willing to see grand conspiracies behind everything, but I'm not. At the moment, all we have is Rio's word that the US took the research and is using it for weapons. How do we know that Doctor Benson himself didn't want to build a weapon with this technology?"

"Doctor Benson is a well-regarded quantum physicist with many papers published, and has a solid reputation in the scientific community," Erick answered. "I find it hard to believe that he would turn his knowledge to weaponry."

"*Could* this knowledge be turned into a weapon?" Ashni asked.

"Yes," Erick answered. "Doctor Benson is one of the few masters of Zero Point technology. Zero Point is when you freeze an atom to almost absolute zero. Once you have achieved such a state you can find a field of subatomic particles within the frozen atoms that have an incredible amount of energy. It is known as the SOE which means the Sea of Energy."

"Okay, but wouldn't it be easier to just build a nuke?" David asked. "We already have plenty of those."

"Easier, yes," Erick said. "But not as effective. With the massive amount of energy found in the SOE, as it is known, you could theoretically cause earthquakes, manipulate the weather, and structurally disintegrate your targets without all the hassle of radioactive fallout."

Nolan turned to Rio. "That sounds pretty damning," he said. "Are you still going to say that Javan didn't want to build a weapon?"

"Energy is not just useful for weaponry, Nolan," Erick said. "There is a serious lack of pollution-free energy in this world, especially in developing countries, and a Zero Point reactor would avoid any of the potential problems of nuclear reactors."

"There is also the reason that Javan began his project," Rio added. "We have already begun to build a Quantum Oscillating machine."

"And the purpose of that would be…?" Nolan asked.

"Teleportation."

A blanket of silence fell upon the room at the utterance of that word, everyone present going over the possibilities in their minds.

"Are you talking about honest-to-goodness, 'beam me up Scotty' teleportation?" Nolan asked. "That's impossible, isn't it?"

"It is not science fiction," Erick explained. "It already happened in a laboratory at the University of California, Santa Barbara, in 2009. Scientists devised the first Quantum Oscillating Machine and used it to cause a small metal blade to vibrate on a molecular level in such a fashion that allowed the blade to 'be' in two different quantum states at the same time."

"Your knowledge is impressive," Rio gushed with appreciation.

"I make it my concern to keep up with the latest in technology," Erick added with a hint of panache.

"I take it, then, that you have already decided to accept this project?" Ashni asked. "You seem to be quite interested in the ideas and the science, Erick."

"I am absolutely fascinated by the science," Erick said, and there was no mistaking the hunger in his expression.

"Yes, it's absolutely fascinating," Nolan sarcastically intoned. "But am I the only one seeing the big elephant in the room?

Actually, two elephants. One: Why do we need to build this machine at all, and directly related to that, how is Javan going to benefit if he's in prison? And a third elephant which I just thought of, how are we going to get the DHS off our butts when we're all done?"

Rio took a moment to compose herself. "For a scientist like Javan, he craves validation of his theories. There is perhaps more to it than simple validation. To be the first to discover something is to go down in history. In addition, if we can prove that the science is sound and that the machine works, we can show it to the world and get Javan exonerated. The government will have to acknowledge that they falsely imprisoned Javan and will be forced to release him, or face the wrath of the world-wide scientific community. We may also be able to get other countries involved in the pressure, especially because Javan is a British citizen. After all, if the US has a huge source of energy and they aren't sharing it, the rest of the NATO treaty countries won't be happy."

"So basically, we exonerate Javan and get him released by proving his theory is correct?" David asked. "That...doesn't make a whole lot of sense."

"It is within the realm of possibility," Erick said. "Even if Javan never gets released from prison, *we* will go down in history as the first people to accomplish true teleportation. Everyone remembers Neil Armstrong, Buzz Aldrin, and Christopher Columbus."

Nolan, unsurprisingly, was the first to object. "Perhaps. But what about the Vikings who actually discovered the American continent? What about the other crew members of the Apollo missions, or the ground crew? Nobody honors them, and that's basically what our situation will be."

"If the PR department of my company wants to earn its paycheck, we will not be relegated to the dust heap of history," Erick pointedly responded. "I will personally make sure of that!"

"Okay, fine, but now we're wanted by the DHS. How are we going to accomplish this while being hunted by the authorities?" Nolan protested.

"First, you will all need to remain incommunicado," Rio answered. "For at least a few weeks. Are you all able to be without outside contact for that length of time?"

"I am often on long Mind Games without contact with my company," Erick stated. "In fact, that is where they think I am right now."

"Nobody outside of this room cares about me or where I am," Nolan said, shrugging his shoulder. "I can live with it."

"My relatives all live in India," Ashni said. "It is often months between contact."

"I think my brother might get suspicious," David said. "But it's not unusual for me to go underground for a few weeks."

"My mother likes texting me a lot, she won't get too suspicious if I don't respond, might just think I am also on a Mind Game," Troy said. "And the less I talk to my father, the better."

There was a brief moment of awkward silence before Rio nodded and continued. "Excellent. In that case, we will need to move to our warehouse and finish construction of the Quantum Oscillator. Once that is complete, we can begin tests before we tell the world about our findings."

"That's if we agree to it," David said. "Have we agreed?"

"I need to know more about the science and the end goal, especially with the Mayan connection," Troy said.

Erick spoke up. "Just to make sure that what you plan is even possible."

Rio pointed to Nolan. "May I borrow your laptop?"

Troy spun on Nolan. "You kept your laptop?! What about Burn Notice?"

"Chill, Troy. I made this thing untraceable the day I bought it. Nobody uses my laptop but me, Rio. Sorry."

A heated argument between all of the SSOSA members and Rio broke out. In the end, Rio managed to win control of the laptop for a few minutes, a hard-fought victory.

"The science involved in this project is advanced," Rio said after she placed the laptop on the end of the bed. "But I believe I can walk you through some of it. One moment..."

She pulled off her necklace, which was a beautiful jewel. With a twist of her wrist it inverted and revealed a USB drive. She plugged it into the laptop, looked at the keyboard, and then raised her eyebrows at Nolan. "What is wrong with your laptop?"

Nolan smirked. "It's a Dvorak keyboard. Get used to it."

She sighed and pecked at the keys. "The most important part of this science is the Sea of Energy. The second most important part is torsion waves."

She spun the screen toward SSOSA. Visible on the screen was a diagram with several pyramids on it, and a lot of lines, numbers, and other jargon scattered liberally about.

"Wait, so the Mayans understood *torsion waves*?" David demanded. "That's impossible!"

"There are lots of things the Mayans understood that don't get enough credit," Troy answered. He peered closer at the screen, trying to understand what all the symbols meant. "One of the very few things my father and I agree on. So, Rio, you think the conical nature of the Mayan pyramids is at such a shape to induce torsion waves?"

"Precisely. The angles of the pyramids are perfect representations of the Fibonacci sequence. By using torsion waves, Javan's experiment will be able to produce Zero Point Energy without reducing atomic structure to absolute zero."

"You'll still need an energy source," Nolan said, uncharacteristically paying rapt attention. "Not as much energy as in a lab, but still a not-insignificant amount."

"We can take care of it."

"Then what do you need us for, again?" Nolan demanded. "You've already got the power and the science."

Rio took a deep breath, and out of the corner of his eye Troy could see her face was troubled. "I need you to build a replica. I cannot do this on my own. I need outside eyes to see what we miss, and only the most intelligent minds behind those eyes so that we do not waste time. With Javan imprisoned, I have no choice whatsoever."

"What did you use for your conductive material?" Ashni asked. "Copper?"

51

"Probably," Troy said. "That is what the Mayans used. Well, it was probably a tin-copper alloy. Did you recreate that detail, Rio?"

Rio's smile brought a small shiver to his stomach. "We did indeed. You people continue to amaze me with your knowledge!"

"Now for an even bigger question," Erick said from the back. "What are you planning to teleport? Surely nothing living?"

Rio laughed. "I would not dare to teleport a living being first. Javan and I worked up a transfer item, as we call it. It is a small iron, copper and gold-meshed cylinder with a message inside of it."

"And where are you planning to teleport this transfer item? Who do you think would exonerate Javan?" Troy asked.

"The University of California at Santa Barbara again," Erick chuckled. "Of course. The site of the very first photon teleportation. An excellent choice. And the message itself?"

"The transfer item *is* the message, but engraved upon the cylinder are a few sentences from Javan explaining his vision. I added some words about him being illegally imprisoned by the US government. That should get the spark started."

"And if it doesn't?" Nolan asked. "What if the transfer device fails to transfer? What if the university refuses to acknowledge the message? What if the transfer device teleports somewhere unknown?"

Rio held up her hand to stop any further questions. "SSOSA's sole responsibility is to help me finish the prototype and teleport the item. If this does not work, you may go your own ways. If it does work, anything after that is my responsibility. It may take years for Javan to be released. He may never be released. But that is *my* goal, not yours. You simply must help me attempt Operation Pakal: true teleportation. Will you help me?"

"It makes sense," Troy pondered. "The Mayan connection will prove once and for all that the ancients knew way more than we give them credit for. Whoever publishes this information will be incredibly rich and well known in the archaeological community."

Troy couldn't keep a smile from his face. This was going to be epic. There were indeed qualms to be had, and difficulties to face, and if it all went up in smoke it would be Troy's fault. If they succeeded it would be the best thing ever, but if they failed it would be quite the crash and burn. Talk about high stakes.

Troy turned to address Rio. "Show us Operation Pakal."

Chapter Seven

Cargo deliveries were a regular occurrence for any military facility, and especially so for a prison. There were always supplies needed: food, clothing, bedding, the list was enormous and seemingly endless. It was not uncommon for two or three huge crates to be brought in on wide load trailers. Four crates in one day was certainly a bit unusual, but not something to make a fuss about.

Which is why the soldiers on the loading/unloading zone were extremely unnerved by the presence of their commanding officer. So much so, in fact, that they weren't paying as much attention as they should have been.

"Move it, soldier!" United States Correctional Commander Colonel Theodore Bonner shouted. "Unless you want to get crushed like a cockroach!"

The soldier in question jumped out of the way of the swinging box just in time. "Sorry, sir," the soldier stammered.

"Didn't your mother ever tell you to watch what you're doing?" Bonner demanded. Being an African-American in the military, he was used to people not giving him much credit, but he was going to make certain nobody got injured on his watch. "And, barring that, didn't Boot teach you to pay attention to your surroundings?"

"Sorry, Sir. No Excuse, Sir."

Bonner waved him aside and looked back at the crates. Yes, this was indeed a special day. After years in development limbo, the latest US Army prototype aircraft was ready for full field testing. Not since the days of the 'Huey' in Vietnam had an aircraft been this important to the Army and that hadn't been stolen away by the Air Force or the Marines. And not since the RAH-66 Comanche had been canceled in 2004 had this much money and brain work gone into an Army helicopter.

"Sir, you cannot smoke around these crates," a soldier on the truck warned. "They are fueled."

Bonner glared at the soldier who'd dared to try and give orders to a Colonel. "It's not lit, *Sergeant*. Get back to work!"

A chuckle sounded from behind him and Bonner automatically knew who'd tried to sneak up on him. "Another soldier trying to warn you of the dangers of smoking, sir?"

Bonner sent a mock-glare at the man. "Always, Lieutenant," he said, some of his ire disappearing. He clenched the cigar tighter in his mouth. He'd smoked from age twelve until just two years ago, a habit spanning over three decades. He still couldn't get used to having quit, so he chewed on cigars all day. It was still an expensive habit, but at least his health was improving. Or so the doctors said. "What do you think?" he asked, waving his hands at the crates.

"I'd rather have to see the contents," Lieutenant McPherson said with another chuckle. "Right now they just look like big boxes."

Bonner shook his head. McPherson's attempts at humor had driven the entire prison mad the first year he'd been transferred - over. Secretly, Bonner thought that might be why the transfer had been affected in the first place. "You know what I'm talking about, McPherson, but have it your way. You and you, soldiers, get that box unlocked and show us our prizes."

The two grunts got immediately to work and within ninety seconds the prestigious contents of the crate was visible for everyone in the warehouse to see. "Say hello to the YUA-50 Arawak. Some people nickname them Yuletides, others call them Wind Slicers."

McPherson whistled softly. "It looks like something out of a video game."

Bonner couldn't disagree with that assessment. The nose and cockpit were a slice-of-pie wedge shape, with the cockpit wrapped in 180 degrees of glass. Sticking out beneath the nose a few inches was a seven-barrel autocannon. The rear stabilizer was actually a dual-wing design, each equipped with blades. The fuselage was where things started to get really interesting: it was a rounded design which led to the wings, which were 90% giant propellers.

"They *are* something out of a video game. And movies. Hollywood beat us to these designs a long time ago, but we're finally getting them."

McPherson pointed at the wings, which were currently in a vertical position. "And those move up and down like the V-22 Osprey?"

"They're more advanced than that," Bonner said. "They move 90 degrees vertical/horizontal like the Osprey, but they also have roughly 45 degree side-to-side capability for more maneuverability. They only go the full 90 degrees like that when they're in storage mode."

McPherson shook his head. "Why design this, then, when we already have the Osprey?"

"Because this is not just a utility carrier, it's armed and highly maneuverable. It's designed for transport and close ground support. So, basically, we get a V-22 Osprey and an AH-64 Apache in one package. The autocannon is an upgraded version of the GAU-8 used in the A-10 Warthogs. This one weighs a third as much, with the trade-off of not packing quite the same punch. But see those holes next to the wings? Those can be loaded with a variety of missiles. You don't want to mess with this thing."

McPherson looked at Bonner with a knowing smile. "And you're just beaming that the Army is getting some technology love, aren't you?"

Bonner grinned and chewed on his cigar a little more. "I was on the ground during Desert Storm, McPherson, barely out of Basic. The Air Force men I know love to claim they were the ones who won the war, but it was the grunts on the ground that did the dirty work. Every time they get a new toy and we don't, I get a call from a General who likes to rub it in. Well, this time *I* get to gloat. Especially with the F-35 fiasco."

McPherson just shook his head and decided to change the subject. "Why are they being stored here?"

"Because this place is about as secure as you can get. We're designed to keep people from getting in or out, and Fort Riley is just a few miles down the road. We'll be delivering this to Fort Riley once they have the necessary facilities installed. The Arawaks are ahead of schedule, for once, and Riley is behind, so we'll have them for a few days until they're ready for us."

"And then, what, you're just going to parade them over to the fort?"

"Why not? It's not like they're a secret. CNN reported on them just last week. Might as well give the good citizens of Kansas something to be proud of. I've already received my flight training and three other pilots will be here in time for the transfer. We'll drive down the middle of town and then launch the birds and shoot on over to Riley. It'll be like an early Fourth of July for the town."

McPherson looked down at the piece of paper in his hands, apparently remembering why he'd visited the Colonel in the first place. "We just received a message that a Kenneth Sims from the Department of Homeland Security is on his way here."

Bonner snapped his head around to stare at McPherson, nearly dropping his cigar. "What? Why? DHS has no jurisdiction here. Wait." He swore loudly, a string of expletives his Drill Sergeant had used to describe a superior officer and had been dishonorably discharged for. "Oh, the irony here is thick. Real thick."

"Care to explain?" McPherson asked.

Bonner waved at the Arawak. "We have a prisoner who helped design these things: Javan Benson. In fact, his first electrical contract work was the remodeling of this very prison. Rick Cannon, one of the big boys at DHS, has been trying to pull Javan out of here for a while now. I guess he's going to try one more time. Deny access to this Kenneth Sims when he arrives."

McPherson looked uncomfortable. "We can't, sir. He's been authorized entry by General Remington."

Bonner let loose another round of swearing before finally calming down. "Well, they still have no real power in my prison. Javan is a military prisoner and a non-US citizen, therefore I have total control. We'll let Mr. Sims have his visit, smile like we're all on the same page, and then kick him out of here faster than an egg boils in a Louisiana summer. *And* we'll keep a very close eye on him while he's here."

McPherson saluted. "Understood, sir. We'll watch him like a hawk."

* * *

Deep in the heart of Vandorph Maximum Security Prison, on subterranean level four to be exact, Javan Benson stared up at the ceiling and attempted to make complex mathematical correlations between the myriads of cracks. He'd already found several representations of the Fibonacci sequence and a few hundred decimal points of Pi hidden in the fractal patterns splayed across the roof of his world. He set about trying to mentally trace a copy of Tesla's first alternating current design when his mind wandered.

He found his mind often wandered lately, and always to the same subject: Operation Pakal. The fools in Washington had buried the project, fearing its power. Always it was the same story: the small-minded ones were the ones in power, and they squelched anything they didn't understand or anything that might be a threat to them.

A small smile managed to crease his face. He was in the same boat as Nikola Tesla, his hero. Hated by those who had lesser minds than his, Tesla had been hounded, labeled a mad scientist, and left to rot in anonymous financial ruin. Unfortunately, Tesla was now a household name and Javan would *really* end up being anonymous. Perhaps, in the minute chance there was an afterlife, he could share notes with his more famous contemporary and see what Tesla thought of the Mayan torsion waves Javan had discovered.

He sighed and his smile vanished. Small men, small minds. They were always the ones in the way of true progress, of true power. Javan had discovered true power hidden in the Mayan structures. Instead of letting him develop the technology to its limitless potential, they'd stuck him down here in this dank cell with a single light bulb, labeled a terrorist. The indignity was almost more than he could bear. He could have strode atop the earth a god, and instead he was buried under the ground like a worm.

He heard the sound of shuffling feet and couldn't keep a grimace from forming on his face. His armed babysitters were here again, ready to escort him for his daily sunshine treatment. To be incarcerated was insult enough, but to be treated like an infant was so much worse. One of the guards punched in the code, the same code that they'd used every time they'd opened his door, by the sound of it.

"Time for your vitamin D, Javan," the taller of his circadian companions said, just like he had every day since the arrival.

Javan sighed and got to his feet slowly. They could force him to walk about when he'd rather be thinking, but that didn't mean they could force him to like it.

They led him from the dank underbelly of the prison up to the roof, through a series of secure elevators and stairwells. All told, the prison was not badly designed. One of his first jobs as an electrical contractor had been to re-haul this very facility, and he'd been impressed then. It was still one of the ''old school' prisons that favored real security measures over electronic ones, with double-backed stairwells, doors that could be slammed shut through mechanical force, and a practical maze built into the living areas themselves.

The sun seared through his eyes as it did every day he came up here. He'd tried to get somebody in power to give him sunglasses, complaining about how the sunlight could trigger severe headaches, but nobody listened. And the view of Kansas left much to be desired. He really would rather just stay in his cell and deal with whatever vitamin D deficiency came his way.

Today, however, something was different and definitely worth going up to the roof for. The large storage hangars on the south side of the facility had their doors open, and sitting inside were the Arawaks.

He stared at them for long moments, feeling very conflicting emotions. On one hand, he was immensely proud of the design work he'd done on those planes. They were truly a step ahead, and a step in the right direction. America had wasted billions on a 'stealth' superiority fighter that wasn't really needed anymore. In today's wars, fought with drones and fire-and-forget cruise missiles that had a range in miles, an air superiority fighter was unnecessary. But wars were always won by the troops on the ground, and the troops on the ground always needed close air support.

He'd helped make that possible. He wasn't responsible for the entire design, of course, but his electrical prowess had helped make certain essential functions possible. That was a nice feather in his cap.

But on the other hand, the incredible vehicle he'd designed was now in the hands of the government that had stolen his other life's work from him. That was very annoying.

So he continued to stare at the aircraft until one of his babysitters noticed his interest. "What are you staring at?"

Javan raised his handcuffed hands and pointed. "I helped design those birds."

The soldier looked over at the Arawaks. "Good for you," he said, his words pure sarcasm. "It's time to go back in."

Javan took one last, lingering look at his work before following the soldiers back down into his dungeon.

Chapter Eight

Gerald Bollinger heaved a sigh of relief when he heard the jail doors automatically opening to release him from his cell. The guard motioned for him to follow him down to a small office. One of the guards handed him a plastic bag that contained his belongings.

Gerald was in a real bad mood. Thanks to the hard work of the SSOSA members, his ill-gotten relics had been confiscated by Federal agents. His high-powered attorney had posted bail and was free to go until he had to face a judge on the charges of stealing antiquities. The FBI and the CIA had been after him for a long time. Things weren't looking good. Soon he would be facing many years behind bars.

Once he had his belongings the guard opened another door that led to a long hallway. Eventually they reached an unmarked door and the guard opened it revealing an interrogation room.

Gerald was perplexed. It was his understanding that he was going to sign some legal papers and then drive away in his sports car and await further legal battles in a future court appearance. Instead, here he was, inside an interrogation room. He saw a metal table and four chairs. He was surprised to see that his attorney was seated in one of the chairs.

When the door closed behind Gerald he approached his attorney and scowled. "What's this about? I thought I was leaving now."

Gerald's attorney pointed to an empty chair beside him. "Just relax and sit down, I have some good news for you."

"Yeah, I heard the good news," Gerald grunted as he placed his belongings on the table and slowly sat down. "You're going to Hawaii on my dime and I'm going to a Federal prison for the rest of my natural life."

The attorney raised a finger. "Somebody wants to talk to you. If you cooperate, the Feds will drop the criminal charges against you. Of course, you can't keep the relics, but you will walk out a free man."

"What? I don't pay you two hundred dollars an hour to joke with me," Gerald snarled. "Who wants to talk to me?"

"This isn't a joke. In a minute a representative of the Department of Homeland Security who goes by the name of Kenneth Sims will be coming in here to ask you some questions. I highly recommend you cooperate and be nice to him."

"The DHS?" Gerald furrowed his brow. "So, what's this about? What do they want with me? I already told the Feds everything about the relics. I'm not a terrorist!"

"I said relax, this doesn't have anything to do with *you* or the relics. It has to do with the people who turned you in."

Gerald was genuinely puzzled. "You mean Troy Rollock and his crew?"

"Yes."

Before he could ask another question the door opened and Kenneth Sims walked in.

Kenneth had a voice recorder in his hand. He sat on a chair opposite the other two men. "Good morning Mr. Bollinger. I'm confident your attorney has briefed you on the purpose of this interview." He turned on the recorder. "I must advise that we will be recording your voice from this moment on. The purpose of this interview is to gather information on the people that contacted you via a holographic image."

Gerald looked at Kenneth and then at his attorney. "Are you guys serious?"

"Just cooperate, Gerald," his attorney grunted as he reprimanded him.

"Why should I cooperate with you clowns?" Gerald growled at Kenneth.

Kenneth leaned forward. "Mr. Bollinger, tell us everything you know about these people. I'm sure you're attorney told you how you would be compensated."

"Yeah, if I cooperate I walk out of here a free man."

That's correct," Kenneth nodded.

"Can I have this in writing?"

His attorney shuffled some papers at Gerald. "It's all here, just do as he says."

"What's the problem? What have these people done?" Gerald asked as he perused the papers and placed them down on the table.

"Let's just say they unwittingly got involved with the wrong people," Kenneth said, not letting out more information than needed. "Anything *you* tell us will facilitate our ability to thwart the terrorists' plans. We need to know who the people are that contacted you so we can arrange a rescue operation. They have no idea they are dealing with dangerous terrorists. If you cooperate I have the power to commute your criminal charges. How does that sound? And yes, we have that in writing too."

The expression on Gerald's face lit up. He felt like he had just won the lottery. He leaned back in his chair and looked at Kenneth. "Yeah, okay, so what's your first question?"

Chapter Nine

Nolan already had his laptop hooked up to the hotel's TV screen, ready for a video presentation.

Rio started. "Operation Pakal is the brainchild of Javan and I. Javan presented this information to the United States government to utilize for peaceful purposes. The powers-that-be had other things in mind. So technically it's Javan's and my property. He's sitting in prison for not cooperating with the government while I'm being hounded as a fugitive from justice."

"Correction, we are now *all* fugitives from justice," Nolan interrupted. "We must advise you Rio that we have all agreed to walk away from this project if for some reason we feel it doesn't serve our collective good."

"I understand," Rio stoically responded.

"If this whole scheme is a ruse," Nolan pointed a menacing finger, "then you lose your two-hundred-thousand dollar deposit and we pack up our toys and go home and apologize to the feds for our exuberant yet naïve spirit."

"Show us the blueprint," Erick said. "We are wasting precious time arguing."

All the SSOSA members looked up at the wall-mounted TV screen, which Nolan had hooked his laptop to. They were filled with great anticipation. The screen came to life when the title of the project was displayed: Operation Pakal Blueprints.

"This program is what we call an interactive blueprint display," Rio explained as a Mayan-type structure appeared on the screen, rotating in slow motion. "You simply click on any location on the screen and the object will move on the screen. Some of the items contain embedded pop-up videos with narration that explain in detail what you are to build. Go ahead, Nolan, click on the pyramid."

Nolan did as instructed on the laptop and the pyramid on the big screen quickly divided into four smaller pyramids that aligned themselves into a four-square pattern and then started rotating clockwise. The voice of a professional narrator was heard through the speakers.

"Torsion wave demonstration in three seconds... three... two... one..."

Suddenly the pyramids stopped rotating as harmonic wave patterns that looked like heat waves swirled above each pyramid.

The torsion waves that emanated from each pyramid moved in a symmetrical motion upwards until all four collided in midair. Eventually the waves conjoined and started vibrating in unison together until it became like a giant tornado, pushing and swirling upwards.

"Torsion waves now vibrating Pakal."

A figure from above the screen descended into view, it was hovering above the massive vibrating-tornado-wave. The figure was a representation of the stone sarcophagus image of the Mayan King Pakal. Only instead of the typical rectangular-shaped sarcophagus it was tear-drop shaped. It seemed to be suspended by a wire as it descended into view.

"It's the Palenque astronaut," Ashni blurted out.

Troy chuckled. "Some *do* say it looks like a Mayan king perched in a cockpit of a spaceship."

"Just listen," Rio admonished them

Suddenly the image of King Pakal started glowing in a bright orange/red color. A bright blinding flash appeared on the screen and to the SSOSA member's amazement the image of King Pakal disappeared.

Nolan moved his head to and fro, somewhat confused. "Where did the image go?"

"It disappeared," Troy said in a low voice.

Erick was the first one to figure it out. "Of course, the conical shapes of the Mayan temples tend to make perfect Torsion Field generators in the Zero Point Field ambiance."

Ashni nodded to Erick. "Please explain."

"In the study of quantum physics, torsion waves were first discussed by Albert Einstein. They are waves found in the Zero Point Field that bend or twist, hence the name 'torsion'. Basically, torsion waves are scalar waves set in motion, spinning and spinning inside a vortex. So those conical-shaped pyramids can get the torsion waves spinning."

"Okay, so what happened to our Mayan king?" David asked.

Erick leaned back in his folding chair, a slight grin on his face. "It went into another dimension just like the experiment at the University of California, Santa Barbara. Only we just witnessed a large object transported into another dimension. And it was all based on the strategically aligned shape of the Mayan pyramids!"

"Is this all true then?" David asked Erick with an incredulous tone.

"Theoretically…yes."

"This is truly incredible," Ashni whispered.

Nolan held up his hand. "Hold it, we have one problem. If we actually build this, how will we generate the waves?"

"We don't have to reduce the atomic structure to absolute zero as one would in a lab," David said.

"I get it, "Nolan nodded. "But you still need a power source."

David turned to Rio, expecting an answer.

Rio looked intently at the crew members. "I will take care of that detail when you build the machine."

The SSOSA members were mesmerized, entranced and amazed. Troy sensed their excitement. Everybody was contemplative for a few moments.

"We have to have one-hundred percent approval," Troy muttered. "Otherwise we dump the operation."

"I go first?" Erick said. He extended his hand in front of him and made a fist. "I am in."

Ashni imitated him. "I'm in….I think."

David gazed around. "I would love to be involved in building the Mayan thing," he extended his arm. "I'm in."

"I don't like this," Nolan let out along breath of frustration. "I have a feeling I'm going to regret this," reluctantly he slowly extended his hand out…then he made a fist. "Fine…I'm in."

"Mr. Chairman?" Erick turned to Troy.

All eyes turned to him.

"This will be an opportunity to prove who *I am*."

"What do you mean?" Rio asked.

"This will finally be my opportunity to prove that I am better than my father. If we get this Mayan science to work, I will go public with the report. I will publish the result and astound the scientific world. Then no one will ever say, 'Oh look there goes the son of the famous archaeologist. No, it will be 'Hey look, it's Troy Rollock, the famous archaeologist who discovered a secret Mayan power!"

Ashni tilted her head to one side and sarcastically smiled. "I assume that means you're in?"

Troy had a large grin. This was the opportunity he had been waiting for. "Of course, I'm in. Let's do it!"

Chapter Ten

Department of Homeland Security
Washington D. C.

The driver dropped Kenneth Sims in front of the Department of Homeland Security building on 7th Street and Virginia in Washington D.C. It was a cloudy, windy day, and Kenneth walked up the seven steps to the entryway. He smelled the pizza from the little Italian restaurant on the floor level to his right.

He always wondered to himself at the irony of the DHS building having such lax security measures. Any would-be bomber could easily place a car bomb near the entryway on the street or in the restaurant, which was open to the public. It would be easy to take the building down.

With these dark thoughts in mind Kenneth entered the building. He was clutching an attaché case that contained confidential documents meant for Rick Cannon. Once he cleared security, he took the elevator to the top, the eighth floor. He saw the sign on the door identifying the office of Rick Cannon, Executive Secretary. Kenneth took a deep breath and knocked.

"Come in," a voice called from the other side of the door.

Kenneth opened the door and saw his boss sitting in his new leather chair behind a large mahogany desk. "Good morning, sir."

Rick leaned back in his chair, his dark eyes scrutinizing Kenneth. "I heard you have something for me."

So much for pleasantries, Kenneth thought as he laid his case on a chair. "I do, sir."

Rick pointed to a coffee maker on a nearby table. "Help yourself to a cup of my finest Colombian coffee."

That's much better. Kenneth didn't have to be asked twice. "It's cold out there."

Rick leaned back in his chair. "The whole world is cold out there, Kenneth. You'd be surprised at all the nefarious things I've learned since I've been in this position. Things that are happening out there in our very own country that, if it were public knowledge, would probably send people into a panic. My job is to suppress the danger so the general public can go along their business buying and selling to keep the economy humming. "

"I suppose so," Kenneth replied as he sat in a leather chair and leaned back.

Kenneth knew Rick wasn't one for small talk. Rick always seemed to have a nervous tic about him, a sense of urgency that permeated his personality as if a great underlying preoccupation was eating at him.

Rick eyed Kenneth's attaché case. "I'm anxious to know what you found out about the recent case in Manhattan."

Kenneth placed his cup on the desk and proceeded to open the case. He pulled out a manila envelope marked *Confidential* and handed it to Rick.

While Rick was perusing the documents Kenneth produced a flash-drive from his pocket, leaned over and inserted it into Rick's computer. He pecked on the keyboard a few seconds until an image came up on a large monitor on the wall.

Kenneth pointed at the monitor. "That's him. His name is Troy Rollock he's the chairman of the organization."

Rick placed the manila folder down and gazed at the image. "Rollock? The name sounds familiar."

"That's because he's the son of the famous archaeologist, Chauncy Rollock."

"Tell me more."

"These other images are the people who are in his secret club. It's called Secret Society of Savant Archaeologists or SSOSA. Apparently they are an underground group that is up for hire to retrieve stolen archaeological items."

"If they are so secret how do they get customers?"

"It's more of a word-of-mouth business, they're known among the elite. The names of the other associates are in the files I gave you. "

"How does the holographic image we saw in New York come into play?" Rick asked. "What were they doing?"

"Apparently they were in the middle of an operation right before Rio alerted them about our presence. The holographic video had a recording of a conversation between Troy and a Mr. Gerald Bollinger."

Rick raised an eyebrow. "You mean the guy that the FBI arrested the other day for theft of antiquities?"

Kenneth nodded. "Gerald's story filled in all the gaps."

Rick rubbed his chin. "So the SSOSA work on the good side of the law? I mean, they aren't thieves, they're more like hired guns to retrieve stolen property?"

Kenneth nodded. "Apparently so, it looks like Rio conned them into running away with her. It was obviously a last minute decision since they left all of their stuff in the rented office."

"The lure of money is a powerful magnet," Rick sighed as he pulled himself out of his chair and walked over to the window, eyeing the thick traffic below. "Javan is still going forward with his plans, even though he was arrested and put in Vandorph... for life. Javan brainwashed Rio to assist him and now she has SSOSA members helping her."

"How do the SSOSA members come into the picture? I mean why would Rio hire them?"

Rick grunted. "The SSOSA group specializes in archaeology. Rio has hired them to continue the experiment. Apparently Operation Pakal is back on the front burner!"

Kenneth sighed with frustration. "If she wouldn't have stolen the blueprints we wouldn't be in this predicament."

"She violated my trust!" Rick said as he turned to face Kenneth. "She's a thief and a liar. I let her borrow the blueprints because she said she wanted to do a little more research. And me, like a complete idiot, let her borrow them. And because of my trust in her, thinking she was done with Javan, I now look like the bad guy to everybody, from the President of the United States all the way to the janitor in this building! Now you see why I'm taking this personally? "

"Yes, I get it," Kenneth nodded. "The big problem is we've lost track of them, every single one of them, they've gone completely off the radar!"

Rick raised an index finger at Kenneth. "We're not without options. We have the SSOSA email accounts. I can send them an email alerting them that they have been tricked. I can give them directions how to proceed so they can turn Rio in and we can have her arrested."

"I have a question," Kenneth seemed genuinely confused. "Why is Rio proceeding with this project anyway? Without Javan, the mission is dead."

Rick turned serious. "This may sound crazy, but I have good reason to believe Javan is planning a breakout."

"A breakout?!" Kenneth's eyebrows shot up. "He's planning an escape from Vandorph prison?"

"It was a mistake to put him in Vandorph, Kenneth, a terrible mistake."

"Why?"

"In his younger years, Javan worked as an electrical engineer. He was the one who drafted the electrical wiring for Vandorph."

"So what, it's a high-security prison—what makes you think he can escape?"

"When he was initially hired to rewire the prison years ago he discovered that a subcontractor, in an attempt to cut costs, had done some shoddy electrical work. The inspector failed to see the mistakes so the project passed the inspection, and back then he basically chose to let it go. Now fast-forward to today. Javan is incarcerated in Vandorph. He knows how to tamper with the electrical system to shut it down if he wishes. He knows where every circuit breaker and every faulty wire is located in that building. There is a reason why Rio and Javan are in an all-fired hurry to start Operation Pakal. Vandorph officials just got a bid from an electrical contractor to upgrade the wiring in the entire facility. Rio and Javan know this, hence why time is of the essence that he take advantage of the weakness in the system to escape!"

"That's crazy!" Kenneth's left eyebrow rose. "What do you plan to do? I mean, what if he actually does escape?"

Rick opened a small drawer in his desk and retrieved a sealed envelope. One side had clear plastic, where a syringe was clearly visible. "I'm sending you to have a small talk with Javan."

Kenneth lifted the plastic envelope and eyed Rick. "What are your orders?"

Rick turned to type on his keyboard and stared at the computer monitor while he talked. "I'm sending you to inject the contents of this syringe into Javan."

Kenneth eyed the envelope, he nodded with understanding. "I take it this isn't medication."

"You're absolutely correct." Rick finished typing and swiveled in his chair to face Kenneth. "Prepare to leave tomorrow. The prison authorities have already been advised of your visit."

"Is there anything else, sir?"

"Yes," Rick lifted the manila envelope that contained SSOSA's information. He pulled out Troy's profile and stared at it for a while. "You need to find Troy's father, Chauncy Rollock. Go visit him and see what you can glean from him. Chauncy may provide us a way to connect with Troy. Meanwhile I'm going to send SSOSA a sternly worded email that will motivate them to do the right thing."

"Yes sir," Kenneth took his leave.

Rick placed the document on his desk and rubbed his tired eyes. Doing the right thing was always his motto. Rick had drilled that motto into all his subordinates from the first day on the job. Ironically they were in this mess due to Rick's over-trusting nature. And now it was critical that all his agents do the right thing to capture Rio.

His job wasn't easy. Having thousands of people under his command was a big responsibility. There was too much bureaucracy in the way, too many middle men and too many egos to deal with that could gum up his plans.

Rick figured that personally taking the reins on this mission was the only way to assure him success, yet doing so was going outside of his boundaries. He knew he had to keep a low profile but this was not going to be easy for a high profile official.

Regardless, stopping Operation Pakal from being used by the wrong people was now going to be his one and only priority.

Chapter Eleven

Gerald stared at the empty shelves that lined his basement. Federal agents had confiscated all of his relics. He still had his millions hidden in foreign bank accounts but his ill-gotten antiquities were gone.

Dublin was busy packing up his furniture. Gerald was going to sell his mansion and go back in hiding. He was thinking of continuing his practice of stealing relics but staying at the present location would only make him a red flag to the authorities, so it was time to go. Thanks to Troy and his crew his cover had been blown so new plans had to be drawn.

Gerald Bollinger hadn't always been a thief. He actually started out well. He started on the lower rung of the business. He was the guy on archaeological dig sites who was always shoveling away the excess dirt to get to the good stuff. But after a few years of tedious work he became tired of it. He saw too many priceless items come and go to museums or into other people's hands. Others were benefiting from the unearthed goods and at the end of the day all he had to show for his hard work was a meager paycheck and callused hands.

Being on a dig site in developing countries afforded him the ability to associate with the wrong type of people. Whether he was working in an arid desert or a suffocating jungle, these places were fraught with danger where a well-placed bribe could get a person anything he wanted. Tomb raiding was like drug dealing, there were billions to be made on the black market, Gerald had wanted a piece of the action and got tired of waiting.

Too poor to attend a university, he became self-educated on the history of antiquities. He hung around plenty of educated archaeologists to understand the lingo of the business. He made contacts with wealthy people who also secretly desired relics and artifacts for their homes.

Eventually the time came for him to try his new venture. Not only had he raided the very sites he was working on but eventually he branched out and traveled the world collecting and stealing items from millionaires to sell to other millionaires. His illegal business made him extremely wealthy.

Gerald acquired an insatiable thirst for more money. He became a ruthless killer if anybody stood in his way. The last person he had stolen from was a tycoon living in Argentina. Unfortunately for Gerald, the tycoon found out where Gerald resided and wanted to teach him a lesson. He hired SSOSA to expose Gerald to the authorities and to squash him for good. And now this business with the censer had made things even worse.

But a twist of fate landed him back on his feet.

"I can't believe I was thwarted by a punk," Gerald sneered as he caressed an empty shelf. "I lost millions of dollars in potential sales on the black market. I swear I'll kill him if I see him again."

Dublin looked up from his task. "I wonder why the Feds were asking about him."

"Apparently SSOSA aren't as smart as they claim," Gerald scoffed. "They've been conned to work with some kind of terrorists. Whatever the case, I got a get-out-of-jail-free card for my cooperation." Gerald twisted his face in anger when he saw the empty shelves, his anger and hunger for revenge started swelling inside. He clenched his fists. "I swear SSOSA is going to pay for almost wiping me off the map."

Dublin wanted to ask his boss how he was planning to do so, but he knew better than to ask him questions when he was in a sour mood.

Chapter Twelve

"I'm continually impressed by your efficiency!" Rio said as she observed how the SSOSA members worked in an orderly fashion.

"Considering how young our business is, I think we work very well as a team," Troy beamed with pride. "As for this building, all thanks goes to Ashni for locating it. Ashni showed up and offered the owner lots of cash for a temporary rental term. The landlord didn't flinch or ask too many questions, after all cash is king."

"Very true."

They were somewhere in an upstate New York commercial structure. It was conveniently nestled in the woods away from prying eyes. The building was constructed in the 1970s, with concrete tilt-up walls. The exterior sported a contractor-white color. The interior was almost empty and devoid of partitions or rooms with the exception of two public restrooms and a shower stall, an amenity that would definitely be appreciated by the future tenants.

It had been abandoned for many years during the economic recession. The new owner had refurbished the building in hopes of having it rented now that the economy was re-surging, but due to the remoteness of the location, he was having trouble finding a suitable tenant.

Troy and Rio watched as the SSOSA crew went about their business setting up shop inside the warehouse.

"Tell me something about yourself," Rio inquired. "How did you recruit your crew?"

"I met Ashni while I was in the university. I was headhunting for talent for the new generation of SSOSA members. Potential members had to possess remarkable skills and possess incredible ability to decipher complex codes similar to the ones that the old

SSOSA used in their Mind Games." Troy turned to look at Rio with a perplexed expression. "I thought you knew all this."

"I'm sorry Troy. Javan briefly mentioned the Mind Games and how much respect he has for your organization, but no details."

Troy gave her a winsome smile. "No worries, I'll fill you in. See that old guy over there fiddling with the IKEA furniture?"

Rio chuckled. "Yes, I know that's Erick Hausen."

"Well he's the one who saw my potential to become a SSOSA member, unfortunately that's where the rift with my father began," Troy sighed.

Rio raised an eyebrow. "I recall you saying that in the hotel. You said you and your father don't get along."

Troy sadly nodded. "It's all Erick's fault."

"Really?"

"Well…not really, but it started with him. My father always secretly desired to be a SSOSA member, but when Erick chose *me* instead he felt slighted."

"Isn't your father smart enough?"

"Oh, it had nothing to do with his IQ. He's just too timid. He's not as outgoing as I am. Besides the intelligence factor, a good SSOSA member has to have an outgoing, adventurous spirit. My dad is just too much plain vanilla, you know what I mean? He plays it way too safe."

"So you and your Dad had a big fight?"

"Oh yeah big time and to be honest with you, I got a little cocky too. Insults were traded, I told him I was smarter than he is and we went our separate ways. I haven't talked to him in a long time. In retrospect maybe that wasn't a good idea."

"I'm sorry."

"Nothing anyone can do about it now," Troy shrugged.

"What about David Nix?"

"David caught my attention as a promising robotic engineer. He has demonstrated a gift for manufacturing things that are needed for the job."

"And Nolan?"

Troy lowered his voice almost to a whisper. "Nolan Smith is a different story altogether, I find him to be irritable and moody. But

I desperately needed a computer engineer in the club. So with much reluctance, I signed him on after he successfully passed the aptitude tests."

Troy quickly changed his mood and the subject. "So what do you think?" he asked as he gestured toward the entire room. "Is the floor area large enough for the project?"

She surveyed the area with a satisfied look on her face. "Yes, I think this is good enough. You have all done a great job!"

"We aim to please," Troy quipped.

Rio sighed and turned to look at him. "I want to thank you for taking on this mission," she said as she pushed her thick black hair back from her shoulder. "I really would have had no other option had you refused to do so."

Troy looked into her dark eyes, he found them mesmerizing. He tried to keep his attention on the conversation at hand. "This was a group decision. If one member had refused we would have scuttled the mission."

"Of course."

Troy ventured with a question he had wanted to ask. "Is it just you and Javan? I notice you didn't bring your boyfriend or husband to tag along, or are you and Javan a couple?"

"No, I'm divorced, hence why I kept my maiden name and I'm currently not in a relationship."

"How did your parents come up with the name Rio? Are you from Brazil? Your accent betrays you."

"How observant. Actually yes, I was born in Rio de Janeiro. My father was born in Israel, his name is Isaac Jordan. He moved to Brazil to do business, he married my mother who is a native of Brazil."

"Ah, I see."

"And you? I figured that a man with your looks would be married or at least have a steady girlfriend."

A man with my looks, Troy was taken aback by the statement. Was she intimating she was attracted to him? Best not go there! "Nah, just broke up with my girlfriend. I'm glad you hired us, this job will keep my mind off of her."

Rio nodded. "I guarantee this job will keep you very occupied."

"How did you get to be a scientist?" Troy asked.

"I've always been interested in science, even as a child. My father noticed it and since he is a wealthy businessman, he sent me to a university in Israel. My specialty was atomic science. I spent years studying the electromagnetic spectrum."

"How did you get involved with Operation Pakal?"

"Some headhunters from the United States were looking for a specific scientific talent. Somehow they found out about me and offered me a job in Washington D.C. That's where I met Javan. We quickly bonded as friends. I was going through a nasty divorce and he was a loner, so we had plenty of time to devote to the project."

"And then it all turned south?" Troy asked. "You guys stiffed the government?"

"You still don't get it, do you?" Rio's mood quickly changed. "Javan's not the evil scientist he's painted to be by the government, Troy. He's got a heart of gold. As I said before, he didn't want to use Operation Pakal for nefarious purposes. But we were too deep into the project to pull out so Javan's unwillingness to continue got him imprisoned."

"That's your side of the story."

Rio's eyes flashed with anger. "Don't you believe me?"

"Hold on!" Troy raised his hands. "Rio, you do realize that we hardly know you. We're forging ahead because so far everything you have told us seems to be true. Besides that, the science intrigues us and the money is great. But we're not idiots, we will pull out if we find you're wrong."

Rio's posture stiffened. "I have told you nothing but the truth."

"For your sake, I hope you have. It would be a shame to leave you and Javan high and dry and in handcuffs with the Feds."

"You don't have to worry about that," Rio's expression turned serious.

Troy smiled in an attempt to disarm Rio's anger. "Rio, as I said, we aren't stupid. But we're still moving forward, so don't get angry."

Rio breathed in deeply. Troy noticed she was genuinely frustrated. He felt bad for upsetting her. He placed one arm on her shoulder as he shifted her toward the workplace. "Look, just to show you that we are really into this project let's go see how our fearless compatriots are faring."

Each SSOSA member, with the exception of Erick, had a shipping container delivered to the warehouse.

David had a container full of construction tools of every sort imaginable.

Nolan had a container of computers, servers and all the IT toys that would make any computer geek drool.

Ashni had her electrical supplies and a mobile office. Troy had an office too and some portable sleeping quarters with inflatable mattresses. To the surprise of the SSOSA members, Rio also had a small container shipped to the office, although she remained secretive about its contents.

Rio noticed they had a fully operational portable kitchen with a walk-in freezer stocked with food. It had been decided that everyone would take turns cooking. Erick had been appointed to make sure the pantry was always properly stocked. He had been chosen to purchase the foodstuffs.

The SSOSA members had emptied most of the contents of their containers and assembled them inside the warehouse. In a matter of hours the warehouse would be a fully functioning company.

Chapter Thirteen

After arriving at Topeka Regional Airport in Kansas, Kenneth Sims drove his rented vehicle at top speed along Interstate 70 westward to the Vandorph High Security Military Prison. He drove the car off the freeway and turned onto a lonely two-lane road. It was nearing harvest time and the cornstalks in the field were brown. Up ahead, the cornfields gave way to the prison.

Kenneth had learned the history of this particular prison in a history class, and it was exciting to see it in person. It had been built in 1854 as a military post when white settlers came westward. It was more famous for its role during the Civil War as a major United States Cavalry post led by General Carl Vandorph. The fort fell into neglect after serving as a military prison during World War II. It was only recently that the Army renovated the building and resumed its function as a prison.

He could almost feel all of the history in the building as he approached it, but the illusion was broken by the heavy duty chain-link topped with razor wire that seemed to extend forever into the horizon.

The first thing he encountered was a booth with an armed guard. The guard stepped out of the booth, waiting for Kenneth to come to a complete stop.

He leaned over to talk to Kenneth. "What is the purpose of your visit sir?"

"DHS," Kenneth replied as he handed him the proper documents. The guard furrowed his brow while he analyzed the document, then he stepped into the booth for a few seconds to check the authenticity of the papers. He stepped back out and returned them to Kenneth.

"Is this your first time here?" the guard asked.

"Yes sir," Kenneth responded. *And hopefully the last,* he thought.

The guard gave Kenneth a plastic card and pointed behind the booth. "Stay on the road at all times. You will reach another set of automatic doors. There will be a freestanding card reader. You must slide this card in the machine in order to activate the gates and enter into the main section. Do you follow?"

"Yes, sir."

"Very well, you may proceed," the guard said in a commanding military tone.

"Thank you," Kenneth replied as he slid the card in his shirt pocket and shifted the car into gear. Two thick iron gates opened.

As he proceeded forward he saw the first obstacle the guard had mentioned. It was another double set of iron gates. Kenneth did as instructed and the doors opened.

The main building was impressively large, surrounded by other minor structures, all of them made of yellow limestone blocks mined from local quarries. Even the ubiquitous guard turrets rising up above the rest of the building were made from the same type of limestone.

An armed guard approached the rental car, apparently he was expecting him. The guard directed Kenneth where to park, then motioned for Kenneth to follow him.

They walked to the main entry on the ground level and stepped into a long hallway where military personnel were moving about. Every forty feet they saw red stripes on the floor with the word *Caution* painted on it. On the walls next to the red stripes there appeared to be slots.

"Mind if I ask what I need to be cautious about?" Kenneth asked the guard.

The guard briefly looked at the lines and nonchalantly answered. "There are iron doors hidden inside the walls. If there is an escape attempt or an emergency, the two-inch thick doors, activated by hydraulic arms, will quickly slide out and shut down each section of the prison—making escape next to impossible."

Kenneth snickered. "Kind of reminds me of the blast doors from the *Star Wars* movies."

The guard smirked too. "Yeah, it's kind of like that, you'd need a lightsaber to burn these open since they are definitely bulletproof."

"Any would-be escapee is literally trapped. Or be would cut in half if he's standing on the red line," Kenneth mused.

The guard nodded in agreement. "Yes, but an alarm should remind one to stay away from the red line."

"I'll keep that in mind."

The men were still on the ground level when they reached Colonel Bonner's office. The guard approached another stationary guard that was standing at the door. They spoke for a few seconds and the first guard was dismissed and returned to his post. The new guard opened the office door and escorted the visitor inside.

They walked into a waiting room and then into the main office. Colonel Bonner was sitting in his chair. He had a scowl on his face. But he maintained a professional stance as he stood up to meet Kenneth.

Kenneth made the first move. "Colonel Theodore Bonner, my name is Kenneth Sims," he said, as he handed him an official-looking piece of paper.

Colonel Bonner made no pretense to even look at the document. He simply thrust it on his desk. "I know why you're here, Sims. Just for the record, let it be known that I do not approve of the DHS or any of its representatives coming into *my* prison and telling *me* what to do. I only let you in this one time due to direct orders from General Remington. Do you understand?" His voice boomed with authority as he emphasized certain words.

Kenneth nodded. "Yes, sir."

"And what exactly are you trying to accomplish today with my prisoner?"

"My orders are to inject Mr. Benson with the liquid that I have in the syringe I brought."

Bonner placed his hands behind his back. "And what exactly are you going to be injecting into him? We have a staff of medics here that have a full range of medications and antibiotics."

"It's a Nano-biotic, sir."

Bonner moved his hands forward, clenching his fists. "What in blazes is Rick Cannon doing?"

87

"The Secretary wants to make sure he can be tracked in the event of an escape."

Bonner's eyes widened as he yelled. "An escape—escape?! Cannon thinks Javan is going to *escape* from my prison? He's an idiot!"

Kenneth raised his hands in mock defense as a slew of profanities exited Bonner's mouth. "Sir, with all due respect, it's all there in the document, I'm simply doing my duty. I have the right to visit the prisoner."

Bonner reached for the document he had thrown on his desk. He quickly perused it and then balled the paper and threw it in the wastebasket. "This is a bunch of hogwash. I will personally call to complain to the general and give him a piece of my mind. And as for Cannon, he hasn't heard the last of me yet!"

"Are you going to permit me to do my job?" Kenneth politely but firmly asked.

Bonner quickly reviewed his options. Fighting an injunction from the DHS and a direct order from the General was not one of them. He briskly walked over to a closet and pulled out a leather belt with a handgun secured in the holster.

"I'm going with you," he growled as he strapped the belt around his hips. He turned to address the guard. "And you, you're coming with us."

The guard snapped to attention. "Yes sir."

Kenneth let out a sigh of relief.

The three men quickly exited Bonner's office and walked down the sleek hallway. Kenneth kept a mental note of all the red caution lines they passed. Even if Javan knew where every circuit was located, how would he ever break out of this ironclad place? The idea seemed ludicrous.

Was it extreme paranoia that had driven Rick to order the injection? It wasn't surprising to Kenneth. He had been noticing the strange behavior in his boss; it was impossible not to notice considering how closely they worked together.

They reached an elevator and entered it.

Before the doors closed, Kenneth noticed a camera mounted on the hallway wall that was directed at them.

"Take us down to Lower Level Four," Bonner commanded.

The guard obeyed and the passengers felt the elevator descend. Bonner kept quiet. Whatever it was that he was thinking at the moment he kept to himself.

Kenneth eyed the electrical panel in the elevator. He attempted to imagine how, many years ago, Javan had designed this very elevator and its electrical components. Could Javan really manage a successful escape? He smiled to himself, now he was becoming paranoid like his boss.

*   *   *

The elevator door opened revealing a stainless-steel clad hallway. The men bypassed two more guards as they headed toward Javan's cell. When they finally reached the door, the guard that had followed Bonner from his office approached a numeric pad on the door and entered the proper code.

The door slowly opened and disappeared into a pocket slot in the wall. Kenneth noted that this style of door must have been the preferred architecture. Javan was definitely a *Star Wars* generation man.

The men squeezed into a room as the door closed behind them. A dim bulb on the ceiling barely lit the room.

Javan was sitting on his bed. He was dressed in the regulation prison attire consisting of a drab gray-colored shirt and pants. His feet were clad in tennis shoes, sans socks.

To Kenneth, Javan's appearance was very different from the last photo he'd seen. He was no longer clean-shaven. He had let his hair grow long and had lost a considerable amount of weight.

Bonner took the lead as he spoke gruffly. "Mr. Benson, you have a visitor from the DHS."

Javan looked up at the men who were trying to fit into his Spartan cell. "Well, well, look at what the cat dragged in," he replied to the colonel in a squeaky nasal tone. "Did he come to wish me well? Or better yet, did he come to release me after finding out that a travesty of justice was committed?"

Bonner got straight to the point. "No. He came with a mandate to see how you are faring."

Javan's eyes brightened with interest. "Of course, Rick Cannon is such a paranoid man," he replied, his voice dripping with sarcasm.

"No, he's an idiot and so are you," Bonner interjected. "This whole operation is a waste of time."

"Let's get this over with then," Kenneth said.

Bonner looked at Kenneth and gestured toward Javan. "Get it done! You've wasted enough of my precious time."

Kenneth retrieved the syringe from the envelope and prepared it as he approached Javan.

"What is that?" Javan recoiled.

"It's a Nano-biotic," Kenneth answered.

"You have no right to do this to me!" Javan protested.

"Unfortunately you have no say in this," Kenneth replied.

Javan turned to Bonner.

Bonner curled his lips in anger. "I have my orders from General Remington. You and I have no choice in the matter."

"These Nano-biotics are designed to track you in the event you escape," Kenneth said.

"This is an outrage!" Javan protested as he reluctantly rolled up his shirtsleeve.

"The imbeciles from the DHS think you're going to escape," Bonner huffed in anger.

"I will escape, Colonel Bonner."

Bonner hissed with contempt.

"Do you really think you can hold me in this prison forever, Colonel?"

Bonner smirked. "No, not forever, eventually you'll be going out feet first…in a body bag."

Javan winced as the needle pierced his skin. "Rick Cannon's fears are not misplaced. I will be leaving this place, Colonel. Let me repeat…I *will* be leaving this place, alive!"

Bonner chuckled to himself and let his eyes wander over the cell walls. Something caught his attention. It was some graffiti that was scrawled on one of the cell walls: *If you amplify the frequency, the structure of the matter will change*

Bonner curled his lips and pointed at the words. "What's the meaning of this?"

Javan tilted his head. "It's the simple formula for all physical matter, Colonel. Nikola Tesla was the first one to coin the phrase."

Bonner shook his head in dismay. "I think you're all crazy. That's what I think, just plain stupid-in-the-head-crazy. I'll make a note to have your crayons confiscated."

When the injection was completed Javan pulled his sleeve down and slowly waved a hand around. "You do realize this is an illusion, don't you?"

"What are you talking about?" Bonner said with a snort.

Javan gestured to his surroundings. "You see these walls, Colonel? Do you really think they're holding me in? Do you really think I can't escape through them whenever I wish?"

Bonner shook his head in dismay. "These walls are made with a steel skin that is two inches thick and beyond that there's three feet of solid concrete. Even if you managed to pierce through the wall, this level was built four stories down *into* the ground. You would have to go up three more levels digging through compacted soil before you even reached the top. And even if you did reach ground level, my men would pump you up with so much lead your body would vaporize into red goo."

Javan nodded. "I know that Colonel. I helped design the electrical wiring of this prison many years ago."

"Then why are you talking like an idiot?"

"Solid matter is an illusion, Colonel—mass and matter are made of molecules and molecules are in reality atoms that move around a nucleus. If I were smaller than the molecules of steel and concrete I could simply float right up in between the atoms and escape this prison."

Bonner cocked his head and sneered. "Is that so?"

Javan glanced at the other men in the cell then back at Bonner. "The problem with you, Colonel Bonner, is that you just don't seem to comprehend the world of physics. You don't understand how the world rolls."

"Oh no, you're sadly mistaken, I know exactly how the world rolls. Let me give you some insight, boy. If you want to keep rolling on this earth then you better obey the rules."

"You will soon see everything I am saying is true."

"I have a notion to have you transferred to an insane asylum," Bonner grumbled before turning to Kenneth. "Are we done here?"

"Yes," Kenneth answered.

Bonner snapped his fingers. "Let's go then."

"Colonel Bonner?" Javan called out as his captors started to leave his cell.

Bonner quickly turned. He instinctively placed his hand on his holster. "What do you want?" he grumbled. "I've had enough of your foolish talk!"

"Do you like the Arawak Wind Slicers?"

Bonner pursed his lips then he relaxed. "I see my guards leaked the information."

"No, I saw them while I was on the rooftop."

"Whatever."

"Well? You didn't answer me. Do you like them?"

Bonner paused for a few seconds before responding. "Yeah—you did a good job."

Javan closed his eyes. "Thank you."

Bonner shook his head. *What a sad, crazy man*, he thought as he left.

Sergeant McPherson noticed Colonel Bonner fuming when he returned to his office. Bonner unfastened the holster and hung it back up in its proper place and then pushed his chair back in a harsh manner. He sat down and gazed out the window.

"Mind if I ask, what's the problem, sir?"

Bonner swiveled his chair to face McPherson. "Do you know what Simmons' parting words were?"

"Hard to say, sir."

"He said 'Oh and one more thing, Colonel, beef up your security because I'm convinced Javan is going to escape.' Escape? How do you like that noise?"

McPherson stifled a laugh. "Really?"

Bonner stood and walked over to his office window and stared at the horizon as he talked. "You don't realize how much work it took for me to make it here, do you, Sergeant?"

McPherson didn't answer; he simply looked at Bonner.

Bonner continued. "It's not easy for an African-American to climb up the ranks in the military. I fought and clawed my way up, every inch of the way. Do you understand what I am saying? Every single inch of the way. It took me many years but I did it, McPherson, I did it! I'm now the *Colonel* of Vandorph Maximum Security Prison!" He turned and made a fist at McPherson and snarled. "I'm telling you this, ain't nobody outside the US Army going to tell me how to run my prison!"

Chapter Fourteen

"What seems to be bothering you?" Troy asked Rio. She looked particularly concerned.

"Uhm, I'm no building expert..." She placed her hands on her hips. "But I was wondering how you're going to manage to move all that heavy stuff. I mean, you have some slabs of granite and a lot of steel beams. Each beam must weigh about a ton!"

"Art will help us," Troy answered in a nonchalant manner as he continued his work.

Rio turned to look at Troy with a perplexed expression. "Who?"

Troy looked at David. "Haven't you introduced her to Art?"

David shook his head.

She raised her hands up. "Who's Art?"

"Art can lift heavy objects, he's strong," Troy responded.

"Troy, why are we bringing another person in? I thought I made it perfectly clear that this is a covert operation. I don't want..."

Troy raised a hand to quiet her. "David, please introduce Art."

With a knowing smile on his face, David picked up a hand-sized, rectangular plastic object and spoke into it. "Art. Please come out, I want you to meet a lovely lady."

Rio was starting to get irked. She was angry to think that there was another SSOSA member hiding somewhere in the building.

There was a strange noise coming from David's container box. It was a sound of machinery moving with the power of hydraulic energy. Suddenly an odd-looking mechanical robot ambled out of the box.

The robot resembled a large scorpion. It was about fifteen feet long. It walked on its six legs and moved its pincers and tail with such dexterity it almost looked like a real insect. The metallic body had a coat of paint resembling the color of the iconic Iron Man in the movies; the segmented plates were alternately red and gold. On both sides of the body were stenciled letters that read: A.A.R.T.

"Say hello to Rio, AART."

AART waved a pincer back and forth.

Rio clapped with delight. "Wow, very nice! You really had me going there for a minute."

"I made him myself," David beamed. "It took me a whole year to design him. The acronym AART stands for *Archaeological Artifact Recovery Tool*. I designed him with the ability to enter dig sites under inhospitable conditions. Due to the design of his legs, he can climb up and down rocky hills without tripping. He can go in cramped tunnels or tight spaces and grab relics with his pincers. He can lift or push heavy objects that weigh up to four-thousand pounds each! The eyes on the head are actually headlights, whereas the stinger on the tail is a camera. That way I can monitor AART from a distance."

"Are all its commands strictly verbal?" a fascinated Rio asked.

"No." David held the box up for her to see. "This control box has dual capability. AART can be voice controlled or manually controlled. With a flip of the toggle switch I can move AART around as I wish. In the real world, my voice commands may not always compute in AART's brain so I need to have an alternate way of moving him around."

"We can also control him via Nolan's computer if needed," Troy said.

"That's true," David agreed.

"He has other unseen features and gadgets," Troy added. "But due to AART's strength, today he will be used as a building supply, load-bearing laborer."

"How is it powered?" Rio asked.

"The main power comes from a rechargeable battery inside the body," David explained. "It's similar to the batteries used in electric cars. The battery, in turn, powers a hydraulic system like the ones seen in small front-end loaders. It has a battery life of about eight to ten hours before it has to be recharged."

A smiling Rio crossed her arms. "You guys continue to amaze me."

Once the introduction was finished, the construction of the project quickly got underway. After studying the blueprints, Erick and David began placing adhesive tape on the warehouse floor to indicate where the structures would be placed.

It took Erick a few tries to get up from the floor. He stiffly ambled over to Nolan's desk. "What this place needs is some life. Let's have some music, shall we?"

Nolan looked up at Erick. "Sure, I have an almost unlimited selection. What's your pleasure?"

"I want to listen to the classics."

"Bach, Beethoven, Chopin?

"No, no, I'm talking about The Rolling Stones, Beatles or Led Zeppelin."

"I got some Led Zeppelin."

"Ah yes, Led Zeppelin," Erick mused. "Our first Mind Game used the music of Led Zeppelin to figure out a clue."

"That was when you were in the university, right?" Nolan asked. "That's where you guys vibrated sand particles on a drum to produce a strange design."

"Yes. It's good to see you know your SSOSA history."

"Of course I do. Do you want me to play Stairway to Heaven?" Nolan chuckled.

Erick waved a hand. "No, try another Zeppelin song."

"Ok, here we go."

The song Nolan played was Kashmir. The music filled the warehouse.

"How apropos," Erick said with a smile. "The lyrics say '*I am a traveler of both time and space*'."

At Troy's command, AART started carrying the heavy steel beams to the center of the warehouse floor. David in turn bored holes at strategic places in the beams then he had AART lift them up at specific angles and hold them in place. Once that was done, David attached the beams together with the nuts and bolts. After a few hours of tedious work, the skeleton of a Mayan pyramid was finished.

It stood twenty feet high at its peak and twenty-five feet at its base.

David stood with Troy admiring the structure.

"Three more pyramids to go and then we layer the exterior with the skin," David announced.

Ashni came up behind them with a spool of thick electrical wire in her hands and started unraveling the spool near the pyramid. "I want to get the wire in the pyramid before you apply the outer layer."

Nolan returned from a restroom break and flopped himself on his chair. He noticed an icon on his computer monitor indicating he had an incoming email. After he read it, Nolan shut down the music and raised his voice for all to hear. "We have some serious problems, people!"

Everyone dropped whatever they were doing and approached Nolan's desk. It became dead silent. He pointed to the email and read it aloud:

"This is Rick Cannon, Executive Secretary of the Department of Homeland Security. This correspondence is to advise all of you SSOSA members to immediately cease and desist from working with Rio Jordan. At this moment she is considered a terrorist and a fugitive from justice. Any involvement with her will be considered an act of treason against the United States of America. The power of our office which has been granted to us by the President of the United States has enabled us to prosecute any criminal activity to the fullest extent of the law. If such action is not taken within four hours from receipt of this notice, all SSOSA members will be considered domestic terrorists."

The mood in the warehouse turned sour.

"I told you guys this was going to happen," Nolan broke the silence with a warning tone in his voice.

"He's pulling out all his stops," David said.

"This really sounds serious," Ashni added.

"Rick Cannon is abusing his position to bully us," Rio said. "Operation Pakal is rightfully mine and Javan's."

"That's inconsequential," Nolan bellowed. "He is the authority and that's all that matters!"

"What if Rio is right?" Troy pointedly asked Nolan.

"What if Cannon is right?"Nolan shot back. "Why should we assist these people if we're breaking the law?"

"What law are we breaking?" Troy asked Nolan.

Nolan pointed to the email. "Hello? Rio is accused by the DHS of being a terrorist."

"I'm not a terrorist!" Rio yelled.

Troy turned to Erick, expecting some sage advice.

Erick stood up and rubbed his chin. "It looks like Rick Cannon is trying to scare us. He's trying to flush us out. The DHS has no evidence we received this correspondence, do they?"

"That doesn't change the charges leveled against Rio," Ashni said, agreeing with Nolan.

"Let's assume Cannon is right," Troy interrupted. "If Rio really is a terrorist, then what is *her* endgame? We are controlling the project, she isn't. We are the ones who can stop anything nefarious from happening."

"Troy has a good point," Erick added. "We have come this far with the project. We haven't seen any evidence of foul play in both the science or on her part, have we? Wasn't that part of the deal when we started this mission? We all agreed to stop if *we* noticed anything wrong."

"Well I think there *is* something wrong here," Nolan shot back. The tone in his voice was becoming more hostile, poisoning the atmosphere.

"I say we continue to go forward with this project," Troy piped up. "If we do find something wrong with Operation Pakal, then I will be the first to turn her in to the authorities. Then we still come off as heroes no matter which way you look at it."

Nolan looked troubled. He stood up and pointed an accusative finger at Troy as he walked backward. "I specifically warned you this would happen. I told you if we kept going forward it would backfire on all of us!"

Troy gritted his teeth. "Shut up, Nolan."

"No! I'm not going to shut up this time. I've had it with you and your eternal optimism when the writing is on the wall," he swung around and pointed an accusative finger at Rio. "We were duped by this woman and now we're all going to spend a lifetime behind bars."

"He may be right," a nervous Ashni added. "We were just warned to back off the project. I don't want to end up in prison or deported to India!"

David came up to Troy. "They will find us. We need to turn ourselves in and confess everything."

"Come on you guys!" Troy bellowed. "We have to finish the project."

"Why are you pushing forward, Troy? Admit it, you're wrong!" Nolan cried out.

Troy looked at Erick, who looked like he was ready to speak but was interrupted by Nolan.

"No, it's over, don't you get it?" Nolan was on fire. He stomped up to Troy. "It's all because of that stupid complex of yours. You had to prove daddy wrong didn't you? You had to prove you were the better SSOSA candidate." He glanced at Rio. "And I wouldn't be surprised if you aren't on a rebound and chasing after Rio...."

Troy lunged at Nolan and grabbed him by the collar and threw him against the wall. "Listen to me you pompous pig! How dare you accuse me of purposely putting us in danger! We all went into this with eyes wide open. If we run into a wall, we find a way around, do you get it? We work as a team! That's what SSOSA is all about! We work as a team and don't quit. We never quit!'"

Nolan pushed Troy away. "You're an idiot. We quit when we sense we are being led to the gallows."

Troy rushed over to his desk and pulled out a checkbook. He scribbled on a check and ripped it out. He walked over to Nolan and handed it to him. "Leave. Here's your share of the profits so far. I added more to purchase your computers. That should cover everything."

Nolan glanced at the check and looked up at Troy. "Are you kicking me out?"

"Yes."

"I'm quitting anyway."

"Get out!"

Nolan fished for his car keys and grabbed his jacket. He looked around one more time. He felt bad for leaving the group, but he had to do what he had to do. "Don't expect me to visit you in prison."

There was an embarrassing silence that hung in the air as they watched Nolan exit the warehouse and slam the door behind him.

Troy was breathing hard. He sat down on a folding chair and pinched the bridge of his nose. He felt emotionally beaten up. It didn't look good for his crew members to be fighting in front of a customer. He was too embarrassed to face Rio. Was this the beginning of the end? Was his company now starting to unravel? He clenched his fist. He regretted hiring Nolan. He regretted not punching him in the face when he had hurled the insult, but most of all he felt stupid for accepting Rio's job offer now that things appeared to be unraveling.

He had no idea how to proceed. He didn't dare look up.

"We have a problem," Rio said as she stared at Troy.

Troy finally lifted his head and looked at her in puzzled bewilderment. "I wish it were only one. So, what is it?"

Rio continued. "We can't go forward with Operation Pakal."

"Why not?"

"You need *all* SSOSA to continue the project. And you told me that unless *all* were in agreement you would walk out. Remember?"

Troy visibly sighed and lay his head down. "Oh yeah, yeah, I did say that, didn't I? I guess you're right, we have to shut down Operation Pakal." This surely wasn't the way he anticipated the operation was going to end. The idea of returning the deposit Rio had given him sickened Troy.

"No you don't," Erick interjected as he slowly lifted himself from his chair, wincing in pain. The arthritis in his knee was starting to act up. "I motion that you accept *me* as an active member of SSOSA to take Nolan's place."

"You?" Troy's face lit up. "Are you serious?"

"Yes I am. I'm not quitting, young man and neither are you. We must go forward, to the bitter end." He turned and stared at all of the other assembled people. "Do you all think the old SSOSA never had problems? Do you think it was always smooth sailing? The answer is *no*!" Erick's voice boomed in the warehouse. "I recall there was a time when we were playing a Mind Game in Greece and the police thought we were involved in terrorist activities. But we came out unscathed in the end. Why? Because we SSOSA stuck with the game all the way to the end and we didn't give up. So now, at this juncture, we are in too deep to quit. We must continue with the mission. If necessary we can stop when we feel like it's time to stop and right now is *not* the time to stop."

Troy smiled at Erick. He admired him. Erick obviously had the courage and emotional stamina that Troy was still trying to cultivate. He stood up and turned to the other SSOSA members. "Do you all accept Erick as a temporary member? If you do, then we can proceed."

The others slowly nodded their approval.

Briefly, Troy was concerned about what had just happened. The mutiny of Nolan was bad enough, but would others follow? Troy swallowed hard, trying not to think negative thoughts.

However, the heroic deed done by Erick had renewed his optimism.

"Let's keep going forward," Troy said.

Chapter Fifteen

Chauncy Rollock was at a local grocery store searching for some fresh produce and other items. This task was usually relegated to his wife, but she was away for a few weeks visiting relatives in Wyoming. When he was finished, Chauncy placed the avocados in a plastic bag and headed for the cash register. As he stood in line he gazed about at the abundance of things in the store. He was always amazed at the extremes in human society. He had spent many years in jungles or developing countries where the basic necessities were hard to come by. He had seen so much human suffering and poverty. And yet here he was, in a Walmart, in the most affluent country in the world surrounded by more things than any human really needed to survive, which consisted mostly of sugar-laden food and plastic junk.

The cashier barely looked up at Chauncy as she checked his groceries. She was a young girl, late teens, with more earrings and nose rings than necessary.

"Did you find everything you needed?" she asked.

"No, I couldn't find any world peace and security," Chauncy quipped.

Unfazed by the joke, the cashier handed him his receipt. "Oh, you'll find that in aisle nine."

"I may have missed it, aisle nine is where the adult diapers are, right?" Chauncy chuckled.

"Have a nice day, sir."

Chauncy took his receipt and groceries and headed for the exit. He felt a brisk cold end-of September wind as he headed for his pickup truck. He fished for his truck keys in his coat pocket. From his peripheral vision he saw a dark gray van pull up beside him. At first he thought the driver wanted his parking space, but the large door slid open and a man wearing a dark suit and tie popped out and approached him.

"Mr. Rollock?" The man discreetly showed him his badge.

Chauncy was temporarily taken aback. "Yes?"

"I'm Kenneth Sims from the DHS. We need to talk to you for a few minutes. Can you step inside the van?" It was more of a command than a question.

Chauncy tried to mentally sort out what was happening. "May I ask what this is about?"

"It's about your son Troy."

That was all that he needed. Chauncy quickly hopped into the van and the agent closed the door. It was warmer inside that was for sure. Chauncy looked around, there was an empty seat. He knew it was for him.

"What seems to be the problem?" Chauncy asked as he seated himself.

"Troy has gotten himself in a serious situation that involves our national security."

Chauncy's eyebrows shot up. "How could that be? He's an appraiser of relics."

Kenneth got to the point. "No Mr. Rollock, he's involved with a group called SSOSA, they deal with archaeological retrievals. The acronym stands for...."

Chauncy chuckled as he raised a hand. "Say no more. I know what SSOSA is. But what does that have to do with our national security?"

"We can't divulge more information except to say that the group that has hired your son has stolen some highly classified material that can do us harm. The point is, Troy and his group of associates have no idea how much trouble they are in. The people whom he is working for are *using* your son to compromise our national security by creating a weapon of mass destruction."

Chauncy leaned back in his chair. "Well, this isn't any good now is it? Have you talked to him?"

"No, that's the problem, these criminals have managed to get him and his associates underground. They've disappeared and we can't locate them. We need your assistance. Can you contact Troy?"

Chauncy took a deep breath. He felt uncomfortable. "This is going to sound strange...but, Troy and I haven't been on good terms lately."

"What do you mean?"

"Well, um...we haven't spoken in months. Let's just say we are rather estranged. He and I had a heated argument last time we spoke."

Kenneth stared at him. He obviously wanted to know more.

Chauncy sighed, he hated airing the family's dirty laundry, but this was a federal agent after all. "You see, SSOSA is a club that only accepts the most brilliant minds in the world. I should know because in the past I was involved with many SSOSA members. Point is, I really wanted to be accepted as a member but they chose my son instead. This made Troy big-headed and we had an argument about why he was chosen instead of me. So I guess you could say we parted ways and I haven't heard from him."

Kenneth looked genuinely frustrated. "Do you have his phone number?"

Chauncy dictated the number, but Kenneth noticed it was the same one he already had.

Kenneth gave him his card. "If you do happen to make contact with him, call me. We are planning to extricate him from this group."

Chauncy looked surprised. "You're going to do a rescue operation for my son and his crew?"

"Yes, but we need to know where they are located."

"Yes, I understand."

"So, you have no idea where Troy and his people are?"

"I'm sorry...I don't," Chauncy sighed with frustration. "I don't even think his mother knows, she's out of town right now anyway, somewhere in Wyoming."

"Keep in mind that these people are terrorists," Kenneth added with a warning tone in his voice. "Any willful cooperation with this group will not be viewed well in the eyes of the law."

"I understand."

105

"Just so you know, we are concerned about your son."

"I am as well...I mean, now that you tell me he's in danger, this isn't good."

"Good day Mr. Rollock."

Chauncy exited the van and it drove away. He shook his head. *I wonder what trouble Troy has gotten himself into? He's a chip off the old block that's for sure.* He looked down at his hands and noticed they were empty. *My avocados, he left with my avocados*!

Chapter Sixteen

Dublin walked into Gerald's office. "He's here."

Gerald looked up from his computer monitor. "Did you frisk him?"

"Yes, he's clean boss."

Gerald quickly pulled his handgun from the desk drawer. He pointed it at the door, his finger not on the trigger but not far from it either. It was, he hoped, a menacing gesture. "Let him in."

Nolan walked in. He was a little surprised to see Gerald pointing a gun at him. But he quickly recovered. They both looked at each other in silence.

Gerald was the first to break it. "Sit down," he motioned his gun to a nearby chair. "We have some talking to do."

"You still don't trust me, do you?"

"What are you talking about?"

"You don't need to point a gun at me."

"I don't even trust my own mother."

"Whatever."

Gerald stared at Nolan for a few seconds, then he spoke. "So out of the blue you email me and tell me you are defecting from SSOSA and want to work for me, eh? What is this, some kind of joke?"

"No, it's not a joke."

"How did you know I was out of jail?"

"We keep tabs on everyone that gets imprisoned by us. My app alerted me that you were released."

"How quaint. So why did you defect?"

"I don't work for that loser anymore."

"So why do you want to work for me?"

"Because I have something you want."

"And I suppose I have something you want."

"I don't want to be under Troy's command anymore. Get it? I've lost faith in him. He's carrying around too much emotional baggage. He's headed for failure. The DHS is after him, too. They have labeled SSOSA as terrorists."

"So why would I want to have any dealings with an ex-SSOSA member?"

"Because I have knowledge," Nolan reached for his car keys and pulled the key chain apart. He lifted a flash drive up in the air. "Can I insert this on your computer and show you?"

"Not a chance." Gerald shook his head. "What if this is a trick and you intend to introduce a virus into my computers? I still don't trust you."

Nolan rolled his eyes. "Please, do you think I'm risking my life to infect your servers? Get me a laptop computer that's not connected to your system."

Gerald motioned to Dublin and he dutifully retrieved a laptop from the closet and after it was turned on Nolan inserted the flash drive and showed Gerald pictures of the pyramids in the warehouse. "These are pictures of SSOSA building Operation Pakal. As you can see they are halfway done building a replica of the machine."

Gerald eyed the screen in deep thought. "So how do you make this work?"

"The blueprint for the structure is located in a flash drive that Rio Jordan has. It's going to happen, Mr. Bollinger, this is the real thing!"

Gerald leaned back in his chair. He pointed the gun at Nolan again.

"Will you stop pointing that gun at me!" Nolan bellowed.

"I'm still not totally convinced you have my best interests in mind."

"Why do you think I came here?"

"So what's your grand plan?"

"I have two options. Option number one: I go to the Feds and spill the beans about the whereabouts of SSOSA and Rio. However, I will be out of a job and worse off financially than when I started. Option number two: We can work together, I can team up with *you* and we can steal the blueprint of Operation Pakal from Troy and Rio. You can sell it for millions of dollars, possibly billions on the black market. I want two million dollars to lead you to the place where they're located."

"You want two million dollars, eh?" Gerald snickered. "You think it's that simple?"

"I know where they are and you don't. At this point even the DHS can't find them. That's the plan. I win no matter which way you look at it and so do you. I don't care if I'm branded as a terrorist in the US. With my millions in a foreign bank account I can get a fake passport, a new identity and retire somewhere in the Caribbean."

"So are you saying we storm their hiding place and take the blueprint?"

"Yes," Nolan eyed Dublin. "You provide the muscle and I lead you to the place. We don't have to kill anyone...just tie them up. They won't dare call the police, they're wanted fugitives."

"Is that so?"

Nolan nodded his head.

"When do we do this?" Gerald asked, slightly more interested.

"Before we take the blueprint I want to make sure the machine works, otherwise we're just stealing something that's useless. We have to wait until they fire up the machine....so, are you in?"

Gerald pondered Nolan's plan. He was having that same feeling he had when he was let out of jail. Another wonderful opportunity was presented to him.

He leaned back in his chair again. He stared at Nolan, scrutinizing him. There were no holes in Nolan's story. Now he understood why the DHS was after Troy and his crew. It all made sense. It was not the first time he had heard or seen the evidence of ancient technology in antiquities. There was no doubt in Gerald's mind that this was going to be the biggest archaeological heist in the history of mankind. And here he was, smack in the middle of it all.

Gerald lowered the gun. His thin smile was all Nolan needed to see to understand that Gerald was in the game.

Chapter Seventeen

Javan slipped out of bed and turned over his cot mattress. He pulled out a plastic baggie that contained metal filings that were acquired by rasping on the metal bed frame for the last few months. He took his toothpaste tube and squeezed the remaining paste into the bag and after mixing the two elements he produced an amalgam of metal paste. With his toothbrush clenched in his teeth, he rolled the metal paste in his hands until it became a snake-shaped tube and then he laid it on the bed. He pushed his bed out into the middle of his cell until it was under the light bulb. Once he was standing on the cot he took the toothbrush out of his mouth. The end of the toothbrush handle had been rubbed and scraped until it was shaped like a flathead screwdriver. With it he unscrewed the light bulb base, exposing some of the interior wires.

He bent down and retrieved the metal 'snake' in a rag with one hand and unscrewed the bulb with the other. The room went dark, but Javan had already mentally noted where the empty socket was, so he slowly lifted the snake and placed it behind the socket, touching the exposed wires creating a short circuit. Javan turned his gaze away as a shower of sparks exploded from the socket into the cell.

In the dark, Javan quickly shoved his cot back into place, threw the rag and bulb in the wastebasket and crawled in bed. The initial plan of short circuiting the electrical grid on Lower Level Four had worked perfectly. This had been the Achilles heel in Vandorph for many decades. And now, Javan had taken advantage of this inherent structural weakness to commence his escape.

It was show time.

The four soldiers at the ground level security station were monitoring the camera feeds. One jolted to attention as he saw a red light blinking on his panel. The cameras monitoring Lower Level Four went dark.

"We have a problem," Private Thomas said.

Private Greer turned to look at Thomas. "What's up?"

Private Thomas pointed at the monitor. "Everything went blank downstairs on Lower Level Four. We lost power."

Greer furrowed his brow. "Call security. I'm sure they can tell us what the problem is."

Thomas slid his headset over his head. He pressed a button. "Security on Lower Level Four, do you copy, repeat, Security on Lower Level Four, do you copy?"

The only response was static.

Greer leaned over to look at Thomas' monitor. "That's strange. We lost all the power and communications to Lower Level Four. I have to talk to Sergeant McPherson. Send some techs with communicators down the elevator."

"Yes sir."

Private Greer rushed over to Sergeant McPherson's office and briskly knocked.

"Enter," McPherson ordered.

He entered and stood at attention. "Sir, we have a malfunction on Lower Level Four."

Sergeant McPherson creased his brow and stared at Greer. "What's the problem, Private?"

He shrugged. "I don't know sir, all power and communications have ceased."

The sergeant quickly stood up. "Show me."

They walked back to the control room. McPherson looked over Thomas' shoulder to view the monitors. All he saw were blank monitors and blinking red lights for Lower Level Four.

"What action have you taken?" Sergeant McPherson asked as he perused the console.

Greer straightened up. "I ordered two techs to go down and check out the problem, sir."

Sergeant McPherson nodded with approval as he started to leave the room. "Very good, keep me posted when you find out what caused—"

112

"Sir!" Private Thomas interrupted. "I found the source of the short. The electrical malfunction started in cell number LL-220."

Sergeant McPherson slowly walked back to the monitors. "Who's the prisoner?"

Thomas clicked on his keyboard. "Prisoner Javan Benson, sir."

Sergeant McPherson froze in place. "Really?"

"Yes, sir."

"Well I'll be a--" Sergeant McPherson's face tightened. "Alert security to be on standby. Cover all elevator exits up on Ground Level. I have to report to Colonel Bonner," he said as he pivoted on his heels and left the room.

"Yes, sir!"

When the elevator descended to Lower Level Four, the two techs exited and headed down the hallway. The hallway was lit by the dim emergency-backup lights.

Corporal Garcia communicated the location via his transceiver. "We've arrived."

A voice was heard through the speaker. "Go to cell LL-220. That's where the problem started."

"Roger."

The two techs reached cell LL-220. "No need to key in the code, the keypads are down," Garcia said as he opened the door, handgun ready. The two cautiously walked into Javan's dark cell. The techs pulled out small flashlights and surveyed the area.

"Prisoner, show yourself now!' Corporal Matthews barked.

"I'm over here," Javan said replied.

Garcia swung his light over to see Javan sitting on his bed. "What are you up to prisoner?"

"What are you talking about? Surely you're not blaming me for this?"

"What happened?"

"I heard what sounded like a loud pop and then the lights went out."

The techs passed their lights around the room until Matthews saw the swinging, empty, blackened socket. "Well, look at what we have here!"

113

Garcia glanced up. "It looks like our prisoner is telling the truth! Let's check it out."

Javan was told to stand at one corner of the room as a guard pulled the cot out and placed it under the socket. Garcia went over to the cot and took a multipurpose tool out of his side pouch. The tool had a small LED bulb on the tip and once he was standing on the cot he used it to examine the socket. "I don't know what caused the problem, but it sure wreaked havoc on this level."

"What do you want to do?" Matthews asked.

"We need to bring in power to see what we're doing," Garcia replied as he jumped off the cot.

The two techs pushed the cot back in place as Javan deliberately bumped into them in the dark.

"Back off!" Garcia shouted as he swung and pointed a flashlight and a gun at him.

Javan jumped back in the dark room, covering his eyes from the glare. "Sorry, man, I can't see."

Garcia pointed a finger at him. "Don't even think of escaping; orders are shoot to kill!"

"Enter!" Colonel Bonner commanded.

Sergeant McPherson looked harried. "Colonel, we have a problem, the power on Lower Level Four is out. We traced it to Javan Benson's cell. Two techs are down there now checking out the problem and I ordered all security personnel to be on high alert. Also all elevator exits are blocked with orders to shoot to kill if any prisoners try to escape."

Colonel Bonner stared at the sergeant as his mind raced with the issue. "What's that clown up to?"

"I don't know, sir."

"What's the status of the techs?"

"Status unknown, sir."

The Colonel shot out of his chair, went into his locker and pulled out his gun and holster belt. He placed it around his waist and buckled it up. "I've had enough of this jackass. Don't you see what he's doing? It's the oldest trick in the book, it's called a diversionary tactic. He sets a bunch of prisoners free while he quietly makes his escape."

"What are you going to do, sir?"

Bonner gritted his teeth. "I'm going to put a bullet between his eyes, that's what I'm going to do. I'm sick and tired of this whole affair, from the DHS all the way down to this, this nut job."

Sergeant McPherson's eyebrows shot up.

Bonner furrowed his brow. "Don't look at me like that, I'm not joking. I'm *gonna* kill him. You know I have every right to stop a fugitive prisoner, even if I have to use deadly force. Come on."

Sergeant McPherson was following him out the door when Bonner abruptly turned. "Wait!" he said and ran back to his desk. He stuck the unlit cigar between his lips. "Okay, now we can go."

Javan waited for the two techs to enter the elevator and then he quickly slipped out into the hallway and walked in the opposite direction. He stopped at a door that had a sign on it that read 'Utility Room.'

Once inside he closed the door and pulled out the multipurpose tool that he had purloined from Garcia. He unscrewed a plate on the door and with the LED light on he unscrambled the wires that controlled the keypad. Once he was done with that task he moved to a panel on the wall. He opened it and started rewiring the system.

The two techs exited the elevator at ground level and they were about to go to Sergeant McPherson's office when they encountered him and Colonel Bonner in the hallway. The two techs quickly saluted.

"What's the status?" Bonner barked.

Garcia spoke. "Sir, we found cell LL-220 with a short circuit at the light bulb. Apparently the system couldn't handle the short and kicked off the breakers, sir."

Bonner placed his hands on his hips. "And exactly how did you determine that, soldier?"

Garcia was starting to sweat as he fished in his leather bag for his tool. "Well, sir, I simply used this...this..." The tech looked stricken as he attempted to locate his multipurpose tool. "Dang! I can't find my tool!"

He looked up at Matthews. "Do you have it?"

Matthews frantically searched his leather bag. "No, sir, I only have mine."

Garcia finally reached the right conclusion. "The prisoner stole it!"

Cursing, Bonner clenched his cigar in his teeth as he pushed the tech away, slamming him against the wall. "Get out of my way, you useless morons."

Colonel Bonner and Sergeant McPherson ran to the elevator. Bonner motioned at the two guards. "Get away! Move it! Move it!"

He summoned the elevator car, but noticed the light on the button was dead.

Bonner swung around to face the guards. "He disabled the elevators! The stairs, he's going to escape through the stairs and the emergency ladders. Send guards to cover all the exits!" He swiftly turned to face Sergeant McPherson. "Initiate Red Alert. I want a lockdown of the entire prison. Do you understand, Sergeant?"

Sergeant McPherson was already running down the hall. "Yes sir!"

Bonner turned back to address the guards. "Have guards go down to Lower Level Four via the vertical stairs and when you find the prisoner shoot him. Shoot to kill!"

The power was eventually restored on Lower Level Four as the techs repaired the damage done by Javan. Bonner, McPherson and three heavily armed soldiers made their way down in the elevators. The soldiers immediately started going from cell to cell to see if Javan was hiding with the other prisoners. But the soldiers came back empty-handed.

"He's not in any of the cells, sir."

"Check the utility rooms and the janitorial closets!" Bonner shouted.

When they did so, one of the soldiers shouted down the hallway. "The door to the utility room isn't responding to the code, Colonel."

Bonner rushed over to the door and entered the code himself just in case the soldier had erred. But the result was the same.

"Blast the door open, he's in there," Bonner shouted.

Everyone with the exception of one of the soldiers stood at a distance. The soldier aimed his rifle at the door keypad and shot the keypad to pieces. The soldier used his rifle as a prying bar to release the locking mechanism from the door jamb since the deadbolts were still activated, which took some time.

"Hurry up!" Bonner yelled.

The door finally creaked open and a soldier flipped on the lights. Bonner pulled his service revolver out and entered to shoot Javan. He was stunned to find the room empty.

Cursing profusely, Bonner replaced his gun in his holster. He saw and pointed to the stacked boxes that led up to the ventilator. "Well, how do you like that? Our monkey has escaped through the ventilator ducts." Bonner walked up to the boxes, cupped his hands and yelled up through the vent. "We know where you are Javan. We're going to flush you out like the rotten mole that you are. Nobody escapes this place, do you understand? Nobody!"

Chapter Eighteen

Bonner and McPherson were back in the security monitoring room up on the ground level. They watched the technician work with a computer program that showed a diagram of the Vandorph ventilation system.

The tech pointed at the monitor. "There. That's Lower Level Four, Sir. The venting system obviously ends down at LL-4 since there are no more underground floors. So the prisoner can only go up."

McPherson shook his head, lips clamped. He saw the maze of vents crisscrossing in many directions. "He could be anywhere. Too bad we can't pump poisonous gas into the vents to flush him out."

Bonner leaned over and stared at the monitor. "Don't tempt me."

"Where in the world does he think he can go?" McPherson said.

The tech scrolled around to show more details. "All the vents lead to the main pump. But before they do, they go off in many directions, sir."

Bonner straightened up and crossed his arms. "Let's concentrate, boys. If you were Javan, where would you go? Now, you wouldn't go into another cell with a prisoner, or into the arms of security? That would be downright stupid."

McPherson pointed at the diagram. "You are correct, sir, the duct work on LL-4 goes to cells, utility rooms, janitorial rooms, restrooms and security. None of those are too inviting if you ask me."

Bonner toyed with his cigar. "Okay, suppose he would shimmy *up* the vent and go up to the next level, LL-3."

McPherson sighed. "Same thing, LL-3 has the same type of rooms, sir."

Bonner clenched the cigar with his teeth. "Scroll to up LL-2," he ordered.

The tech did so. "Here it is, LL-2. It has the cafeteria for the soldiers, uniform rooms, showers, rec room, computer room—"

"Hold it!" Bonner yelled, pointing at the monitor. "Look. That duct goes to the computer room right?"

"Yes sir, it shares the same venting system, why?"

Bonner put his hands on his hips. "Because, if I were him—"

Suddenly the computer shut down and then the bank of security monitors went dark.

The tech raised his eyebrows. "The server is down and so is the security video computer, sir."

Bonner's eyes widened and then he slammed his fist on the wall and cursed. "I knew it. He's in the computer room. Let's go!"

Javan finished entering his commands on the keyboard then quickly shut down the file he was working on. He heard commotion and yelling outside as Bonner, McPherson and a soldier jiggled the handle to open the door, but like on Lower Level Four, he had electronically jammed the keypad. This gave him enough time to jump on the desk and climb up on a chair atop the desk and pull himself back up into the venting system to his next destination.

A large blast from a rifle blew up the keypad and after struggling with the jammed deadbolt, Bonner and his crew finally stormed into the computer room.

"He's gone up the vents again!" McPherson said.

Bonner sighed with great irritation. He returned his handgun to his holster and paced like a caged lion. He walked up to the vent and yelled. "All right, Javan. You want to prolong the inevitable? Go ahead. But I'm going to get you, no matter what you do."

"What do you suggest, sir?" McPherson asked.

Bonner stared at the floor for a few seconds. "Get another technician to unscramble the damage done to this computer," he said. He turned to the tech. "How many ducts do you think there are in Vandorph?"

The tech hesitated. "Sir, there could be hundreds of vents—"

"I mean on ground level, soldier!"

The tech hesitated. "I'm sorry, sir. I have no idea. The computer is down and—"

Bonner interrupted again as he raised a finger. "Okay, listen up. He can't escape from any of the lower levels, right? So, if we guard *only* the vents up on ground level he's bound to show up when he shimmies out a vent. Let's go catch him, boys."

All personnel to Ground Level, All personnel to Ground Level, a voice boomed from the loudspeaker in the prison. Meanwhile Bonner's tech was furiously scribbling lines and arrows, indicating the location of each vent on a hardcopy architectural plan of Vandorph.

"Obviously I can't recall where every single vent is, sir, but I'm doing my best," the tech said.

Bonner ignored the statement; he simply concentrated on the drawing. "I think we have just about every vent covered by a soldier up on ground level."

McPherson said, "Let's suppose he doesn't emerge from the vents—where else would he go?"

"That's the million-dollar question, Sergeant," Bonner said.

McPherson pointed to Lower Level Two. "If he were to drop into any of these rooms he would be immediately apprehended."

Bonner clenched his teeth. "Unless..." Anger rose in Bonner; he felt he was always a step behind Javan. The answer suddenly came to him. He privately berated himself for not thinking faster than his adversary. He cursed and slammed his fist on the desk, then he quickly went for the door.

McPherson looked up. "Where are you going, sir?"

"I know where he is!" Bonner yelled as he stepped out into the main hall. A river of soldiers passed by dressed in combat gear, carrying rifles and wearing helmets, responding to the alarm that echoed through the hallways.

McPherson followed Bonner into the hallway. Bonner turned to face the soldiers, and some of them bumped into him as they rushed to their stations to cover all the vents.

One specific soldier that was coming in his direction caught his attention. There was something about his eyes that registered in Bonner's brain.

The soldier brushed by him.

That's him! Bonner swiftly pulled his revolver out and swung around and aimed. Not wanting to hit the other soldiers he yelled at the top of his voice. "Hit the ground! Freeze! Hit the ground!"

A loud alarm sounded when the iron blast door that was hidden in the wall slid out from its wall-pocket and shot across the hallway into the slot in the opposite wall, thus sealing Bonner and McPherson in the hallway.

But Bonner had already squeezed the trigger and the bullet hit the iron door, ricocheting in the compartmentalized area.

McPherson grabbed his shoulder and grimaced in pain as blood oozed out. "I'm hit!" he yelled.

Bonner clenched his teeth in anger then turned toward the sergeant. "I have a first aid kit in my office, let's go."

McPherson protested as he examined his shoulder, realizing it wasn't a serious wound. "No, I can take care of it, it just grazed me. The prisoner is escaping, sir."

Bonner suddenly looked up as he heard a series of loud thundering sounds.

He knew what had happened. Now it made sense.

As Javan was running down the hallway, he had activated the iron doors with a remote control device he had stolen and modified in the computer room. Thus, one by one, he was sealing the soldiers in hallway compartments just as he had done with Bonner and McPherson. The soldiers who were trapped inside the hallway compartments meant fewer soldiers to capture him as he made his escape outdoors.

Bonner's mind raced with the possibilities.

And then it hit him.

"He's going for the Wind Slicers!" he yelled.

"But we're stuck in the hallway," McPherson grimaced in pain.

"Oh no we aren't! Come on!"

Colonel Bonner raced back to his office where a tech was monitoring a computer. The colonel violently pushed the tech off of the seat, sending the hapless man to the floor, while McPherson arrived and observed the colonel's actions from the doorway. Bonner lifted the heavy chair up over his head and hurled it through the office window. The glass exploded outward onto the sidewalk. Bonner climbed on his desk and prepared to exit through the window opening but stopped short. "Not again!"

McPherson stepped aside while Bonner ran back into the hallway and picked up his cigar from the floor and placed it between his teeth. He then ran back into his office, jumped on his desk and climbed out the window. He landed on the sidewalk, slipping on the glass shards until he caught traction, then he ran in the direction of the Hummers.

The tech slowly lifted himself off the floor. "With all due respect, sir, that man is insane."

McPherson, still holding his injured shoulder, walked to the window and looked out. "You can say that again."

The tech sat on Bonner's desk, gazing out the broken window. "Our prisoner has escaped. This will be the first time in modern history."

"And he did it using only a multipurpose tool," McPherson added, shaking his head with both consternation and awe, reaching for the first aid kit.

Javan was already seated inside one of the parked Wind Slicers when Bonner hit the tarmac. Javan nervously worked the switches and controls. The engine fired up and the rotors started to turn.

Bonner quickly ascertained which Wind Slicer Javan stole and ran faster toward it.

A soldier who was outside aimed his rifle and started shooting at the aircraft as he saw it rise up.

"Stop shooting!" Bonner yelled as he passed the soldier and pushed him aside. "Those things aren't affected by small-arms fire. Don't waste your ammunition."

By the time Bonner was seated in his own aircraft, Javan was already flying away. In a manner of seconds Bonner got his aircraft rising above the prison grounds, grateful that these specific machines were equipped with a rapid-startup feature.

Javan surveyed the view below: the Kansas fields were brown and the farmers were riding in their combines harvesting their crops. But this was no time to admire the fall scenery. He noticed that Bonner was quickly gaining on him.

Each Wind Slicer was equipped with two rockets. The current position he was flying was going to make it easy for Bonner to pluck him out of the sky.

He weighed his options.

Javan pushed his controller stick forward and the Wind Slicer nosedived beyond the fields below into a heavily wooded area. He whisked around the trees attempting to shake Bonner off. But the stubborn colonel kept trailing him as if the aircraft were connected by an invisible line.

You're a good pilot, Javan silently nodded to Bonner.

Bonner muttered obscenities. He pressed a tracer switch on the instrument panel that pinpointed a laser on Javan's craft.

Javan heard the beeping sound warning him that Bonner had a lock on him. It was just a matter of seconds before he would be blown to smithereens. He had to think fast.

He swerved to the left, exited the forested area and buzzed a cornfield. Ahead of him was a red combine moving at a slow speed.

The farmer inside the combine happened to look in the rear view mirror and saw the two strange aircraft coming upon him. Terrified, he opened the door and jumped out. He fell unceremoniously to the ground in between the cornstalks while the large, unmanned combine kept moving forward.

Bonner fired a rocket, leaving a contrail of white smoke behind it. Javan turned hard right just in time and the rocket slammed into the combine. The agricultural machine died an ugly death as it exploded in a large fireball.

Bonner turned to the left, barely missing the debris and shrapnel from the explosion. Looking behind, all he could see was a black plume of smoke rising up out of the field.

Bonner pulled a 180 and saw Javan's Wind Slicer going into another cluster of trees.

Completely stunned and disheveled, the farmer saw the two planes disappear into the forest. He turned to the other side and saw his combine being consumed by big red and orange flames. *How am I going to explain this to the insurance company?*

Bonner rose higher up in the air to see if he could spot Javan. Sure enough, once Javan ran out of forest cover, he was visible again over the cornfields.

Like a hawk hunting a dove, Bonner descended on his prey.

Up ahead Javan saw a very large red barn, the front doors were open. The word *barnstorming* came to his mind when he decided what he was going to do. He launched a rocket. It shot out and entered the open barn doors and hit the rear wall, easily leaving a gaping hole. Javan flew in the barn and exited the rear perforation into another forested area.

Bonner turned sharply to avoid hitting the barn, since he was temporarily blinded by the shower of wood splinters and smoke. He almost slammed into an oak tree but he quickly turned to avoid it and maneuvered the craft upward again to get a better view.

He finally saw Javan flying low, hugging a road in a wide open field. There was no place for Javan to hide now, the forested area was behind him. He focused his attention ahead of the road Javan was flying over.

Bonner's laser tracer honed in on the target. He fired his last rocket.

Javan didn't see it coming because the rocket wasn't purposely targeted on his craft, hence no tell-tale warning alarm went off in his cockpit. The rocket flew past him and blew up on the gravel road ahead of him.

A tremendous shockwave with a shower of gravel slammed into the Wind Slicer causing it to wildly twist around like an errant, twirling arrow. Part of the canopy glass shattered around him. Blood started running down his forehead and Javan screamed in pain as he held on to his face. He was disoriented and no longer in control of the vehicle.

"I gotcha, sucker!" Bonner yelled in triumph, figuring he was going to have the satisfaction of watching Javan's plane crash and burn.

But the triumph was short-lived. Bonner stopped smiling. Watching the Wind Slicer right itself, he recalled a feature that

VTOLs were equipped with for situations like these. It was a temporary, automatic-self-flying mechanism in case the pilot was injured in combat. The computer in Javan's aircraft sensed the erratic flying pattern and automatically took over the controls, straightening the Wind Slicer into a proper flying mode.

Bonner cursed again.

Javan found the first aid kit above his head, barely able to see what he was doing due to the flowing blood from his forehead. After he wiped his face he was relieved to find lacerations but no deep wounds. He hurriedly placed a bandage on his forehead.

Bonner was out of rockets.

He had only one option left.

He pushed the throttle higher, and the engine whined as his craft lined up with Javan's craft. He automatically lowered a small side window. This was a built-in feature to allow a pilot to talk to personnel on the ground without lifting the entire canopy. He took his handgun out and aimed at Javan through the window.

Javan felt a sharp pain in his left hand.

Bonner smiled as he aimed one more time.

Unlike Bonner, Javan still had one rocket left.

Up ahead on the road was a cluster of tall grain silos. Thinking quickly, Javan had an idea. He aimed at the biggest silo. Bonner was too busy focusing his aim at Javan so he failed to realize what Javan was preparing to do.

Javan clenched his teeth, fired his last rocket, then turned a hard right.

Suddenly realizing the situation, Bonner grimaced and quickly pulled back on the throttle with all his might, making the craft slow down, so that it was almost hovering near the silo.

That move was a big mistake.

The rocket reached the target. There was a loud explosion and the silo burst open like a popcorn bag. The shock wave slowed Bonner's craft causing it to tilt up a few degrees.

4,500 tons of dry corn grain poured out like a river. Bonner's rotors caught the shower and became weighed down by the flowing corn. The Wind Slicer appeared to have come to an abrupt standstill midair. Bonner was pushed forward by the inertia and momentum. He struck his head and was knocked unconscious.

The Wind Slicer went down.

Two farmers who were unloading their corn in one of the other silos saw the whole affair. They looked at each other in shock and then back at the strange looking aircraft that was slowly being buried under an avalanche of grain.

"Wow! Did you see that?" the first farmer asked.

The second farmer started running toward the damaged silo. "Come on, we gotta help that pilot!"

Seeing that there was no fire or imminent explosion, they clambered up the corn hill to reach the pilot. It was difficult to walk up the hill of corn as they sank up to their hips in the grain more than once; they were taking great care to not be engulfed by the grain. When they finally reached the craft they used their hands to dig toward the cockpit. They found Bonner slumped over the control stick, it took the two of them to pull him out. The three men started sliding down the corn hill until they reached the ground.

The first farmer gazed at Bonner. "He's from the military."

The other farmer nodded as he recognized the insignia on his uniform. "Yup, he's an Army colonel!"

Bonner started to move, and corn sputtered from his mouth as he tried to talk. He opened his eyes and sat up. "Where...where am I?"

"You're in Kansas, sir," the second farmer answered.

Looking around him and coming to his senses, Bonner started flailing wildly. "Let me go, I gotta get him. Let me go, let me go!"

Concerned for his welfare, the farmers tried to keep him from leaving, but Bonner wouldn't have any of it. He pulled away from the two men and started climbing up the corn hill, yelling all the way up. "I'm going to get him! I'm going to get that sucker!"

More than once he slid down or sank in the grain hip-deep, but he finally managed to reach the Wind Slicer and pulled himself into the cockpit. He frantically searched until he found what he was looking for.

"I got him!" Bonner yelled as he waved the cigar stub. He started laughing hysterically. "I found him...ha-ha-ha... yes, I got him!"

And with great finesse he placed the cigar in his mouth, exited the craft and folded his arms as he sat on the grain. Soon he started sliding down the hill.

The farmers looked at each other in dismay.

Chapter Nineteen

Javan let out a sigh of relief as he continued flying. While looking down at what was now becoming hilly terrain he realized he was lost. His initial plan had been to reach the local airport after his escape from Vandorph, but he had lost his bearings during the aerial fight.

He keyed in the coordinates in his GPS system to see his present location in reference to his next destination, which was the Manhattan, Kansas airport, where his private plane was stowed. The display showed him to be ten miles off course. Not bad in itself, except for the fact that he was a prison escapee wearing a bloodstained Army uniform and he was flying a strange looking aircraft on a clear day.

This was certainly no way to be inconspicuous.

But Javan had not left the prison escape to chance. The plan was that once he had escaped Vandorph he was to use a car that was hidden in a forested area near the prison. In the vehicle were a change of clothes and a small supply of snacks to carry him through the ordeal and to help him get safely to the airport.

However, the air battle had taken him farther west than he had anticipated and flying *back* toward Vandorph to locate the vehicle was no longer a viable option. The seconds were ticking away and Javan was aware that the Vandorph officials were actively looking for him everywhere. So now he had to quickly come up with an alternative.

Rummaging through the storage compartments he found a loaded handgun. He weighed his options. He would have to fly closer to the airport than he had planned and commandeer somebody's car.

Flying in a westerly direction, Javan eventually came over the city of Manhattan, Kansas, home to Kansas State University. He keyed in: Aviation Field, Kansas State University." The GPS system automatically guided him to a small airfield near the school campus.

Down on the airfield, three students had just retrieved a prototype airplane made of balsa wood from a trailer and carefully placed it on the runway. One of the male students tweaked the solar-powered panels that were mounted on the wings and fuselage, making sure that they were tightly secured.

The students heard a strange sound, looked around them, then up at the sky.

"Whoa, check it out!" a student said as he pointed at the source of the noise.

The second student yelled, "What's that?"

The Wind Slicer quickly descended onto the field, with all three students recording the event on their phones. Javan crawled out of the broken cockpit and jumped on the grass while the rotors were spinning to a stop. "I have an emergency, people," Javan announced. "My aircraft experienced some serious problems and I got hurt—that's why I have all of this blood on my uniform. I need to use one of your vehicles to get to Fort Riley immediately."

The students were too stunned to react. One of them thought Javan looked familiar, but she was too dumbfounded to put a name to the face.

"I'll trade my aircraft for a vehicle," Javan said. He was wondering if he was going to have to show the gun and use some force. "We can settle this with the Fort Riley officials once I get there."

One of the students threw him his keys, keeping his eyes on the alien-looking craft in front of him. "Yeah, sure, sure, I own that beat up Chevy pickup over there."

"Thanks man," Javan said as he ran to the truck and started the engine. The spinning tires kicked up some dirt as he made his getaway.

"You better say goodbye to your truck, dude," the other student said.

The owner of the truck quickly approached the Wind Slicer, eagerly inspecting it. "Who cares? That truck is a piece of junk. Check this out."

Located near the university, Fort Riley was already in lockdown mode, but it didn't matter to Javan, since his destination was the airport only minutes away. Apparently the civilian population had not yet been warned of the prison escape, but that was about to change real soon.

Javan turned off the highway, and parked the truck on a grassy embankment that was near the hangars. He noticed the only obstacle between the road and the hangar was a six-foot-tall chain link fence. The lack of a high security fence had already been noted by Javan and Rio when they were planning the escape.

Javan exited the truck and clambered over the chain link fence and walked up to his private airplane.

"Halt. Don't move!" Javan heard a harsh voice behind him. "Raise your hands above your head. Don't try anything funny, you're surrounded. Turn around, slowly."

Javan slowly obeyed, expecting to see federal agents with guns pointed at him. Instead he saw a smiling older man pointing a gun at him

"Dr. Benson, I presume?" Erick said with a wry grin. "I am Erick Hausen, of SSOSA."

Javan's jaw dropped. "SSOSA? But...how did you find me?"

"Do you seriously think I swallowed Rio's story? Oh, she's an intelligent person but a bad liar. Perhaps the explanations she gave were enough to convince Troy and his crew, but not I. I did not reach this age in life and not learn a few things along the way."

"So, what tipped you off?"

"The story about teleporting an object to the university in California in hopes of moving the good hearts of the government to release you was the first tip. Second, this operation is way too elaborate to think that it was based on pure altruism. I'm sorry, but people nowadays aren't very altruistic. I smelled something bigger."

"How did you know I was planning to escape and end up here at the airport?"

"I hacked into Rio's computer and read the escape plans. I made up a story to Troy telling him I had to leave to get some food and supplies for the crew and followed you here. I must admit you did an admirable job of escaping."

"Thank you. It wasn't easy." Javan's expression turned serious. "So that's it? Are you going to turn me in to the authorities?"

Erick lowered his gun and holstered it. "No, you're coming with me. Rio is waiting for you."

"What?" Javan slowly lowered his hands, yet still incredibly perplexed. "I...I don't understand..."

Erick placed his hands on his hips. "Look, Javan, maybe the two of you are terrorists, maybe you are not. I have done my homework, and as far as I am concerned you are not a danger to me."

"I appreciate your appraisal of my character. I have been horribly wronged by the United States government."

"Perhaps you speak the truth," Erick added. "You are not the first person to ever be wrongfully convicted and you will not be the last. I know how governments work.

"But what if we are terrorists?"

"If you and Rio are terrorists, we still have a cover story to protect us."

"Why are you risking it then? That would make *you* altruistic, right?"

"Not at all. I believe in the *science* more than I believe in you, I want to see this experiment to its completion. It will be a once-in-a-lifetime experience to see Operation Pakal work."

"So you are going ahead with the mission even though there is a possibility you and your friends may end up in a federal prison?"

"Do you really think this is the first time I've been in danger?" Erick smirked. "I've been playing the Mind Games for decades and I have been in some extremely precarious situations. If this turns out to be a fluke we can claim you held us at gunpoint to finish the project. Don't underestimate us, Javan, I already have Plans B, C and D in place in case this thing go south. As for the DHS, they don't scare me. So no matter what you do, we are one step ahead."

"I admire your character, Erick."

"Thank you, but we better go now."

"Unfortunately the authorities have pinpointed my exact location and are on their way over to arrest me."

Erick raised an eyebrow. "What are you talking about?"

Javan looked visibly nervous. "I have some bad news for you."

"Speak."

"Before I escaped the prison I was injected with a Nano Bio GPS tracker. We are being tracked as we speak."

"Did they inject a capsule? If so we can surgically remove it."

"No, it was introduced into my bloodstream."

"Ah, I see," Erick had a crooked smile. "Well it looks like we are going to have to do some quick thinking. Now you get to see how a *true* SSOSA mind works." Erick motioned to Javan. "We are not leaving in your plane." He pointed to his jet that was at a short distance away. "We are going in mine...and while I fly I want you to tell me everything...I want the entire story, you understand?"

"Yes, sir."

"Lead the way, I will follow."

Javan jogged toward the hangar where a larger corporate-sized jet was waiting for them. They both scrambled on board. Erick quickly pointed out the restroom facility, the small galley area and the first aid kit. He apologized for not having any spare clothing to fit Javan due to the great height disparity between them. He then went to the cockpit, took control and taxied out onto the tarmac.

Once they reached a good altitude, Javan went to clean up and then re-bandaged his injuries. He then ate a small meal in the kitchenette and staggered back to the cockpit. He sat down in the co-pilot seat and took a long drink from a water bottle he had brought from the mini fridge. He was exhausted and the droning of the jet engine was threatening to put him to sleep. But the mission wasn't over and this was no time for letting his guard down.

It was time to tell Erick everything.

Chapter Twenty

Rick Cannon was filled with two contrasting emotions as he rode the elevator from his office down to the basement. The first one was the feeling of vindication. He had predicted Javan was going to escape from prison. The second emotion was anger because Javan *had* escaped even after he had dutifully warned Colonel Bonner to beef up security. He hated failure. He also hated the fact that he couldn't control every single situation. He tried to, but there was too much bureaucracy and too many egos to deal with.

And now that the news headlines were screaming about the escaped terrorist from Vandorph, all eyes were on *him* to fix the problem. He still couldn't understand why SSOSA members had chosen to ignore his email. What was it going to take for these people to do the right thing?

Maybe they were being held at gunpoint. Maybe Rio was a good liar. Yes, that had to be it. One person couldn't hold off multiple people with just *one* gun. Operation Pakal was too complicated to put together unless they were willing partners. She would have had to conceive an elaborate story to convince a group of extremely intelligent people to attempt to fire up the most dangerous weapon since the atomic bomb.

Rio had already made a major blunder by using her phone to contact Troy. She had alerted the DHS of her and SSOSA's whereabouts. But was it really a blunder? No. She wasn't stupid. It was a deliberate ploy to entrap SSOSA and use their fear of persecution to get them to cooperate.

And it worked.

Unfortunately this was not going to end well for SSOSA. They were going to need an intervention, a rescue operation was already formulating in Rick's mind.

The elevator doors opened and Rick walked into the basement. The entire place was an operations command room. The lighting was kept low to better view the monitors. There were three men hunched over their keyboards typing commands as they watched a giant TV screen mounted on one of the dark walls.

Kenneth was overseeing the men and he quickly turned around when he saw Rick walk in. "Hello, sir."

Rick nodded his acknowledgment, more interested in what was on the large screen. "Is there any coffee?"

"Yeah, I'll get you some."

Rick waved him off. "I'll get it myself. What's the latest?" He walked over to the refreshment station and poured himself a cup.

"The Manhattan, Kansas airport said the pilot of a corporate jet belonging to Erick Hausen took off an hour ago."

Rick turned around and sipped his coffee, eyes still glued to the big TV screen. "And that moving icon on the screen represents his jet I presume?"

"Yes, we've tracked Javan in midair. They are headed toward the east coast. Should we have the FBI arrest them when they land?"

Rick lowered his coffee cup and took a deep breath. "Not yet. Nabbing Javan is no longer priority number one. Let them land."

"I...don't understand, sir." Kenneth was truly perplexed.

"If we arrest Javan and Erick, the others will be alerted and they will scatter. We need to follow Javan and Erick to their home base. I'm more concerned about getting the machine in our hands and those two *will* lead us to it. Get a SWAT team together, we're going to raid their hideout and arrest everyone. If SSOSA won't come to us, we will come to SSOSA and rescue them. Then we will arrest Rio and Javan and put an end to this once and for all."

*   *   *

The GPS signal emanating from Javan was weak. Rick's men had a hard time tracking him as Erick and Javan weaved through traffic in a New York suburb. There were some erratic movements from Javan that puzzled the trackers but they doggedly kept an eye on him. After a while they noticed Javan's signal stopped at a certain geographical spot and remained unmoving for at least one hour. That meant the two men had reached their destination.

Now was the time for action.

The local SWAT team in that specific jurisdiction was summoned to action. Most SWAT personnel were assigned one of three roles—negotiator, sniper, or entry officer. For a typical hostage situation, the sharpshooters were deployed to sniping positions in pairs while the entry team contained the area. As the negotiators worked from the SWAT command post, some members of the entry team prepared for an emergency assault on the hostage-takers, called a"crisis entry."

This specific mission required a briefing of the SWAT members to remind them to refrain from touching any machinery or strange looking devices found in the warehouse. Anything they saw was classified information. Operatives from the FBI would be standing by to secure the machine after the terrorists and hostages were removed from the site.

Four armored vehicles left the compound and headed for their destination. They eventually reached the warehouse and the armored vehicles easily surrounded the building and the agents jumped out and took their respective positions.

The entry officer took the lead and had two other operatives ram the front door. The hallway was dark. The team turned on their helmet lights and proceeded with caution.

When the lead operative reached the desired door where the GPS signal was traced, he looked behind at his fellow operatives. He motioned with his head to go.

They rammed the door and rushed in, guns pointing in all directions. Two officers rushed in and checked the bathroom. "Clear!"

The agent walked around the room, circling the only objects in sight. The middle of the room was dominated by a table. On the table was a foot-high plastic Mayan pyramid and on top of the pyramid was a mechanical Hawaiian hula dancer. The agent swept the doll across the room, breaking it into pieces. He reached for a small item that had been under the doll. It was a GPS capsule.

He looked up at his men and gave them a wry smile. "We've been spoofed!"

Chapter Twenty-One

Dublin was in Gerald's office double checking the firearm inventory as Gerald pored over the handwritten schematic of the warehouse that Nolan had provided.

Gerald tapped on the drawing with his pencil. "So there are two access doors on the east side and three large delivery doors?"

Nolan peered from behind his shoulder. "Yes. The access doors should be easy to break into."

Gerald leaned back in his office chair still pondering the plan. "How many people did you say are in the building?"

"All SSOSA members, and Rio Jordan." Nolan pointed at the TV screen. "But according to the news, Javan Benson has escaped a maximum security prison. Guess where he's headed?"

"Incredible," Gerald looked up at the TV monitor that was showing the CNN newscast. "The news of the prison escape is dominating the day. So we can conclude Javan should be arriving there soon."

"So this was Rio's plan all along?" Nolan shook his head in dismay. "I knew something fishy was up. She was using SSOSA to assist Javan. Troy was too blind to see the facts."

"So what's Javan going to do?"

"Possibly assist in weaponizing the machine. He knows how it works."

"How can Javan be useful to us?"

"We need him so he can explain how the machine works."

"What if he doesn't cooperate?"

"I'm sure you have ways of persuading him."

"What if he fails to make it to the warehouse?"

"You can hire another scientist to explain the science."

Gerald grimaced. "That's easy for you to say."

Nolan straightened up. "I saw the videos on the blueprint. It's somewhat self-explanatory."

"Yeah, 'somewhat' is the key word."

"Look, once you have the flash drive in your hands what difference does it make if you know how to operate it or not? Just sell the dang thing to a rogue scientist or whatever."

"Then why were you so bent on coming here to find a working machine?"

"Having a working machine would be the ideal, but if not, at least having the blueprint will suffice."

"You sound like you have all the answers," Gerald huffed.

"It's called Plan B and Plan C, that's how we SSOSA members roll. Well, former SSOSA."

"Yeah whatever," Gerald hissed as he stood up.

"I'm serious. You can find another scientist to assist you.'

"SSOSA members, current and former, apparently operate on stupid logic. It's not as simple as it looks."

Chapter Twenty-Two

Erick had orchestrated the spoofing plan to hinder the SWAT team. When he was done he informed SSOSA members he was on his way with Javan Benson.

The news of his prison escape and the fact that Erick was arriving with Javan deeply troubled the remaining SSOSA members. Some even accused Rio of lying and misleading them. Troy tried to assuage their nerves by assuring them that Erick would not mislead them by bringing Javan into their company.

There was no festive party waiting for Javan when he finally arrived at the warehouse. The mood was tense. Everybody had been warned beforehand that Javan had nano GPS in his blood. If anything, they were keenly aware the DHS would figure out they had been outwitted by a misleading GPS signal and perhaps trace them to the warehouse.

The SSOSA members approached Javan when he entered the room. He was still wearing the stolen military uniform albeit torn and bloodied.

"Javan! It's so good to see you!" Rio ran over to Javan and hugged him tightly. She then lightly touched his face. "You look so pale and thin…"

Javan looked at her with sad eyes. "Prison wasn't a picnic, my dear friend. Besides, I had to lose weight to fit into the air ducts."

Rio nodded her head. "I understand."

Troy went up to shake Javan's hand. "It's a pleasure to meet you. I don't know if I should feel proud or guilty. We just assisted a condemned criminal to escape prison."

"You did the right thing. I have been a victim of a great injustice," Javan remonstrated. "It is a pleasure to meet you. Thank you so much for assisting us."

"So, this entire plan is to send you to another dimension?" Ashni asked as she approached Javan. "That's why you escaped prison and that's why we built this machine?"

Javan nodded. "That is the plan."

"Why?" David asked.

Javan's face turned serious. "Because it's the only way I can escape my persecutors. My other choice is to rot in prison. But with this technology I can escape to another dimension."

Rio looked proud as she summed up the plan. "We knew Javan would never be released from prison. So he and I devised a clever plan for him to escape and use Operation Pakal to send him off from here."

"Why not just escape and disguise yourself and go into hiding?" David pointedly asked.

"Go where?" Javan answered. "With our modern technology it would only be a matter of time before they located me. I could not and will not live in fear, looking over my shoulder for the rest of my life."

"What exactly do you expect to find there? Is there a parallel universe?" David asked.

"That's possible. However what I have been telling you is pure theory, the other dimension may be totally different than what we experience here."

"Will you feel any pain?" Troy asked

"The molecular and atomic level of my body will vibrate at such high levels I may not appear human in the other dimension."

"This is crazy," David said. "You may enter the other universe as a...a spectrum of light!"

"Exactly"

"No pain, no suffering," Erick mused. He appeared to be lost in deep thought.

"You will be like an angel!" Ashni said.

Everyone became pensive for a moment.

"This is truly ground-breaking science," Erick remarked.

"However, there is a dark side to all of this," Ashni pointed out to Javan. "So we are a bit leery of you."

"You should be leery of your government!" Javan shot back. "They want this energy to create a super weapon and cause mayhem."

"If it's not a weapon for you, then how would you describe it?" Troy asked.

Javan became animated. Operation Pakal had that effect on him. "Imagine finding an ancient tuning fork. Now imagine finding a way to make it vibrate. The result is an awesome tool that can change the world as we know it if used properly."

"That's where I come in," Rio piped up. "Once Javan is gone, I can use this machine for the benefit of mankind. The way Javan wanted it in the first place."

"I would love to continue this discussion," Erick said nervously as he glanced at his wristwatch, "but we are running out of time. Spoofing the Feds with a fake GPS signal will only last so long. Rick Cannon will be re-calibrating Javan's GPS signal and find us here. Let's get started."

The SSOSA members were psychologically on high alert. The previous night they had all privately talked about sabotaging Operation Pakal if anything nefarious was detected. They surely didn't want to be responsible for opening a Pandora's Box of destruction on New York City. However they still wanted to look like heroes in the government's eyes if they succeeded in thwarting what might be an evil plan. But foremost on their minds was to see the machine actually work. At this juncture of the operation they felt they could still claim innocence in continuing with the project.

But now the moment of truth had arrived.

Nerves were a bit on edge, but they were ready. All the SSOSA members knew their particular responsibilities. David lowered the cable containing the rain-drop-shaped throne until it was level with the floor. Erick monitored the computer terminals, Troy watched from the sidelines in case anything suspicious took place. Rio and Ashni started the quantum oscillation generator.

David strapped Javan into the throne and with a remote-control mechanism slowly raised the throne to a predetermined height. Once he was done David moved to watch with the others.

"Start her up!" Javan yelled.

143

Rio approached the oscillation generator and pushed a large lever forward to a predetermined energy level.

Everybody in the room held their collective breath. Emotions were running high.

"This is it," Rio whispered.

There was a low rumbling sound that started vibrating everything inside the large warehouse. Everybody gazed about, wondering what was going to happen next. The rumbling sound with the accompanying vibrations became so intense somebody's plastic Coke bottle vibrated off a desk and fell onto the floor.

The noise startled Ashni.

Erick stood up from his chair and motioned to Troy to get ready. Troy nodded in acknowledgment. They knew this was the critical point. The plan was to lunge at the oscillating generator and shut it down if something went wrong.

As the rumbling increased heavier objects in the room began to rattle. The torsion waves started emanating from the four pyramids and converged at Pakal's throne. From the viewer's point of view, Javan looked like a shimmering mirage as strong magnetic waves washed over his body. But instead of smiling, Javan's expression seemed like he was being tortured by unseen forces. His facial expression was that of pain and anguish. He appeared to be saying something but his words were convoluted and distorted.

Troy turned to Rio, her expression was that of concern.

Everybody sensed something was wrong.

Suddenly small items started rattling off desks and falling to the floor. Lighter items such as paper clips and plastic cups started floating in midair. Troy was going to say something to Rio but he noticed his feet were no longer touching the warehouse floor.

Troy gasped in astonishment. Looking about he noticed Rio and his fellow crew members were also starting to levitate.

Now heavier items were also levitating. An empty folding chair started rising up in the air. Everything and everybody floating were slowly gravitating toward the four pyramids.

David saw AART rising. "AART, grab the storage container!"

AART did as commanded. It thrust a pincer out to keep itself pinned down to the container.

Everyone else had to hold on to heavier objects to avoid levitating. It was an eerie sight to behold. The machine was acting like a magnet, like a black hole that was sucking in all of its surroundings toward the throne.

Javan seemed to be yelling something at Rio but his face was contorted with pain.

"Turn the machine off!" Troy yelled at Rio. But it was obvious Rio was having a difficult time keeping herself anchored as she frantically reached for the power level.

"What's happening?" somebody yelled, but the voice was muffled by the thundering noise.

Something was wrong. Terribly wrong!

Chapter Twenty-Three

Though it felt like an eternity, the anomaly only lasted about fifteen seconds, but it was fifteen seconds of trepidation. When Rio finally managed to shut down the quantum oscillating machine all the floating objects, including the humans, came crashing down to the floor.

It took a few moments for everyone to get their bearings. All the SSOSA members were still on the floor, breathing heavily.

"That was a truly magnificent phenomenon!" Erick exclaimed. "At least you did not blow up New York City."

"You just can't get it out of your head that we're not terrorists!" Rio angrily retorted.

She turned her attention to Javan. He looked pale and his head was bobbing. She rushed forward to help him, with David and Troy right behind her. They helped him off the platform while Erick manually controlled the cable with a joystick. Ashni ran into one of the tents and pulled out an inflatable mattress. They laid Javan's limp body on it and checked his pulse.

Ashni looked up and smiled. "He's alive!"

Rio let out a sigh of relief. "Thank God."

"What went wrong?" Erick asked, looking genuinely bewildered.

Rio looked equally confused. "I...I don't know. We followed everything according to the blueprint. I didn't add more energy than what was needed."

Javan was starting to come to. He coughed and asked for some water. When he was done drinking he forced himself up on his feet. He looked dazed and confused. "What...happened? Why am I still here?"

"Good question," a baffled Erick blurted out.

"How do you feel?" Rio asked anxiously.

Javan shook his head. "I felt like I was being crushed, but at the same time, like I was being ripped into a billion pieces. What went wrong?"

"I don't know," Rio answered. "Everything started vibrating and levitating."

"And we were being sucked into the middle of the pyramids like a vortex," Troy added.

"Instead of acting like a true oscillating machine it acted like an atomic vacuum cleaner," Erick noted.

"What?" Javan clenched his teeth. "That makes no sense." He walked over to David's workbench and grabbed a retractable measuring tape. He wobbled over to the pyramids and started taking measurements.

"I made sure everything was built to specs," David said in a defensive tone.

Troy grabbed a folding chair and sat down. He felt like a deflated balloon. Things weren't going right. First there was the issue with Nolan and now this. Without a functioning machine, Troy was going to look like a colossal failure. Not only was he going to lose out on any potential revenue for the group but he most likely was going to have to answer to the authorities for cooperating with wanted criminals. He anxiously rubbed his temple with his hand.

Javan finished measuring then stepped back from the pyramids. "It can't be so, the machine wasn't supposed to act like a vacuum."

"What's the matter?" Erick asked.

Javan shook his head then went over to the computer to check the blueprint specs. When he was done he sat down on a nearby chair. He seemed to be truly perplexed. "Something is wrong. All the measurements are correct. But why...why didn't it work?"

Troy looked up and shook his head. He looked bewildered. "I don't know."

Erick raised his hand to interrupt anyone who might comment. "Before we start investigating I recommend we shield Javan. The nano GPS is still active."

"What can we do about that?" Troy asked. "We need more time to figure out this dilemma."

"He needs to be concealed in the walk-in freezer," Erick said. "The steel box and freezing temperatures should impede the GPS signal. Ironically it's thicker and more insulated than my jet and more so if you take into account the concrete walls of this warehouse. We can keep him warm with heavy coats but he *must* stay in there until we come up with a viable solution to make this machine work properly."

They all looked at Javan and he nodded without saying a word. His mind was racing, trying to find a solution to the dilemma. The DHS was hot on his heels, Operation Pakal had failed, so being locked up in a freezer was the least of his problems.

"We can outfit him with a communicator so he can hear our conversations," Troy said.

"We can also outfit him in some clean clothes," added Rio.

In matter of minutes, Javan was outfitted with ill-fitting but clean clothes and all the jackets and gloves SSOSA members were able to scrounge up among themselves. As Javan entered the freezer, Erick promised he would go to a store and purchase proper clothing to help him survive the extreme cold.

Troy sat down at the computer terminal and started checking the blueprint. "We had to have miscalculated something somewhere and I'm going to find it."

David and Erick walked around the structures looking for anomalies or anything that could have been connected wrong.

"Don't get too discouraged," Erick reassured Javan. "The machine *almost* worked! That in itself makes me believe in the science now more than ever, but...but something is missing."

"What could it be?" David asked.

There was a brief moment of silence.

"I think I know what it is," Javan finally said, his voice coming out of nearby speakers. "We are missing one vital piece of the puzzle."

"What piece would that be?" Troy asked.

"The machine is missing a working part and we don't have *that* part here with us."

"You are correct," Erick said to Javan as he walked up to one of the pyramids and caressed the cold stone. He turned to look at everyone. "And *that* missing part is down in Guatemala."

Everyone turned to look at Erick.

"Erick is right," Javan intoned over the speaker. "My machine was patterned after the pyramids. The Mayans knew what they were doing. The missing part is down at La Danta! We need to find it to make it work properly."

Slightly more encouraged, Troy pulled up some pictures of La Danta on his laptop computer. "The entire place is covered by vegetation. It has been that way for centuries. Even if we went down there we wouldn't know where or what to look for." He pulled back from the monitor and rubbed his forehead. "This is an exercise in futility."

Everybody became silent as they pondered Troy's words. They considered the immense task at hand. The solution seemed impossible to figure out and time was running out.

Finally, Erick broke the silence. "Troy, I have a suggestion."

"Speak."

"Your father has been in Mexico, near Guatemala, hasn't he?" Erick asked as he ambled toward Troy.

"That was about 16 years ago. I was eight at the time. My father was abducted by drug lords and held hostage there."

Erick waved a hand. "Yes, I know, but...he spent some time with one of our old SSOSA members, did he not?"

"Yes, he was with the late Dr. Rene Sova."

Erick waved an emphatic hand again. "I know, I know...my point is, Rene taught Chauncy how to read the Mayan glyphs, right?"

"I believe so, why?"

"Rene studied the pyramids down there. He was the one that figured out the code to a Mayan treasure, correct?"

Troy nodded. "Yes, he realized that King Chac left a code on some glyphs that were engraved on a temple in Palenque. What's your point, Erick? Dr. Sova is dead."

"Yes, I know, but your father is not dead. Since he spent a long time with Rene, he may be able to offer some answers to this enigma."

"What?" Troy looked at Erick askance. "Are you asking me to go see my father? Are you crazy?"

"Yes, I am. I mean, no I'm not crazy, I'm serious."

Troy shot out of his chair. "No way!"

"Why not?" Rio asked.

No not my dad, there is no way I can go see him Troy thought as he made a fist. He turned away from everyone as he spoke. "You already know why my father and I aren't on speaking terms. He's a control freak. Besides, I'm making my own way in the world. I don't need him. We need to figure out this enigma ourselves!"

"Troy," Erick said in a softer voice. "Your father and Rene knew what was going on down there. He should have something to offer us to understand why the machine won't work. Can't you see?"

"You guys don't understand!" Troy raised his voice. "I…he…it's just too complicated!"

"Troy," Rio approached Troy and placed a hand on his shoulder. "Erick is right. Your father may have something to offer. What other alternatives are there? We are running out of time. Javan can't stay in the freezer forever. We need your help."

Troy turned and looked at her. He gazed into her pleading eyes. He swallowed hard. His father most likely had some information. But going to him would require he humble himself before his father. But here he was, between a rock and a hard place, with no other apparent solution.

Rio continued. "Look how far *you* have brought us. You believed in us Troy. We believe in *you*. Please consider Erick's advice."

"What if he comes up empty-handed?" Troy pointedly asked, still trying to find a way out. "Then we will have wasted precious time."

"That's a risk we are all willing to take," Rio said.

"We have no alternative," Erick reminded Troy.

Troy inhaled deeply. He thought he was finished with his father. He had placed enough emotional and physical distance from his father as possible. And now here he was, being asked to rebuild the bridge he had burned some time ago. This was not going to be easy. Why couldn't they see? Why couldn't they understand his feelings? How could they ask him for such an emotional sacrifice? On the other hand, Operation Pakal was at an utter standstill. Doing nothing would be more disastrous than going to his father with his figurative tail between his legs. He knew they were right. On behalf of Javan, Rio and SSOSA, he would have to swallow his pride. Doing nothing would be worse. Much worse.

Troy glanced at the hopeful expressions on the faces of Rio, Javan, Erick, Ashni and David and exhaled in surrender. "Okay, fine…I'll go see my dad."

"Do you need my help?" Erick asked. "He knows me very well. I can go with you. We can both convince him."

"I can go with you, too," Rio offered with an eager smile.

Troy shook his head. This wasn't going to be easy and he certainly didn't want anyone to witness his submission to his father.

Troy shook his head. "I appreciate your offers but no, I have to deal with this myself."

Chapter Twenty-Four

"All I wanted was to be the one who caught all the bad guys," Rick bemoaned as he and Kenneth were sitting in the DHS basement break room.

They were drinking coffee and chatting. The technicians in the control room were desperately trying to relocate Javan's GPS signals. The spoofing had thrown them off and now they were attempting to re-calibrate Javan's location.

"It started years ago after I was promoted to this position," Rick reminisced as he took a sip of the hot brew. He leaned against the wall and closed his eyes. "I wanted to be the hero for my country. The guy who would crush the terrorists that threatened our way of life. I wanted to defeat the enemies of democracy and freedom." He chuckled at the thought as he opened his eyes and looked at Kenneth. "That sounded so naive, didn't it?"

Kenneth looked back at him. "I don't think so. You had good intentions."

"Good intentions mean nothing to me anymore." Rick slowly shook his head."I guess you can say I'm jaded...I can't get anything done. I'm tangled up in so much bureaucratic tape it has practically handicapped me. I wish I had more authority."

"And then this happens," Kenneth reminded him.

"Yes, and then this happens. Ironically, it's under my watch. It all started when Javan approached me with a unique experiment. He found some strange correlation between antiquated Mayan structures and torsion waves. He said it was like finding an ancient tuning fork and connecting it to our modern machines and amplifying the waves. At first it sounded so crazy...but then he showed me the plans. It was then and there I realized what great potential this technology was for our country. The United States government would benefit greatly from this newfound source."

"Did Javan prove he could replicate the experiment?"

"On paper and computer models only, but he needed financial backing to actually build a working model. That's where the government came in, or shall I say where *I* came in. He convinced me to ask the government for funding to develop and improve the technology. I'm the one who sold the idea to the President of the United States. We sponsored his project yet he stole the money and the technology right out from under our noses. When we finally caught him it was too late, he had deposited the money in a dummy bank account. We never recovered it."

"And that's how he is funding SSOSA."

"Yes, Rio Jordan controls the money. She is the one leading SSOSA by the nose. I can't fathom how such intelligent people can be so stupid. I sent them an email and how did they respond? They spoofed my GPS signal and mocked us with a Hawaiian figurine."

Kenneth nodded while he suppressed a snicker. The image of a Hula dancer came to his mind. "I can see why you're taking this project so personal."

Rick snorted. "More than you know."

"This reminds me of the Philadelphia Experiment conducted in 1943," Kenneth mused.

"That never happened, as far as the public knows, of course. Come to think of it, Operation Pakal *is* similar to the Philadelphia Experiment. Both projects were based on an aspect of Zero Point Field theory, which was discovered by Albert Einstein."

Kenneth stared at his boss. Rick Cannon was a tireless worker. He was going beyond his duties in getting involved with the capture of Javan. Being recently divorced and without any children, Rick now had the time to dedicate his entire energies to hunting down Rio Jordan and the SSOSA members. Yet, in Kenneth's opinion, Rick seemed obsessed with the hunt. It made sense. After Rick's explanation of how it was his pet project and how he had sold the idea to the President, it was no wonder he was doggedly pursuing the terrorists. But it wasn't just the pursuit of the people, it was the machine and the implications involved if used improperly by terrorists bent on destroying the United States.

"We have something!" one of the technicians shouted out.

Rick jumped so quickly from his chair that he spilled his coffee. They both ran into the control room.

"What do you have?" Rick asked.

One of the technicians pointed at the monitor. "We just got a major spike from Javan's nano GPS and another strange anomaly happened at the same time!"

The technician pointed to the screen. "There was a brilliant flash on the screen coming from Javan's location. I've never seen anything like it."

Rick bent down to get a clearer sight of the monitor. "Where is he?"

"That's the problem." The technician looked confused. "I'm...not sure, sir. It was a large flash, an unnatural surge." He pointed at the screen/map. "We know it was somewhere in New York City, however we couldn't pinpoint his exact location. It's as if...as if he became a giant lighthouse...then, bang a few minutes later he disappeared!"

"Can you triangulate the position?" Rick asked.

"We're working on that as we speak, sir."

"So help us God," Rick muttered to Kenneth. "They fired up the machine, Javan wants to blow up New York!"

The two men were glued to the monitors as they watched the technicians.

Ten minutes later they found what they were looking for.

They watched a video display of the GPS tracking system. Rick had the technician replay the abnormal event that had been captured on the computers. He pointed at the monitor. "That's the point where the machine was started. It caused a spike in Javan's GPS signal. Something happened to the machine. It didn't work."

"Show me again," Kenneth said.

Rick had the video replayed and stopped at a specific point. "Right after the big flash, his GPS coordinate was still emitting a signal, then it returned to normal levels. See?"

"But then the signal disappears," Kenneth noted. "Maybe the flash killed him."

"No, it took about five minutes for the signal to vanish *after* the big flash. That means he was still alive. And even if he died, his

155

nano-GPS would still be functioning, it would still be emitting a signal."

"What are your thoughts?"

Rick stood up and paced the floor. He put his hands in his pockets and became pensive. "There are various possibilities. The best one I can think of is that the machine didn't work. Yet somehow they managed to neutralize his signal."

"In other words, something went wrong with the machine," Kenneth added. "So they hid him in a place where his signal could not be traced."

"Bingo!"

One of the technicians placed his phone receiver down and looked at Rick. "Sir, we are getting reports of some anomalies in the area where the flash occurred."

"What do you mean?" Rick furrowed his brow.

"There are reports of objects and people levitating in the target area and power outages. People are freaking out."

"Of course they are!" Rick retorted. He turned to Kenneth. "I need you to go do some damage control ASAP!"

Kenneth dutifully nodded. "Yes sir. I'll tell the media it was a temporary anomaly. I will tell them the government was working on some scientific experiment or whatever."

Rick snapped his fingers. "Make it happen." He turned to look at the computer screen as he made a fist. "Sooner or later Javan will have to reappear in order to make the machine function properly. Then I'll have him."

Chapter Twenty-Five

In New York City there were plenty of dilapidated cars to hot-wire. He drove his newly-stolen car north to the hamlet of Bedford Hills, New York. Nervously, he checked the rear view mirror in case he was being followed. There was no reason to believe the FBI knew he had stolen the ugly car. To any observer he was just another driver in the neighborhood. As long as he didn't stop in front of his parents' house he was incognito in the dark.

He parked two blocks from where his parents lived and snuck through the alleyways. He took cover behind trash cans and bushes. As he glanced down the alley behind his parent's home he determined it was too narrow for agents to be parked in. Good. They were most likely half a block down the street monitoring the front yard. And they were very likely bored out of their minds.

Troy finally reached his destination. He managed to jump over the backyard fence, grateful his parents no longer had the annoying, yapping dog from years ago. He quietly climbed the rear cement stairway that led to the back door of the two story house. He opened the screen door of a back patio enclosure and closed it behind him. He took a deep nervous breath as he knocked on the door.

Through the curtains he could see the hazy figure of his father walking toward the front door. Perhaps Chauncy had thought the knocking was coming from the front.

Over here you big dummy! Troy thought as he knocked a little harder.

Naturally confused, Chauncy slowly walked over to the back door. "Who is it?" he voiced with concern.

"Dad, it's me, open the door!"

"Troy!" Chauncy gasped as he obeyed the order. "My goodness, what on earth....why didn't you use the front--"

157

"Shhhh," Troy hissed as he pushed his way into the house. "Close all the blinds," he ordered his father. "The FBI or DHS is monitoring you half a block down from here."

"Yeah, they accosted me at Walmart!" He quickly went about closing some of the window shades. When he was done he turned to look at his son.

Chauncy was able to see his son's face better. He had a haunted, tired look about him.

"Troy what have you been up to? The DHS says you're in trouble."

"What did the Feds tell you about me?" Troy asked as he sank into a nearby sofa.

"They told me you were involved in some big trouble. They used words like 'national security', 'weapons of mass destruction' and something about terrorists."

Troy looked around the living room with a worried look. "Where's Mom?"

"She's visiting your aunt."

Troy looked askance. "In Wyoming? Without you?"

"Yeah, she's going to be gone for three more weeks. I told her I thought that was too long but she said it's payback for me being gone so long when I was involved in my archaeological digs."

Troy managed to smirk. He remembered the heated discussions of long ago when Chauncy was gone for months at a time. He looked at his father. His once blond hair was graying, his once stocky frame was slightly softer with age, but he still had those piercing blue eyes.

"Dad..." He swallowed hard. He was having a difficult time finding words. "Dad I...I'm here because I need your help."

Chauncy wanted to say something sarcastic about how much time had gone by before Troy had finally communicated with him, but the look in Troy's eyes convinced him to keep quiet and listen.

"Come into the kitchen," Chauncy said.

They both walked into the kitchen. Troy sat down on one of the hand-crafted walnut chairs. Chauncy retrieved two water bottles from the fridge and set them on the dining table.

Troy took a big gulp of water. When he was done he ran his hands over his head and looked at his father. "Dad, I'm sorry for acting like a jerk and treating you badly."

"You did act like a jerk," Chauncy said as he sat at the table.

"I'm...I'm sorry. I just wanted my independence. I wanted to prove I was better than you, plus I wanted to join SSOSA. But you were so determined to stop me. You were jealous because they chose me over you."

"Can you imagine how I felt?"

"Yeah, but it was my time to shine, you have no idea how it feels to live in your shadow!"

"And you have no idea how it feels to be overlooked after all my years of associating with them."

"They saw greatness in *me,* Dad."

They saw greatness in me, too!" Chauncy stood up from his seat and pointed at his chest. "I was the better choice. Are you calling me stupid?"

"No Dad, you *have* the brains," Troy got out of his chair and closed the gap between them. He felt his temper flaring so took a deep breath to calm himself. "Why don't you face the facts Dad? The truth is Mom would never support you being an active SSOSA member. She didn't want you playing the Mind Games and running all over the world, especially after what happened to you in Yucatan. She said she was never going to have you put your life in jeopardy again. I had to lie to her when I was chosen. She has no idea how we run SSOSA today."

"Yes, I guess that's what it boiled down to, didn't it? Your mother didn't want me to join. I supposed I understand her viewpoint, but I don't necessarily agree." Chauncy sat back down on his chair. He looked frustrated.

Troy sat down as well. A few moments of silence passed.

"We let too much time pass before resolving this, Dad," Troy said quietly.

"Too much time, Troy and time waits for no one."

"We should have spoken about this sooner. We should have cleared the air."

"Well, what is done is done. And we're talking right now."

"I'm sorry."

Chauncy raised a hand. "Say no more, Son. To be honest, my father and I had a falling out too when I was a kid. I understand."

"You mean Grandpa Daniel?"

"Yeah," Chauncy nodded. "I didn't talk to him for a long time. Finally when he was a very old man, I returned to his house to apologize, only to find out he had died of cancer. So I never did get to tell him anything."

Troy looked at his dad. "I understand," Troy whispered. "I'm sorry."

Chauncy looked at his son. "Let's talk about something else. How's Sheila?"

Troy shook his head. "We broke up."

Chauncy sighed. "I'm sorry to hear that. Your mother had high hopes you would marry this one."

"Typical of Mom," Troy shrugged. "I'll get over it...just like I did with the others."

"I don't understand girls nowadays. Why would they leave a handsome man like you?"

Troy wanted to change the subject, so he glanced at his wristwatch. "Dad, listen. I came for help. I need you to help me."

Chauncy stared at his son. "Tell me what's bugging you, son. Why is the FBI or the DHS or whatever after you?"

Troy related the entire story to his father. He told him everything from the beginning, starting with the job of the holographic image and how Rio contacted them and how they ran from the DHS and started building Operation Pakal. He explained the science and the details of building the machine and how it failed. Chauncy clung to every word he said. It seemed like the spark of adventure was lit in his eyes.

He leaned back in his chair when Troy was finished with his account. "You SSOSA guys never cease to amaze me! Do you believe Rio and Javan are telling the truth?"

"I do and so does Erick. He seems to know something I don't know."

"Why do you say that?"

160

"Erick is the guiding hand that keeps us pushing forward to the end. Nothing is deterring him from finding out about the machine. He even re-joined the SSOSA group to keep the head count up after Nolan quit."

"Erick is a fanatic about science, but he's *not* an idiot. I'm glad Erick sent you here to me. His intuition will pay off well."

Troy tilted his head to one side. "You mean you can help me?"

Chauncy lowered his voice as if he thought he'd be overheard. "I know a lot more about those pyramids than you think. Do you recall my time with Dr. Sova?"

Troy leaned forward. "Of course I do."

"That genius of a man knew more than any other man alive. There are deep, dark secrets down in Mayan territory that I haven't revealed to the public."

"Do they involve La Danta?"

Chauncy simply nodded.

"What did Dr. Sova know about La Danta? Tell me! I need to know."

"Rene was a reader of Mayan glyphs. He understood the secret code of the Mayas. Not only did he correctly decipher and break the code of the glyphs that were on King Chac's temple steps, but in his travels to La Danta in Guatemala he discovered something else about the glyphs there as well."

"Wait, are you telling me that the answer to how to operate the machine is on a glyph in La Danta?"

"Sort of, yes."

"You're being rather vague, Dad."

There was a glimmer in Chauncy's eyes. "Come upstairs to my office, I will show you."

Troy was so excited he felt like bounding up the stairs and skipping some steps along the way but instead he kept pace with his father. Chauncy's office was just as Troy had remembered it. There was a clutter of books on the shelves and many pictures on the walls of Chauncy's past visits to archaeological digs. Troy walked up to a cluster of pictures where he was seen shaking hands with various dignitaries. One of them caught his attention. It was a younger Chauncy standing next to a Mexican military officer.

"That's Gustavo De Leon, isn't it?"

Chauncy was busy looking through some documents and turned to look at Troy. He smiled. "Yes, that's him. You were only eight years old then."

Troy had a weak smile. He placed his hand on the picture. "Yeah, I remember it well. I remember when your Jet Ski washed up on the beach in Cancun and you weren't on it. Mom was so distressed. I wish I could have gone in the helicopter to rescue you," Troy bemoaned.

"Yes, so do I, but you were just a boy."

Troy looked at the other pictures. "My father, the famous archaeologist," he mumbled. "I've heard that my entire life."

Chauncy patted Troy on the shoulder. "Someday you will make a name for yourself. It just takes time."

"That depends. If you help me with my quest. If I can make this machine work I *will be* the most famous archaeologist ever. More so than you!"

"Don't start that again," Chauncy chuckled. "Come here, Son."

He led Troy to a window niche in the office. There was a small sitting bench near the window, Chauncy pushed aside a stack of magazines and pulled the bench's seat up. With one hand on the seat he fished his other hand around the storage space located under the seat and retrieved a small wooden box.

After putting the seat down Chauncy motioned for Troy to follow him. Placing the old wooden box on his desk he opened it and retrieved a small copper key from inside. "Move Dr. Sova."

Troy lifted an eyebrow. "Excuse me?"

"Move the picture of Dr. Sova away. Better yet, take the picture off of the wall."

Troy immediately understood and did as ordered and removed a picture that had the image of Dr. Sova. A small door had been hidden behind the picture.

Chauncy inserted the key into the tiny keyhole and turned it clockwise. The door popped open. He put his hand inside the safe and pulled out an old weathered manila envelope. He held it up for Troy to see. "This is the unpublished manuscript Dr. Sova wrote. The title is 'The Secret of La Danta'. Let's sit down at my desk."

Troy was filled with excitement and was intrigued by the manuscript. He sat in front of Chauncy's large mahogany desk filled with anticipation.

Chauncy went around the desk and sat down on his comfortable leather chair and placed the envelope on the desk. "You realize, don't you Troy, that what I'm about to tell you is extremely confidential. Well, until now. I gave my word to Dr. Sova that I would never tell a soul about this secret. But Dr. Sova is dead and you...you my son, are in extreme danger, so I'm only doing this for *you*."

Troy was at a loss for words. "I'm...I'm extremely grateful."

Chauncy leaned back in his chair, then started his explanation. "As you know, many years ago, when Dr. Sova and I were on the Yucatan peninsula, he taught me how to read Mayan glyphs. While we were down there we did some forays into Guatemala to study other temples. Dr. Sova was obsessed with La Danta. He loved the fact that La Danta was the largest known pyramid in the world, even larger than Giza in Egypt. It still is. Speaking of Giza, you may recall I did a thesis on Giza and all of its hidden wonders."

Troy nodded his head. "Yes, you called it 'The Missing Capstone'."

Chauncy smiled. "Anyway, while down at La Danta, we discovered a series of interesting Mayan glyphs at the foot of the temple. We spent some time attempting to decipher them to understand what the ancients were trying to tell us. Dr. Sova was astounded by what he found."

Chauncy pulled out a picture from the manila envelope and placed it on the desk. "We found one interesting glyph, see?"

Troy picked up the picture. It was rather faded, but he could clearly see it was a series of Mayan glyphs. "What's interesting about this?"

"Dr. Sova said the word in Maya for door is '*Honah*', that glyph has that distinctive word on it."

Troy furrowed his brow. "Door?"

Chauncy slowly nodded. "You may recall that besides the Indians and the Babylonians, the Mayans also "invented" the zero to use in their elaborate calendars. Think about it. Zero is a very

163

strange number, it's a dichotomy. A separation into two divisions that contradict each other, a yin and a yang, a dual personality, an opposite yet a parallel! All by itself zero is nothing. Get it? *Nothing*! Absolutely nothing. But put the zero next to number one and bang! The number becomes a ten. Add another zero and it becomes one hundred, then a thousand, ten thousand, a million and so on and so forth into infinity. Suddenly, the zero changes from a worthless number to the most powerful number in the universe. Understand?"

"Okay I get it, but what does the number zero have to do with the word 'door'?"

"That same glyph contains a series of numbers on it, the number zero being the most prominent, see?" Chauncy pointed to the glyph. "That shell symbol represents the number zero. But a careful examination of that glyph shows that the engraved numbers are in reality a mathematical algorithm."

Troy grabbed the picture and examined it. To the untrained eye it looked like almost any other Mayan glyph. But upon closer examination he could see what his father was telling him. "What does this algorithm show?"

"It's a mathematical equation, the number zero, as in the Zero Point Field theory."

"Seriously?"

"Yes."

"Okay, I get it. Rio and Erick explained the theory to me. It means that scientists attempted to freeze the atom thinking they would find *nothing*. So they took the temperature down to nothing -to zero- and what did they find? *Something*! Something so grand, they found limitless energy. A field of energy composed of electromagnetic waves that Javan can employ to ride off into the sunset."

Chauncy banged his fist on the desk. "Yes! It's just like the number zero, it can mean nothing yet it can be the most powerful number in the universe. Javan is correct. He figured out that the Mayans had knowledge of a powerful energy."

"That's why he built the machine to resemble the pyramids in Guatemala. But how did the Mayans know this?"

"Think about it. The Mayans became such a powerful civilization that they managed to build a city the size of modern-day Los Angeles. They built the world's largest pyramid, too. What other secrets are hiding in La Danta just waiting to be discovered? Could they contain more knowledge than the pyramids of ancient Egypt?"

"We've been looking in the wrong place!" Troy blurted out. "The answer to the riddle is not outside the temple but inside. The word 'door' means the glyph is a *door* to go *inside* of the pyramid!"

Chauncy nodded. "Yes."

"But why didn't you and Dr. Sova go inside the temple?"

"There were many reasons. One being that the glyph was big and seemed to weigh at least two tons. Second, we were already contracted to do work in Palenque and third, you need funding to do a job like that one. We simply ran out of time and we had no money to continue, we had to go back to Palenque...and sadly, Rene died."

"Can you help us find this glyph again?"

"Me? Oh I don't think so, it's been what...fifteen or sixteen years and the glyph most likely has been covered by overgrowth. It's not easy to approach the temple since the jungle is very thick. And don't forget you will eventually bump into drug smugglers, tomb raiders and dangerous wildlife."

"What will I find if I open the Mayan door?"

Chauncy raised both hands up. "I don't know. You need to present this to the other members and figure it out. I gave you the key to start, you need to finish it."

"No. You're coming with me."

"Me?"

"Yes, you, come on Dad, you can add important details as we uncover the secret of La Danta. You were *there*, you can guide us!"

"But..."

"No buts, Mom is away anyway, she can't stop you. Just leave her a note saying you and I went off to appraise an archaeological item. That's not really lying because that's exactly what we're

165

going to do. Besides, I can tell your life has become boring, hasn't it?"

Chauncy stuttered. "Well…you see…I uh."

"Dad….I *miss* you. Please assist me. This is a great opportunity for us to work *together*. It's the adventure we've never had."

Chauncy sighed, he saw the pleading in Troy's eyes. That was all it took. After all this time living as estranged family members, Troy was asking him to come along.

Chauncy stood up. "Okay, let me pack my things."

"No just bring your passport. We can provide the rest."

Chauncy turned to look at Troy. "Are you serious?"

"We are fully funded," Troy nodded. "And we are not leaving in your car. The stakeout agents will see us."

Chauncy looked confused. "I suppose we are leaving in yours? Where did you park?"

Troy stood up and pointed toward the back door. "We are going to walk into that dark alley a few blocks down. Come on Dad…adventure awaits!"

Troy had texted the crew at the warehouse that he and his father were on their way. The mood of the people in the warehouse significantly improved. Once they arrived, Troy introduced everyone to his father.

Erick hugged Chauncy. "It has been a long time since I last saw you, my friend."

Chauncy pulled away and looked at Erick. "Yes, last time I saw you I was accompanying Rene on a Mind Game in Quito, Ecuador. Man, I sure miss Rene."

"I miss him as well," Erick sadly remarked.

David tapped on Chauncy's shoulder and took him over to the miniature pyramids. "These are the replicas we manufactured."

"Impressive," Chauncy exclaimed as he placed his hands on one of the pyramids. "And you generated energy from these structures?"

"Yes, with Rio's generator we created some awesome power, but unfortunately we weren't able to accomplish our goal."

"What a pity."

166

Ashni approached Chauncy. "Please excuse the interruption, but Javan wants to speak with you and Troy. He says it's important." She then handed them winter jackets and gloves. "You'd better wear these, it's really cold in there."

After dressing in the outerwear, Troy and Chauncy entered the walk-in freezer to meet Javan. This time Javan was dressed like a Himalayan mountain climber.

"Mr. Benson, I'm Chauncy Rollock."

Javan held out a gloved hand. "It's an honor to meet you, please call me Javan. I wish we were meeting under better circumstances...but I suppose this will do."

"No worries."

"I was briefed about the information you gave Troy and I'm very excited about your discovery."

"You mean about the Mayan glyph?"

"Precisely. Tell me more."

Chauncy gave the same detailed information he had given Troy. Javan listened with great interest.

After a few seconds of silence Javan spoke. "I think that's a solid lead. We need to go to Guatemala to find the missing part of my machine."

"Erick was spot on," Troy added. "He's the one who recommended we go down there."

"I hope it's the key you are looking for," Chauncy said.

Javan stared at Chauncy and then at Troy. "I figured out why my machine is malfunctioning and you, Chauncy, provided the missing link to find what I needed."

"Are you serious? What is the missing link?" Chauncy asked.

Javan patted Chauncy on the shoulder and pointed at Troy. "Your son has a presentation to give. Please exit the freezer and take a seat, I will listen from here with my communicator and respond accordingly."

Troy and Chauncy exited the freezer. One of the desks in the main area was cleared and chairs were assembled around it. Since he was the chairman, Troy commenced the meeting. "Okay people. It looks like we may have a breakthrough in the case as to why the machine didn't work. I've been mapping out a plan in my head but

I want some input from all of you to see where I need to modify it. My father was gracious enough to lend us the manuscript Dr. Sova prepared many years ago," Troy pointed at his father. "Listen to my father."

Chancy stood up and gave the same discourse about the glyphs he had given Troy and Javan. He explained everything about Dr. Sova's knowledge of the secret Mayan door.

"This is amazing!" Ashni said. "So the glyph is a door that will let us into the temple, how cool."

David raised his hand. "So, are you saying that the machine can only work *inside* the temple?"

Troy nodded. "That seems to be the consensus. That's why it didn't work here in the warehouse."

"Well, it did work," Erick corrected him. "But rather erratically. There is something *inside* the temple that will make it work properly."

"The machine was acting like a black hole. It started sucking everything toward the four pyramids," Ashni said to Chauncy.

"And to be perfectly honest, for a few moments I thought it really was a weapon of mass destruction," David said.

"That is what the DHS would have you believe," Javan's squeaky voice was heard over the speaker.

"Don't forget I was sucked into the vortex too, David," Rio shot back. "We would all have died there."

"Javan, what could be different inside La Danta than inside this warehouse?" Troy asked, wanting to avoid an argument. "What can happen at the real pyramid that we couldn't replicate here in New York?"

Javan was silent for a moment. "I know why the machine didn't work."

Everyone became silent, ready to listen to Javan.

"It has to do with ions. Apparently when the torsion waves start moving they need to react with positive ions. Otherwise it turns into an atomic vacuum cleaner by sucking in all matter surrounding the machine."

"So why did the model work on the computer but not in reality?" David asked Javan.

"Computer models work on theory. The computer video in the blueprint demonstrated how the machine would operate if all the components had been present. I added the equation of working ions in virtual blueprint, but in the real world I assumed the ions would be present when the machine was energized. But I was wrong."

"So, in essence, what we are saying is that we have to go to the temple, open the glyph door, go inside and find out what component can create ions, then return with the answer and add it to the machine or something like that. Am I understanding you correctly?" David asked.

"That's too complicated and time consuming," Ashni interrupted. "By the time we figure it out, and *if* we figure it out, Javan will be a human Popsicle."

"Too late," Javan replied.

David scratched his chin. "Another idea is that these small pyramids must be taken to La Danta."

Ashni shook her head. "Do you realize what a logistical nightmare that would be? We would have to dismantle the four pyramids and ship them to Guatemala. How in the world are we going to do that?"

"Javan, do you think we need to move all of this machinery to La Danta and set it up inside the temple?" Troy asked.

There was more silence as Javan pondered the idea. "I think the Mayans built the four small pyramids and left them *inside* the main temple, otherwise they wouldn't have left a glyph for future generations to read."

"So all we need to take is the quantum oscillating generator, some cables and David's tools?" Rio asked.

"Yes," Javan answered. "But we still need a power source."

"I wonder what the Mayans used as a power source," Erick mused.

"We have another problem," David commented. "I did some research on the temple and it's enormous! It's about 230 feet high with a massive base covered by the jungle canopy. You can't just walk up to it and knock on the glyph door and hope it opens."

Ashni turned to speak to Chauncy. "Didn't you say you actually saw the glyph? You would know how to get there, right?"

Chauncy cleared his throat. "Well yes, but that was fifteen or sixteen years ago. I couldn't just go in there today and say 'there it is'. As I told Troy, by now it must be covered with vegetation so thick I couldn't identify it even if I tripped over it." He looked around with a sad expression. "I'm sorry."

"Well that kills the mission," Ashni said in a sad tone. "We can't see through jungle canopy, now can we?"

"Maybe we can," Troy snapped his fingers. "I have an idea, why don't we use IKONOS imaging? NASA has the IKONOS satellite camera. It's a special camera that has multi-spectral sensors that allow us to produce high resolution images of earth scenes. Basically speaking, the camera can see through vegetation and produce high quality photos of stone and rock."

"That's nice, Troy, but what are we going to do, ask NASA to hover their satellite over Guatemala for a few hours?" Ashni answered. "That's not going to happen."

"We can hack into their computer system and make it go over Guatemala," Troy said enthusiastically.

"Oh, that's a wonderful idea," David retorted sarcastically. "We have the FBI and the DHS after us, why not include NASA?"

"It's a gamble, but it just might work," Troy said in an optimistic tone.

"I don't think it will work," Ashni piped up.

"Ashni is right," Erick added. "It is too risky and we do not need the attention of another government entity."

Everyone became thoughtful at Erick's somber words. If Erick was against it then it was a done deal.

"However," Erick paused for dramatic effect. "I have another idea and we do not have to use IKONOS."

Everyone turned to look at him.

"We can use LIDAR," Erick said with a grin.

Chauncy's eyes lit up. "Of course! LIDAR technology is better. That's how scientists discovered La Danta!"

"Actually, IKONOS did," Troy answered.

170

"Yes, Troy," Erick acknowledged. "IKONOS did it first, but LIDAR technology perfected the ability to see through vegetation."

"Yes," Rio said. "I believe LIDAR uses a form of pulsed laser to measure the topography."

"Correct, and the machine is only about two feet long," Erick said, again his telltale grin revealing more. "The LIDAR instrument can be attached to the belly of a helicopter or a small aircraft and fly over the desired area to create three dimensional pictures of the pyramid."

"And I suppose you have that technology," Troy said.

"I do. My company in Germany has one in storage," Erick said. "I can have it delivered overseas on my orders ASAP."

A knowing smile came from Chauncy. He recalled that Troy had mentioned that Erick was pushing ahead and overcoming all obstacles.

"Excellent!" Troy stood up and walked over to a white board. "Here are the basics, we can always hammer out the details later." He picked up an erasable marker and started drawing a graph as he spoke.

"We can take the quantum oscillation generator and the wires and ship them to Guatemala." He drew a map of Guatemala. "Rio, Javan, Dad, AART and I will go to Guatemala to receive the container and haul it on a special four-wheel-drive truck to La Danta." He drew a Cessna airplane. "Meanwhile, David will get the LIDAR that Erick will deliver to Guatemala and he will hire a pilot to fly him to take overhead images of La Danta. He'll have to strap the LIDAR on the bottom of the airplane hull. David will then relay the images to those remaining here in New York. While we are in La Danta they, in turn, will tell us the location of the glyph. Because the glyph is too heavy for us to move, we will have AART open it and then we enter the temple. What do you guys think?"

There were a few objections and some pointed questions. After a few tweaks to his plan everyone seemed satisfied it would work.

Chauncy nudged Erick's arm. "That's my boy."

Erick nodded and whispered back. "That is a real SSOSA mind at work. Now you know why I wanted to train him."

"You could have trained us both," Chauncy chided him.

"Your wife would not approve."

"Bah!" Chauncy waved a hand up, but didn't argue with Erick.

Ashni raised her hand again. "As the project manager, I have a question. How in the world will you travel? You can't purchase plane tickets with your real passports because you won't make it past security. Unless you forgot, we're all labeled as terrorists."

Troy turned to look at his father. "Dad, I assume you still have Jake Thrasher's number?"

Chauncy pulled his wallet from his pants pocket. "Of course I do. I've been carrying his number for twelve years ever since you were abducted in Turkey."

Troy briefly related the story to Rio and Javan about the incident in Turkey. Everybody on the SSOSA team was acquainted with the ordeal Troy had gone through as a twelve year old when he was abducted by some evil cultists and how Jake Thrasher had rescued him.

When he was done he addressed his father. "Do you think he's still alive? He must be an old coot."

"Who are you calling an old coot?" Erick protested. "He's about my age."

"Call him and find out, Dad," a smiling Troy said.

Chauncy retrieved the business card out of his wallet and dialed the number using his new phone. "He lives in San Diego, he's probably on the beach sunning himself as we speak."

"In September?" Ashni asked.

"It's warmer in California than New York this time of the year." Chauncy pressed the speaker icon on his phone for all to hear. The number he was calling rang a few times then a gruff voice was heard. "Hello, who's this?"

"Hey Jake, we all had a bet going to see if you were still alive."

"I said who's this?"

"It's Chauncy Rollock."

There was brief silent moment. "Who?"

"You heard me."

"It's been years since I last talked to you, you son–of–a–gun! What are you up to man? Please don't tell me you're in trouble!"

Chauncy chuckled. "No, no. We were just wondering if you're retired."

"Well I am almost eighty years old! I should be, right?"

"Where are you right now?"

"I'm sitting on a beach in La Jolla. It's kind of chilly today."

Chauncy looked up at everyone with an I-told-you-so expression. "Did you ever get that mansion up on the La Jolla bluffs?"

"Nah, I let that dream die years ago. I live at the marina, I own a private yacht. That way I'm not tied down to any real estate. I move as I please."

"Hey Jake, are you looking for any work?"

"That depends. What do you need?"

"No, you tell me, what do *you* need?"

"I need to remodel my yacht."

"I have some work for you then."

"What's up?"

"We need five fake passports and a fake company that wants to ship some goods from New York to Guatemala. No questions asked."

"Guatemala? What are you up to now, Chauncy?"

"More than you want to know, that's why I said no questions."

"Yeah, yeah, yeah."

"But that's okay at least I don't have a gun pointing at my head."

"I heard you say 'we', is one of the passports for Troy?"

"Yes."

"Lovely, you guys can't stay out of trouble, can you?"

"What can I say, it runs in the family."

"So does insanity."

"You want the job or not?"

"Of course I do. Email me passport quality photos of the five people. I will text you the other info I will require later on. Wire me 60K up front. I want all of my money now in case you get yourself killed in the jungle."

"I'm pleased to see you still have the greatest confidence in me."

"Goodbye Chauncy. I need to get back to my solar radiation treatment."

"You're going to get skin cancer."

"I don't mind, you should see the dermatologist I visit, she's real cute."

"Goodbye Jake." Chauncy hung up and looked at the crew and smiled.

Troy jumped up out of his chair and raised both hands in the air. "We're going forward." Even though there were still many obstacles ahead and many things that could thwart his plans, his spirits were soaring again.

Chapter Twenty-Six

Dublin made his F-250 truck come to an abrupt stop in front of the warehouse, making the tires screech.

Gerald gave him an evil glare. "What's the matter with you, you idiot? Are you trying to spook the people in the building?"

"Sorry boss," Dublin grimaced.

"Get the crowbar and let's go," Gerald growled.

Nolan, who was sitting in the back seat, glanced at his wristwatch. "They should be making dinner right now."

"I wonder if their little jail bird has arrived yet," Gerald remarked.

Nolan pursed his lips. "We don't know if he made it or not. The news has been silent...but we are about to find out, I hope he's in there."

Gerald pulled a handgun out of its shoulder holster. "You're not getting a gun, you stay behind me and Dublin."

"You're not going to kill anybody are you?" Nolan asked. His conscience was flaring up again.

"No of course not, this is just to scare them," Gerald lied. "Where did you say the flash drive is located?"

"Rio keeps it on as a necklace."

Gerald opened the truck door. "Excellent, let's get this over with."

Dublin approached one of the small entry doors and wedged the crowbar between the door and the casing. His muscles bulged as he pried with all his might, then there was a loud cracking sound as the metal door gave way to the pressure. Dublin dropped the crow bar, grabbed his handgun and opened the door. Dublin and Gerald led the way with Nolan trailing behind.

Nolan became apprehensive. The chance of somebody getting killed was high if Gerald encountered any real resistance. Knowing the SOSSA members as he did, they weren't going to go down without a fight.

Nolan was so lost in thought that he hadn't noticed that Dublin and Gerald had come to an abrupt stop once inside the warehouse. This made him bump into them.

"What's up?" Nolan asked as he quickly backed up.

He didn't need an answer.

When he went around the two men he saw that the warehouse was empty of people.

Nolan was in complete shock. He walked up to the area that had once been the center of operations. The only thing left were the four large pyramids in the middle of the large floor and the hanging throne. All of the equipment was gone. All of it.

"What the...where did they go?" Nolan gasped in bewilderment.

Gerald pursed his lips. "That's a good question kid. I was hoping you would have an answer."

"I...don't understand," an astonished Nolan said as he turned to the former workstation that had held his computer. With the exception of the four pyramids nothing was left but strewn garbage on the floor and empty tables. It looked like there had been a hasty exit.

Gerald approached the four pyramids and touched each one as he spoke. "So this is the replica? Apparently they left in a hurry and didn't have time to dismantle it."

Nolan was still trying to grasp the reason the warehouse was abandoned. He turned to gaze upon the pyramids. "It looks like they fired up the machine... but something must have gone wrong," he said almost to himself.

"How do you know that?" Gerald asked.

"We were supposed to dismantle the pyramids after the operation was over. We weren't going to leave any trace of Operation Pakal behind, nothing...but...it looks like they left in a hurry. This isn't like SSOSA." A thought came to him. "Of course, it was that anomaly that the news was shouting about! It was in this area where there were reports of objects levitating and then..."

"That explains everything," Gerald interrupted him. "Something misfired...but what happened?" He looked at Nolan. "You better

176

come up with an answer. I'm losing my confidence in you really fast."

Frustrated and anxious, Nolan brushed a hand over his straggly hair. "We need to go back to your home. I can use my computer and gain access to their computers to see what they were researching."

Gerald turned to look at Nolan. "If you SSOSA guys are as smart as you say you are, do you really think they would leave an electronic trail for you to follow?"

"Oh, I know they'd try to block it. But I left a special backdoor app on my computer before I left SSOSA. Trust me, I can find out what happened."

He furrowed his brow at Nolan. "This is getting really old. I'm tired of pointing my gun at you. I want answers not promises, boy, and so far all we have is an empty warehouse and empty promises."

Nolan spread his hands out. "Then take me back to your place so we can find out!"

Gerald motioned for Dublin to follow him to the vehicle.

Chapter Twenty-Seven

"They're going to Guatemala," Rick said confidently. He threw a document on Kenneth's lap.

Kenneth looked surprised as he picked up the paperwork. "Are you sure?"

Rick nodded as he looked out of his office window. The Washington traffic was thick this morning. "Oh yes I am, look at the picture. What does it say?"

"It says *The Secret of La Danta, Author Dr. Rene Sova*. Where did you get this?"

"An operative got it from Chauncy Rollock's office last night."

Kenneth looked surprised. "What? Did Chauncy put up a fight?"

Rick chuckled. "No, we had small cameras in the alleyway. He and Troy escaped thinking we weren't monitoring them."

Kenneth's shock left him momentarily speechless. He had just heard Rick say they knew where Troy was and yet he allowed him to slip away. It was an incredibly lost opportunity.

Rick continued talking as he pointed to the document. "That's the front cover of a manuscript that Chauncy had in his office. Chauncy took the rest of the manuscript with him, but in his haste he dropped the first page. But that's enough to convince me the reason Troy was visiting his father was for assistance. My investigations show that Chauncy Rollock spent some time in Palenque with Dr. Sova. The two deciphered some Mayan glyph about sixteen years ago. Think about it, why else would Troy seek his father's help?"

"To see how they can make the machine work?"

"I do recall Javan telling me the machine is patterned after the ones in El Mirador, especially La Danta," Rick said while turning around.

"What do you think they will find?"

"I don't know. But whatever it is, I'm betting they're going down there to find the answer."

"With all due respect, sir, you could have had Chauncy and Troy detained last night. What seems to be the problem? Why did you let them escape?"

Rick got closer to Kenneth. He had an extremely serious expression as his breathing became labored. "Listen to me, getting the machine in *my* hands is of the utmost importance. Arresting all of those characters really doesn't amount to a hill of beans to me. I *must* have that machine. I must be able to have control of it. Javan stole the blueprint from me! The national interests of our country are way more important than putting people in prison. Do you understand? We have to have a working machine. They will lead us to it."

"Yes, sir, just tell me what I need to do."

Rick straightened up. He wiped some perspiration from his forehead. "Keep following them. Let me know when they leave the country. Meanwhile, I'm going to have a serious talk with the President."

Kenneth was secretly wondering if the stress of recent events was taking a toll on Rick. His concern for the mental health of his boss was rising each day.

Chapter Twenty-Eight

When Alexander Rodriguez was inaugurated as the President of the United States, most of his thick hair had been a rich dark brown. Now that he was two years into his second term, the stress of the Office was not only noticeable in his prematurely graying hair but the lines on his face were deeper.

It wasn't easy being the first US President with Hispanic heritage. Winning two terms came with a price. The Hispanic vote from his constituents was easily won in the first term, it had been a landslide victory. He had a winsome way of speaking in both English and Spanish. When he spoke to the people, they felt at peace after hearing his engaging words.

But the cracks in his administration were starting to show. His detractors blamed him for being soft on illegal immigration due to his heritage. The Mexican border was porous as ever. He was popular in Latin America but was seen as weak in other countries. Russia and China were aggressively taking over their neighboring countries making America seem ineffective.

The war on terror in the Middle East was still raging with no end in sight. And now there was this recent news event of escaped domestic terrorists running around somewhere in New York.

"Mr. President?" the attendant said in a soft voice.

President Rodriguez was sitting at his desk at the Oval Office. He looked up from a letter he was reading. "Yes?"

"The Executive Secretary of Homeland Security, Rick Cannon, is here to see you."

The President placed both hands on the desk. "Show him in. We will need a few moments alone."

"Yes, Mr. President."

The door softly closed behind Rick as he entered the office. He was dressed in a fine three-piece suit. "Good afternoon Mr. President."

He waved a hand and pointed to a nearby chair. "Have a seat."

"Yes sir," Rick complied.

The President leaned back in his nice leather chair as he stared at Rick, there was a troubled expression on his face. "It's been a difficult week, Mr. Cannon. We have two terrorists on the loose and people are scared. New York is still reeling from the strange phenomenon that started levitating things and spooking the entire nation. We are running out of excuses and have no answers."

Rick held both hands up. "Operation Pakal has been severely compromised, Mr. President."

"So I heard," he answered in a semi-sarcastic tone. "What happened? *You* were in charge."

"I understand, but mistakes were made, but not by me."

"Yet I hear the DHS operatives had more than one opportunity to capture the fugitives. Rumor has it *you* ordered them not to be arrested."

Rick gritted his teeth. He hated information leaks, yet they were impossible to prevent. He secretly wondered if Kenneth was leaking the information or dozens of others who worked around him. "It was a purely tactical maneuver, sir."

"Really? So, you did it at the expense of the security of the people of the United States?"

"Short term yes, but long term no."

"Please explain yourself."

"The good news is that the machine has been activated, sir."

"I'm aware of that." The President raised an eyebrow. "Did Doctor Benson make it work?"

"He did. But thankfully it failed."

"How do you know?"

"Because New York City is alive and well."

"Don't joke with me."

"That's why I have refrained from storming in and arresting everybody. It would be a failure on our part to arrest Javan and his cohorts and capture a non-working mechanism. Once the machine is in full operating order, then we make our arrests. Then all the things we spoke about in the past will be a reality."

"Do you really think it can do what he said it would do?"

"Oh yes," Rick nodded. "The incident in New York City was a small-scale example. Javan made it work for a few seconds before it failed."

"I'm sure you learned from this experience. Tell me more."

"There were some strange electromagnetic disturbances in the area where the machine was activated. You heard about the reports of objects levitating in the New York area. The Internet was blacked out and some cars wouldn't start. You are correct, people were spooked, but since it only lasted fifteen seconds we ordered the media to squelch the reports."

"Now I understand Dr. Benson is gone."

"We lost track of his GPS location because the disturbance was so intense it messed up our tracking devices. All of this happened in a span of fifteen seconds. Imagine what we can do if we had *unlimited* time with the machine?"

The President seemed more interested. "Imagine it for me."

"If properly controlled, we can make enemy airplanes fall out of the sky. We can destroy their means of electronic communication. The Zero Point Energy can boil the seas where enemy ships are floating. Javan once described it as an ancient tuning fork that can vibrate to disturb molecular wave patterns. It's the kind of power that can bring enemy nations to their knees Mr. President. Just think about the power *you* will have in your hands! You will go down in history as being the first president to harness this awesome power!"

President Rodriguez pondered Rick's words for a few seconds before he spoke. "You do realize don't you that Operation Pakal is a hard sell."

"I'm sorry sir, I don't understand."

"You are asking me to convince my generals that merging some ancient Mayan technology with modern science can create a powerful weapon."

"What if we wrap it in a stainless steel package, will that convince them?"

"I told you to stop joking with me."

Rick leaned back in his chair and raised his hands. "I'm sorry, sir, but I am telling you the truth. This machine can work."

"Yet, you tell me that the machine failed. Why?"

"Javan just escaped from prison. I'm thinking he must be suffering from the stress of isolation, but once he gets his bearings he will figure out how to operate it."

"What does Javan think he's going to do with the machine?"

"He wants *complete* control of the power. He doesn't care about the interests of the United States government, he never did. All he wanted was for us to fund Operation Pakal, and after we did, he ran off with the technology to use it for himself. If he does get full control of the machine....then imagine the destruction that he can cause."

"What's his next move?"

"He's headed with his motley crew of associates to Guatemala, apparently they hit a few learning curves in New York and now they most likely will find a way to make it work down there. I came to ask for help, Mr. President."

"Hmmm...what is your proposal?"

Rick leaned forward. "We can't just waltz into Guatemala and grab the machine. I'd like you to authorize a Spec Op down there."

"Be more specific."

"I need operatives to assist me in a covert operation in Guatemala to track down Javan, Rio and their associates. If we need to use lethal force, so be it. Then we secure the working machine and bring it back to the States."

"It seems too messy."

"Spec Ops rarely fail."

"The key word is *rarely*."

"We're talking about a backwater country like Guatemala Mr. President, not some advanced country like China or Russia. Plus, most of the action will take place in the jungle, away from a lot of prying eyes. The point is we *need* to get our hands on that machine."

"No, we can't just march down there, there must be a better plan and I think I have one." The President stood up from his chair and paced the Oval Office. "You don't know this but the President of Guatemala has been requesting technological assistance in the fight against illegal drugs."

Rick chortled. "Since when has the President of Guatemala been concerned about fighting drugs? That's how he makes his millions."

"Let me put it another way, he wants to *make a show* of fighting drugs, so he wants to parade our stuff in front of the public to look good."

"That makes sense."

President Rodriguez continued. "I was thinking of offering him a chance to see the new Arawak fliers."

Rick smiled with understanding. "Ah, what a brilliant idea Mr. President, that way we can use the Arawaks in the jungle. There will be no need for clandestine maneuvers, all we do is embed our Spec Ops in the military group that is presenting the aircraft. They make a pretense of flying into the jungle to test the machines but in reality they are hunting down Javan and company."

"Yes, you are correct. That way I have a cover story in case something goes wrong. You realize don't you, what you are asking is fraught with many negative scenarios. However…doing nothing can open us up to a more dangerous situation if Doctor Benson actually makes the machine work."

"Exactly."

The President pinched the bridge of his nose to relieve some tension. Then he walked over to the large window and spoke as he looked out. "If I authorize this mission and you fail, I will be as responsible as you."

"I understand sir."

"I don't think you understand. If you fail, I will distance myself from you. Do you understand now? It will be your head that's going to roll, not mine."

Rick stood from his chair and shook the President's hand. "Thank you Mr. President. I will not fail."

Chapter Twenty-Nine

"Okay this is really strange," Nolan huffed as he read the information on his laptop computer while sitting in Gerald's office.

Gerald looked up. "What have you found?" He was watching Nolan closely to make sure he wouldn't do something stupid.

Nolan kept a steady gaze at the monitor as he spoke. "They were doing research on Guatemala."

"Be more specific," Gerald grunted.

"They were researching information about La Danta."

"La Danta?" Gerald stood up from his chair. His eyes lit up. "That's interesting. I was there a year ago. We stole some glyph fragments from a dig site. Three years ago some archaeologists found a series of glyphs on the foot of that pyramid that just might explain the entire history of the Mayans. That stolen fragment alone fetched me three hundred thousand dollars on the black market!"

"Well that's what they were looking at."

"What else did you find?"

Nolan kept typing. "They were looking at airfare prices for Guatemala."

"For once you were right," Gerald scratched his chin. "Apparently something went wrong here in New York. So now they're going down there to either get something or do more research."

Nolan leaned back in his chair and stared at the ceiling. "Javan got his ideas from Mayan pyramids. The machine didn't work because there *had* to be something missing." He looked at Gerald. "And that *something* is definitely down there in Guatemala. Whatever it is, they quickly abandoned everything to pursue the clue. And that's where *we* have to go.

"If that's the case, I'm reducing your pay."

Nolan squirmed in his chair. "That wasn't our agreement!"

"Our agreement was that we would find them here in New York."

"Yeah but it's not my fault they left...."

"This is going to take longer than I expected," Gerald interrupted him. "It's going to cost me more money to hunt them down in Guatemala."

"Come on, give me a break."

Gerald approached Nolan, his nostrils flaring with anger. He had had enough of Nolan's condescending attitude. He grabbed him by his shirt collar, pulled him out of his chair and slammed him against a wall. "You got a break when I didn't shoot you on the spot. I'm the one footing the bill to travel down there. I'm gonna have to rent a Jeep and purchase guns on the black market down there because I can't transport arms from here. And I'm doing all of this with absolutely zero chance of success. Do you understand what I'm saying? And you're asking *me* for a break?"

Nolan twisted away from Gerald. "Fine. I get it."

"I'm leaving Dublin here but you're coming with me to Guatemala, the more people that come on a mission the more liability I incur and I'm not in the liability business." Gerald released Nolan and walked away. "On top of that, I have to get a fake passport for you because they don't let terrorists fly, just in case you were wondering."

Nolan didn't answer, he simply rubbed his neck.

Chapter Thirty

The Wind Slicer filled the air with noise as it hovered above a clandestine military camp at White Sands, New Mexico. A banner fluttered in the breeze as the aircraft gently landed on the ground. The letters on the banner read USSOCOM which represented the United States Special Operations Command.

Once the aircraft landed, the canopy of the cockpit clicked open and a solitary pilot jumped out.

The Special Forces soldier snapped to attention and saluted him. "Good afternoon, Colonel Bonner."

Colonel Theodore Bonner returned the salute and removed the unlit cigar from his mouth. "At ease."

"That's a nice looking aircraft!"

"It's a state of the art flying machine, soldier."

"No doubt about that, sir."

"Mine's a two-seater. It has a larger fuel tank and it can carry another operative, unlike the smaller one-seaters."

"I'm sorry to hear about the incident at Vandorph, sir."

Bonner adjusted his aviator sunglasses and snorted. "Yeah, well, it is what it is. I'm facing a jury review in two weeks to discuss the incident."

"I'm sorry to hear that too, sir."

"I've been released from duty at the prison because the commander ordered me to bring the Wind Slicer here to this camp. After this, my future service to the greatest nation on earth is in jeopardy and in the hands of judges who don't know the difference between their...." Bonner interrupted himself when he saw other Arawak Slicers being released from their transport compartments. "What's going on here?"

"We were ordered to bring *all* the Arawaks here, sir."

189

"*All* of them! Why?" Bonner furrowed his brow.

"We have a special detachment, sir."

Bonner furrowed his brow. "Just exactly where are these birds going?"

"I don't know, sir, it's classified. We will be briefed tonight. We will start packing the Wind Slicers into those containers over there."

Bonner shook his head. "Well, my job is done."

"Actually sir, I have orders to direct you to Building C. Somebody wants to talk to you."

Bonner stopped in his tracks, more confused than ever. "Who wants to see me?"

"A representative from Washington sir, he has an important message to deliver," the Special Forces soldier said as he guided him to a portable camouflaged building.

After the operative watched Bonner enter, he took his leave. The room was a little dark and his eyes had a hard time adjusting.

Bonner saw Rick Cannon starting to stand up from his chair.

Bonner made a fist. "What's all this about? Is this some kind of a joke?"

"It's not a joke," Rick said as he stood and faced the colonel.

"What are you doing here at White Sands?" Bonner bellowed.

"I will get to the point. I know where Javan Benson is."

Bonner stepped forward. "Where is he? I want to get my hands on him!"

Rick made a hand gesture for him to stop. "Hold on. He's not here. Your jailbird has landed in Guatemala."

"Guatemala?" Bonner furrowed his brow. "What's he doing down there?"

"He's in the jungle near a pyramid. He's going to activate a weapon."

"So you've come to blame me again?" Bonner yelled.

"On the contrary," Rick replied, raising a hand to calm him. "I came to help you. I came to vindicate you. If you assist me in Guatemala I will see to it that you get exonerated from the fiasco in Vandorph. I have the power to do that."

"Oh, is that so?"

190

"I have the influence."

"What are you talking about?"

"I'm going to Guatemala with the operatives and we're taking the Wind Slicers with us."

Bonner tried to shake his confusion. "Since when does the Executive Secretary of the DHS accompany a Spec Op force on a clandestine mission? And who gave you authority to take the Wind Slicers? You have a lot of explaining to do."

"You may recall Javan was placed in Vandorph for stealing the blueprint to a secret weapon that belonged to the US. He's down in Guatemala trying to activate the weapon."

"Why would he want to go there?"

"It's hard to explain. Let's just say it's a convenient place to do it. We worked together on this weapon, therefore, I feel a personal responsibility to get the weapon back."

"Well it's my responsibility to get my prisoner. I'm going with you to get him whether you like it or not."

"Yes you are," Rick smoothly replied. "And you can also get the people who assisted him in escaping. They will be down there with him."

Bonner chewed on his cold cigar as he pondered the information. "Why did you bring the Wind Slicers here?"

"With the permission of President Rodriguez, I made an appointment with the President of Guatemala. I am going down with the pretense of showing him the Wind Slicers. The story we told him was that we would like to sell him the aircraft to assist in fighting the war on drugs."

"Is that so?"

"Yes. The planes are highly mobile and can work really well in the jungle. So we're going to give him a free demo. The Wind Slicers will be shipped to a base in Guatemala City tonight. After the ceremony I will climb aboard the double seated aircraft that you will be flying along with the others to Javan's hiding place. The pilots of the Wind Slicers will be highly trained Spec Op forces. The Guatemalan government will think we're testing them in their country to see how they perform."

Bonner paced the room. He stared at Rick. "If I go with you, then we'll both get what we want, won't we?"

Rick held out his hand. "I will see you in Guatemala City, Colonel."

Bonner refused to shake his hand, instead he swiveled on his heel and walked away.

Chapter Thirty-One

It didn't take Ashni long to find a suitable place. She located a smaller building on the outskirts of New York City that had office space for rent. It was a fifteen by fifteen room where all the computer equipment fit rather nicely. She chose a suite that was adjacent to vacant offices for the sake of privacy. All the tenants had to share the same break room and restrooms so it was inevitable that they would eventually rub shoulders with other tenants. When questions arose about the nature of their business their rehearsed answer was that they were running a start-up staffing company. Even though that seemed to satisfy curiosity, they made it a point to avoid the break room as much as possible. Thanks to Rick Cannon, the news was already saturated with information about the prison escape and the people assisting Javan so the last thing they wanted was to draw attention to themselves.

David was already in Guatemala having caught an earlier flight but Troy, Chauncy, Rio and Javan also flew out of the same airport. To keep from being noticed by the FBI or DHS, they had traveled separately from New York to Guatemala City, where they had met up and chartered a plane to the airport in Lake Petén. Thanks to the work of Jake Thrasher, their disguised faces matched their fake passports, so they had no problem passing through customs.

A lifted, black, four wheel drive Ford F-350 with a special cargo box in the bed and an enclosed trailer had been shipped to the Mundo Maya International Airport. Troy received it and once everything was ready he and the others traveled via Highway 14. It was going to be an hour and a half journey to Carmelita, the most northern outpost of the Guatemalan Mayan biosphere.

Troy was driving with his father riding as the front passenger. Rio and Javan were in the back seat.

"So far so good," Troy spoke with enthusiasm.

"Don't get too excited," Javan warned. "I am still emitting a GPS signal."

"Yeah but we may have thrown them off with the two spoofs we created in New York," Troy answered.

Javan shook his head. "Momentarily perhaps, but most likely a spoof would work only once. Reminds me of the old saying, 'fool me once, shame on you, fool me twice, shame on me'. They most likely picked up my signal at JFK."

"That's true," Troy said. "But your signal isn't super strong, once we became airborne they might have lost it."

Javan was feeling nervous so he drew a deep breath then slowly released it. He looked out the window but hardly took note of the thick forested jungle they were passing. "I wouldn't underestimate Rick if I were you, Troy. I have a funny feeling that he knows where we're headed. He wants to get his hands on a working machine."

Rio patted Javan's hand. "It's okay, Javan, Troy is right, let's try to stay positive. Consider all you've been through to get to this point. You escaped a maximum security prison, made your way to the airport in New York and now you're in Guatemala heading to La Danta."

"Even if he does know where we're going, we have a lead on him. We can still get to La Danta and do what we have to do," Troy reassured him.

Javan finally grinned. "True, thanks for the pep talk. After all that time I spent in prison, then in a freezer, I guess I should consider this an upgrade and not worry so much."

Rio glanced up at the rear view mirror and caught Troy looking at her, she smiled. He smiled back then returned his attention to driving. Then suddenly his ex-girlfriend came to mind. He wondered why he was feeling guilty. Sheila had left him, not the other way around. Maybe it was time to move on. If so, was Rio the one? He mentally shook his head. No. This was business. It wasn't right to get romantically involved with a client. Yet Rio was different. He remembered back at the warehouse how she had shown him compassion when he'd been upset. That was a quality his ex-girlfriend never showed. At the same time he had a strange feeling that Rio liked *him*. Was it his imagination or was he really picking up on the vibes? But this wasn't the time to explore any potential possibilities because there was a job to complete.

Troy motioned to his father. "Hey Dad, we need to communicate with the guys in New York and tell them we arrived safely. There's a hat in the glove compartment, will you please pass it to me?"

Chauncy did as requested. He removed a thick, black baseball cap and took a moment to inspect it. On the right side of the hat was a small cylindrical object pointing forward.

"Is this a camera?" Chauncy asked.

"Yes, it has a satellite hook-up device that sends a live video feed. It also has a small microphone embedded on the side so we can communicate with SSOSA in New York."

"You seem to have covered all bases. Oh wait, what about David?" Chauncy asked. "Can we communicate with him?"

"No, he has to relay a message to New York and then New York relays it to us once we're in communication with New York. This works more like a satellite phone connection than a three-way communicator."

"Ah, I see." Chauncy handed the cap to Troy who took it and put it on his head. He then pushed a small button to turn on the camera.

Back in the New York office, Erick was monitoring the computer terminal awaiting a call from either David or Troy. With only a one hour time difference between New York and Guatemala they didn't have to worry about losing sleep.

An audible beep was heard and Erick came to life. "We have something from Troy!"

Ashni rushed over to the computer terminals.

"Hello Troy," Erick answered. "Can you hear me?"

Troy's voice came through the speakers. "Loud and clear, we are headed toward Carmelita.

"Excellent."

195

"Have you heard from David?" Troy asked.

"Not yet. But we should soon."

"Hey Troy, turn your video button on. We can hear you but do not have a visual," Ashni said.

"Oh, sorry." Troy did as ordered and the computer screen filled with the view through the windshield.

"So that's what the Guatemalan jungle looks like," Ashni muttered.

"It's going to get thicker once we leave Carmelita," Chauncy explained. "I've been here before."

"Okay, I'm going to save some battery power on my hat," Troy said. "We will get in touch soon and let you know when we leave Carmelita."

"How's AART?" Ashni asked.

"He's just fine, he's sleeping in the trailer."

"You better take care of him, he's David's baby."

"Yeah, I know. See ya later, Troy out."

The screen went blank and Erick leaned back in his chair, a sad expression on his face. "Operation Pakal is in full force. I wish I were there to see the machine work."

"I'm sorry you couldn't go," Ashni said with a sorrowful tone. "It's not your fault, you got old."

"Yes it is," he quipped, "I took care of myself all these years, which is why I made it to this age."

"Oh, you know what I mean," Ashni giggled.

Erick rubbed one of his knees. "My arthritis would kill me if I went trekking into the jungle."

Ashni tried to sound upbeat. "I'm sure Troy will get some good video."

"He will."

So far we've had no opposition," Ashni mentioned.

Erick hesitated before responding. "So far."

*   *   *

Rick, Kenneth and entourage had flown from Guatemala City and then went north to Lake Petén where Mundo Maya

196

International Airport was located. After conferring with Javier Espinosa, the president of Guatemala, Rick had advised him for this specific demonstration he wanted to keep a low profile. The United States government wanted to fly the Arawak Wind Slicers for two days in the jungle without Guatemalan officials along to see if they were fit for the job. If they weren't up to snuff then they would spare Mr. Espinosa any embarrassment if he had accepted the aircraft prematurely.

President Espinosa agreed, so he discouraged the media from following Rick and his associates and he granted permission for them to go up north. Even though it wasn't a big secret that numerous North American cargo planes were on the tarmac in Petén, the locals took it in stride.

Rick privately mentioned to the Spec Op soldiers that this was probably the first time in US history that a covert mission was being undertaken in broad daylight and in plain view. Everyone had a good laugh. Rick's jet, still sitting on the tarmac, was outfitted like his operations room in Washington, only it was much more cramped. Each of his two technicians was in front of a computer, one of them had locked onto Javan's GPS signal and he was monitoring his location.

"What's Javan's status?" Rick asked the technician as he tried to squeeze in the aisle to see him working on the computer.

"We've locked onto his signal, he's headed for Carmelita."

Rick nodded. "Good. We've got him!"

Kenneth opened the cabin door and approached Rick. He was holding some documents in his hands. "I have something for you, sir."

Rick motioned for him to move forward near the cockpit. "I miss my office!" he groaned.

They both sat in the front row seats.

Kenneth handed him the documents. "I had to grease a lot of hands to get this information."

"What is it?"

"I bribed one of the airport workers to let me see the bill of ladings of the most recent shipping parcels and containers. I found this! It's the document for the Ford F-350 delivery and the contents of a box that has a robotic insect and a strange machine that the shipper declared as a generator."

"Isn't that the truck Javan is in?"

"Yes, but I also have this."

Rick grabbed the document and read it. "One LIDAR camera and it's from Future Engineering Technology in Germany," he turned and smiled at Kenneth. "That's Erick Hausen's company."

"Yes it is."

"Excellent! The pieces of the puzzle are starting to fit together. But I wonder why they need something like that?" Rick turned his head around to address his technicians. "Hey you guys, any idea what a LIDAR camera does?"

"LIDAR is an acronym for *light detection and ranging*. It's like a laser scanner that reads the topography below for taking high definition terrain pictures."

"Be more specific."

"It can see through vegetation and only take pictures of the actual ground below."

"Thank you." He returned his attention to Kenneth and lowered his voice. "Kenneth, I need you to get to Washington before we take off."

Kenneth's eyebrows rose. "What? Are sure?"

"Yes, I can handle it from here." Rick stood up, his body language said it all, there was no arguing. "The fewer people I have hanging around here the better. The operatives will help me finish the mission. Thank you for your assistance. I will be back in Washington soon."

Kenneth knew better than to argue with his boss. He stood and shook Rick's hand. "Very well, sir. See you in Washington. I wish you success."

Rick gave him a smile and patted him on the shoulder. "Don't worry, I'll get the bad guys. It's my job."

Chapter Thirty-Two

The crew in the black truck finally arrived at Carmelita. It was a small town, population under four hundred. Most of the buildings were one-story wooden shacks with corrugated iron or palm thatched roofs. Those who were better off financially had houses built of adobe with plaster-coated overlay and painted bright green or blue.

Most of the indigenous people made a living in the thriving tourist industry. Carmelita was the closest town to La Danta and after the discovery of certain Mayan glyphs at the foot of the temple had made international news, business was good in the small town.

In the middle of the town was a large clearing that served as a grungy soccer field or a makeshift airstrip. It was in the middle of this crushed rock strip where the black Ford came to a stop. The locals came out to greet the newcomers. Children laughed and touched the large tires. The teenagers admired the truck's design. The four people climbed down from the high profile truck, dressed in safari-like clothes and sturdy hiking boots.

Chauncy took in the scene. "Wow, this place brings back a lot of memories. Things haven't changed much since I was here."

Troy looked at his watch. "We should probably get going."

Chauncy nodded. "From here on the roads will be dirt or mud if it rains. Dr. Sova and I rented a Jeep and we had a tough time getting in."

"It's a good thing we brought tents," Javan remarked.

Chauncy agreed. "It won't be easy. We had some hardships in the jungle. This is one of the most ecologically diverse regions in the world and dangerous, too. It's home to a variety of mammals, reptiles and birds, including jaguar, puma, howler monkeys, the giant anteater, the deadly fer-de-lance snake, oh and the stinging ants, watch out for the stinging ants! On top of that, we may even run into tomb raiders. Drug lords also like to use this route into Mexico."

Rio became apprehensive. She was a scientist, not a jungle trekker.

Troy noted her nervousness and stood beside her. "Don't worry. I got your back."

She looked at him and smiled. "I appreciate that."

A few of the local men came up and interrupted their conversation.

One of them, a thirty-something man who spoke English, took the lead.

"*Hola amigos*. My name is Samuel. I will be your tour guide."

Troy was expecting this. He pulled out some forged documents and waved them in the air. "I'm sorry, Samuel, but we are going in alone. We have permission from the Guatemalan government."

Samuel waved a hand in disdain. "We do not care what documents you have. You need a guide into the jungle."

"We're on a private tour. My father will be leading the tour. He has been here before."

Samuel angrily waved a finger. "You cannot enter the jungle without a proper guide!"

"But I have these legal papers that give us permission." Troy said in a louder voice.

"This is a protected area we cannot allow just anybody to enter the biosphere."

Realizing things were rapidly degenerating, Chauncy took Samuel to the side and spoke to him in Spanish. He pulled something from his pocket and talked to him and the other men for a couple of minutes. When he was done the men had smiles and took their leave.

"What on earth did you tell him?" an astonished Troy asked.

Chauncy had a large grin. "My documents speak louder than yours Troy."

Troy was truly perplexed. "What documents?"

Chauncy crossed his arms. "I showed them some little green papers. It's amazing how motivational American greenbacks can be."

"But…Dad, you didn't have to…."

Chauncy patted Troy on the back. "Sometimes, a simple brain can be just as effective as a SSOSA brain. Let's go, we're burning daylight."

Chapter Thirty-Three

Bonner was standing on the tarmac at Mundo Maya airport watching while the Wind Slicers were being fueled. He slowly walked up to the two Special Forces operatives who were in the process of finishing. Due to the engine noise they didn't hear him approach.

"The turboprop that left an hour ago was transporting one of the guys who assisted in getting Javan Benson out of prison," one said to his companion. "He's got a lot of guts, his photo has been all over the news."

"Yeah, I heard he has a special camera mounted on the plane," the other one noted. "He's headed to La Danta to take some pictures of the pyramid."

Cursing up a storm, Bonner pushed the two astonished men out of his way as he climbed into the Wind Slicer. "I swear that jackass Rick is going to pay for his incompetence!"

The two operatives tried to prevent Bonner from starting the machine. The wind blast from the fans on the Wind Slicer caused them to stagger backward.

Bonner typed in the coordinates for La Danta and the aircraft quickly became airborne.

*   *   *

The Embraer EMB 110 general purpose 20 passenger turbo-prop airplane flew a thousand feet above the steamy Guatemalan jungle. David worked his laptop computer in the last row of the airplane. He chose that seat because he figured the farther away he was from the pilot least talking he would have to do. While the LIDAR instrument was strapped to the underside of the plane, the pilot did his best to maintain constant altitude as David took a stream of digital infrared images of the temple below.

David was feeling good. The picture taking operation was successful. He didn't know which glyph was the key to gaining entry to the temple, that job was for the crew in New York.

"How much more ground are we covering?" the pilot asked as he warily eyed the fuel gauge. "We have about twenty minutes worth of fuel left."

"I'm almost done with the entire grid-work," David said as he turned his attention back to the laptop. "My boss is going to love this."

"He'd better. You've spent a lot of money already."

"What are you complaining about? It's easy money for you,"

The pilot shrugged. "True. It sure beats dealing with noisy tourists."

David grinned for a second before becoming serious. He recalled seeing the Wind Slicers at the airport. He was so focused on taking his pictures he forgot to alert Erick. He made a mental note to send him an email.

"All right—the entire grid pattern has been documented and stored in the files. We're done," David finally announced.

The pilot was about to give a thumbs up, when from the west he saw a Wind Slicer coming at him at a good clip. His voice was grim. "Uh, oh, we have company and it doesn't look good."

David turned to face the window. He was shocked by what he saw. "It's one of the US military planes from the airport!" David swallowed hard. "Can we lose him?"

"I don't think so," the pilot shook his head. "He's coming in way too fast!"

"Do something. Let's get out of here!"

The pilot maneuvered the plane to bank at an awkward angle.

David grunted as he fell back and slid onto the hard steel floor.

"Hang on!" the pilot yelled.

"Too late," David painfully winced as he crawled back into his seat.

"I'll radio them. I'll tell them we aren't drug dealers." The pilot immediately started his communication. "This is Flight 140, I repeat, this is Flight 140. We are on a peaceful, scientific mission. Do you copy? I repeat, this is a peaceful, scientific mission." There was no radio response from the pursuer. "Wait a minute. Why would a US plane be flying in Guatemala? This doesn't make sense, what's this all about?"

Without warning and before David could offer up an explanation, a barrage of bullets from the Wind Slicer hit the fuselage and shattered the windows of the fleeing plane.

The pilot screamed while David threw himself on the floor. He crawled back to the computer as fast as he could. Thankfully the computer was secured because there was an important task he desperately needed to perform.

"You lied to me at the airport!" the pilot yelled, warily eyeing his instrumentation panel. "He's after *you!* Are you a fugitive?"

David cursed as he continued typing. He was out of stories and didn't know what to tell him, not that it mattered. He pulled up the file that contained the digital recordings of La Danta.

Another barrage of bullets hit the turboprop. Alarms sounded inside the cabin.

The pilot cursed in Spanish at the military craft. He glanced at the dials on the dashboard indicating critical areas. "He hit the fuel line!"

David sent the files into cyberspace then he quickly opened a large duffel bag and retrieved two parachutes. He threw one at the pilot. "I highly suggest you get this on. We're going to jump out of this plane together."

"Are you crazy?"

David quickly pulled his parachute on but noticed the pilot had refused to do so. "Didn't you hear me? Get the parachute on!"

The pilot picked it up and looked at it incredulously due to the small size of the parachute.

"It's a specialized parachute, compact yet efficient for low altitude jumps. Get it on or else," David said urgently.

The pilot was still in emotional shock. The idea of losing his plane had put him in denial.

David rushed for the door hatch. He turned and saw the pilot finally come to his senses as he raised the parachute up.

"Come on! Follow my lead!" David yelled as he opened the hatch. A stiff warm breeze wafted into the cabin.

A white contrail of smoke followed the fast moving missile as it slammed smack in the middle of the fuselage.

The explosion was deafening. The airplane split exactly in half as if it were a fragile eggshell. The resulting force of the explosion made the two pieces of the fuselage spin in different directions. The centrifugal force of the spinning pieces threw David and the pilot out of the plane.

Both men screamed in fear for their lives. But only one was wearing a parachute.

Even so, David's instinct was to grab something. So he vainly grabbed empty air as he saw the jungle floor coming at him. Fortunately for him, the parachute was designed to sense a free fall. An automatic timer suddenly deployed the parachute and David heard the comforting snapping sound of his canopy catching air, he also sensed he was slowing down. As he did, fiery plane parts fell past him and crashed onto the jungle floor below. He didn't want to look down to see the pilot crashing into the canopy of trees.

He hoped his death was quick and painless.

Now he had another deadly dilemma. The pilot flying the Wind Slicer had seen him slowly descending. That made him an easy target. The pilot did a turnabout and followed David's descent. This wasn't going to end well for David, all the pilot would have to do is shoot him with another barrage of bullets and make him look like a slice of Swiss cheese. He had regained enough of his senses to realize he had only two options. Neither of them was good. But timing was always everything.

He looked down and saw the tops of the trees coming at him. He looked up and saw the Wind Slicer heading for him.

Wait for it…wait for it…now.

He quickly pulled a red cord that was attached to the harness near his chest. Suddenly David was released from the parachute canopy and he started a fast free fall straight into the trees. Just in time because the pilot of the Wind Slicer shot a shower of bullets at him.

The Wind Slicer flew past David. Bonner had just squeezed the trigger and the bullets sliced David's parachute to shreds. He saw David release from the parachute so he pounded on the control board and used every curse word known to the English-speaking man and then some.

David went crashing into the trees. He twisted and flipped as he fell, hitting branches on the way down. He tried to catch a branch but he was moving too fast to break his fall. He fell onto the ground with a hard thud and immediately went into shock. Something was wrong but he couldn't pinpoint what it was.
Everything went dark.

Bonner did a 360 and fired the rest of his bullets into the foliage. He was hoping that at least one of them would find its target. He had three more missiles and didn't hesitate to use them. He put the Wind Slicer in hover-mode above the treetops and fired one by one. The jungle became an inferno of burning trees. He peered down at the jungle as he hovered in his aircraft. Black smoke swirled upward. Was his target dead? There was no way to know. He clenched his cigar and cursed some more as he threw the controls forward and headed back to the airport.

*   *   *

The chime on the computer startled Erick while he was looking at some Mayan glyph drawings from Dr. Sova's unpublished manuscript. "We have a message!" Erick declared. But it really wasn't necessary to raise his voice since they were both on high alert.
Ashni hurried to Erick's workstation. He opened the email file and saw marvelous photos of the Mayan temple, minus the vegetation.
"David made it!" Ashni gushed with enthusiasm.
"Apparently so," Erick said as he tapped on the keyboard.

"Wow!" Ashni said. "Those are some impressive photos. Only problem is there are thousands of glyphs surrounding the pyramid. Why don't you scan a copy of the key glyph from Dr. Sova's manuscript into the computer?"

"I already did, but it may take over an hour to completely download all the photos. I will start a comparison exercise to find the right one."

Ashni was going to say something in return when another chime interrupted him.

"It's another message from David," Erick stated.

Under attack…Wind Slicers here

"Rick Cannon is down there!" Erick exclaimed. For once he was truly astonished.

Ashni bit her lip. "This is awful!" As the project manager, Ashni was feeling as responsible as Troy to pull the job through. This didn't bode well.

Chapter Thirty-Four

Troy and his crew were deep in the jungle trying to maneuver around potholes or the muddy, swampy road conditions. The foliage was so thick it seemed to swallow them up. There were areas in the road where the truck barely made it through, either because of the encroaching jungle or the large water and mud-filled potholes.

"Whose idea was it to come during the rainy season?" Troy joked.

The laughter was short lived. Chauncy pointed ahead of the road. "There are some people over there, Troy."

Troy furrowed his brow. "We have trouble," he cautioned.

A few yards ahead they saw what appeared to be a hazy outline of two people. They were blocking the dirt road and looking straight at the truck. It was difficult to identify them due to the shrubbery and the trees but there was no doubt that those were rifles in their hands.

"What do they want?" Rio asked with a nervous voice.

"Could be bandits," Troy said.

"Possibly tomb raiders," Chauncy added.

"Should we gun it?" Rio nervously asked.

"Try to run them down," Javan added.

"No." Troy shook his head. "We can't go any faster than this. They seem to know it too. They're standing behind a large puddle and there are trees to the right and left of the puddle. I don't have time or space to make a U-turn either."

"We're corralled," Chauncy mumbled.

"What are we going to do?" Rio asked. As they got closer to the men Rio put a hand over her mouth. "That's Nolan!"

"And the other one is Gerald Bollinger," Troy said as he gritted his teeth. "He's the guy we turned over to the FBI."

"He's just an art thief, though, isn't he?" Rio asked.

"No, he's a tomb raider and a murderer. Let me handle this." The truck came to a stop near the men and Troy rolled the window down, he was the first to speak. "Well look who we have here, Judas Iscariot and the Devil himself!"

Gerald pointed his rifle at Troy. "If you make a wrong move I'm going to find out if you're a hologram or not. Get out of the truck...now!"

Nolan walked over to the passenger's side and pointed his rifle at Chauncy. "Everybody else get out of the truck, now!"

Chauncy looked at Troy, his son nodded. "Do as he says, Dad."

When they had all exited they were ordered to walk to the back of the truck with their hands up on their heads.

"You don't know how to handle a rifle," Troy taunted Nolan.

"Shut up!" Nolan said as he nervously pointed the rifle at him.

"It was all a lie," Troy said. "You weren't afraid of getting caught by the DHS. You've been embezzling money from our company since day one. I discovered it on the computer files you left behind. You were creating this aura of fear to dissuade us from figuring out that *you* wanted to get out of our group so you could join forces with Gerald to help you take over Operation Pakal."

"Mr. Genius is finally figuring things out," Nolan smirked. "It took you a while."

"Enough chit-chat," Gerald said. "Here's the plan, Javan is going to take us to the pyramid and show us how to run the machine. As for the rest of you, well it's been nice knowing you." He motioned to Nolan. "Tie them up."

"You don't know what you're getting into," Javan said.

"Oh yes I do," Gerald snapped back. "I have wonder-boy Nolan to help me figure out the other details and you're going to take us to the machine." Gerald pointed his rifle at Troy. "Open the back door of the trailer. I want to see what you have."

Troy complied with the order. He nervously fiddled with the keys until he found the right one and swung open the door. "Go ahead, go in there and see what we have."

Gerald peered in and saw AART and a mini trailer. He climbed into the trailer to get a closer look. "Well, well, look at this."

Nolan was about to tie Rio's hands when he looked up and saw Gerald near the cargo unit. He panicked. "Gerald, no!"

"AART! Grab intruder now!" Troy yelled.

AART suddenly came to life and thrust his pincer out and grabbed Gerald's arm. Gerald went down on his knees howling in pain as AART latched onto his arm with an ever tightening force.

Completely surprised, Nolan scrambled to get his rifle that was lying on the grass where he had put it.

Troy quickly snatched Gerald's rifle from his free hand and swung around and aimed it at Nolan.

He pulled the trigger and a bullet pierced Nolan's earlobe. Nolan swung around and instinctively grabbed his ear, screaming in pain as blood gushed out, then he dropped his rifle on the ground.

Chauncy lunged for the firearm and pointed it at Nolan. "I got ya boy."

"He's breaking my arm-" Gerald screamed. "Tell...him to....let me go!"

"AART, release arm now," Troy commanded him.

The robotic insect did as ordered. Gerald dropped to the floor wincing in agony.

Troy pointed the rifle at Gerald. "I'm giving you five seconds to get out of here, both of you, get back to the hole you came from."

Gerald staggered out of the cargo unit, holding his injured arm. "You don't have the guts to shoot me," Gerald sneered at Troy.

"Don't tempt me," Troy responded as he aimed at him.

"This isn't the last you've seen of me," Gerald muttered under his breath. He turned and motioned with his head to Nolan, they both disappeared into the jungle.

Troy was breathing heavily. The adrenaline rush was leaving his body. He leaned against the cargo unit, sweat was running down his forehead, his hands were trembling while still clutching the confiscated rifle.

"That was awesome," Chauncy said as he placed his hand on his shoulder. "I never knew you could fire a real gun."

"Neither did I," Troy gave him a weak smile.

"Thank you, Troy. That was quick thinking," Javan said with a sincere smile and then he looked up at the sky. "We need to get going, it will get dark soon."

Chauncy and Javan walked back to the bed of the truck. Troy finally regained his composure and started locking up the trailer.

Rio quickly came up to Troy and kissed him on the cheek.

Troy eyed her suspiciously. "What was that for?"

"For being brave," she smiled at him and then walked away.

Okay, there's the answer, she does like me. Troy thought. *She's the perfect woman, too.* His gaze landed on the place where Gerald and Nolan had disappeared. Unfortunately, as much as he wanted to dwell on the subject, now was not the time for romance. He had almost been killed by Gerald and his one-time friend turned traitor.

Chapter Thirty-Five

David finally came to. He lifted his wobbly head and gazed at his surroundings. It was a surreal view. The area was strewn with burning airplane parts that created a heavy, smoky mist around him.

He tried to get up but a terrible pain in his right leg made him collapse back onto the ground. Wondering what the problem was, he pulled up his pant leg and saw his mangled leg. He fell back and cursed his predicament. There was no way he was going to walk on a damaged leg.

Suddenly he felt a burning sensation on his skin. He looked down and saw ants crawling all over him. He swiped at them, then started dragged himself using his arms and good leg. He needed to get away from the stinging torture. Once he was clear of the anthill, he sat back against one of the remaining trees. *Shoot! I need shelter, water and food until I'm rescued, but where can I go?*

He took a deep breath but coughed as his lungs filled with acrid smoke. Things were looking bleak for David. He knew he wouldn't survive long in this place without protection.

Nobody would.

Fortunately, the big predators were most likely scared off by the explosions and the fire, but the need for shelter and sustenance was becoming a paramount concern. The animals would eventually return. They always did.

Something way off in the distance caught his eye. There were too many trees in the way to discern exactly what it was. But due to the light emanating from the fires he was able to see what looked like a white, shimmering, oblong object. He had to get a closer look.

He dragged himself across the jungle floor, wincing in pain. As he got closer to the object he realized what it was. It was the broken rear fuselage of the turboprop that had crashed on the ground.

Finally there was a glimmer of hope in David's heart. If he could reach the plane, he would have some semblance of shelter from the elements. It took him about thirty minutes of painful dragging until he reached the fragmented plane. There was still enough fuselage area left to cover him. He crawled in and laid on his back until he caught his breath.

A thought came to him.

He recalled while he was in training to use the parachute, the instructor had told him that the harness had a distress beacon that was easily activated by simply pushing a red button that was located under a flap on the chest part of the harness. The beacon was encrypted so that only the SSOSA people in the New York office would be able to decipher his location.

He deftly located the flap and pushed the button. A small LED red light blinked silently on the harness. If he lay still, the pain in his leg wasn't so bad, at least for now.

*   *   *

Rick was fuming when he saw Bonner return and land the aircraft on the tarmac. He wanted to berate the man for his impetuous behavior. But he still needed Bonner for the most crucial part of the mission.

Rick gritted his teeth and approached Bonner. "Did you kill him?"

Bonner spat on the ground. "No, but the jungle will. It won't be long before he dies of exposure."

"What happened?"

"He bailed in a parachute."

Rick sighed in frustration. "Okay."

Bonner furrowed his brow and pointed at him. "Why didn't you send a detachment to pursue the enemy?"

"I told you already. I need a *working* machine and those people will lead me to Javan."

214

"Let me tell you what you can do with that working machine, Mr. Cannon."

Rick clenched his jaw.

"You already know where Javan is!" Bonner yelled. "Your techs have already locked in on his GPS. Had you planned this in advance two operatives could have taken the two-seater and one could have rappelled down into the jungle to put a bullet in the guy's head. But you know what your problem is? You're way out of your league. This dog ain't gonna hunt. You should leave this to trained professionals because you ain't the person for this job."

Rick ignored Bonner's rant. "You need to get all the Wind Slicers ready, I'm going with you in the two-seater to La Danta. It's time to stop this nonsense and go claim our prize."

"For the record, I am doing this under protest!" the colonel angrily huffed as he quickly walked away to refuel and arm the aircraft.

*   *   *

"That's him!" Ashni yelled. "David deployed his parachute, he's still alive."

Erick rubbed his chin. "We do not know his condition. But at least he is alert enough to activate the distress signal, I think I located him!"

"Rick must have ordered him shot down," Ashni said. "He's not too far from La Danta."

"But technically, he is in the middle of nowhere," Erick added. "He is far from civilization."

"We have to get him rescued before the Guatemalan military finds him," Ashni pleaded. She straightened up and paced around. "We have to find a way to get to him somehow. I can arrange for a civilian outfit in Guatemala to rescue him."

"No," Erick shook his head. "By the time you do that he will be dead from exposure. We have no idea how he is going to survive the night in a dangerous jungle, do we? He probably has no food, no water and no shelter. He may also be injured. How badly injured is he? We simply do not know all the details, do we?"

215

Ashni had a worried expression. "We *have* to find a way to reach him."

"I told you already, we simply have no time to assemble a rescue." Erick shot back.

"Do you expect me to do nothing?" Ashni said with an anguished tone. "I'm the project manager and he's my responsibility. We leave no man behind."

"Let this be a lesson for you SSOSA kids," Erik stood up from his seat and walked away.

"What lesson is there to learn Erick?" Ashni angrily responded. "David could die out there!"

Erick swung around and stared at her. "I can see you still need more training. Dr. Sova was one of the smartest men in the world. He taught us a vital lesson when we played Mind Games with him. He said "Always have a Plan B"."

"I had a Plan B," Ashni interjected. "I had him trained at a skydiving school. I also had a Plan C, I provided a smart parachute for him that had a free fall detector and a distress beacon."

Erick stance softened. "Let me tell you something, I said Rene Sova was *one* of the smartest men in the world, I am another."

"What are you talking about?" Ashni responded with a puzzled expression.

"I already have Plan D in place," Erick responded with a smug face.

"What? Why didn't you tell us?"

"Because you needed to learn a lesson," Erick mused. "There was a time when we thought SSOSA members were invincible. We thought we could conquer the world. But we are not invincible," Erick's eyes moistened as he turned to address Ashni. His hands were clenched in fists. "All of my contemporaries are dead, I am the last surviving member of the old SSOSA and it is my duty to make sure you succeed. SSOSA will never die on my watch."

Ashni was in quiet awe of her mentor. Just like Troy she too finally realized how determined Erick was to continue the mission to the end. Whether it succeeded or failed was inconsequential. Nothing mattered to Erick except the mission.

Chapter Thirty-Six

Gerald and Nolan eventually stumbled into base camp. Their Jeep was parked deep in the jungle to avoid being seen by anyone else. There was a small remnant of a campfire and two tents that were erected near their vehicle.

After he had taken some extra strong painkillers and bandaged his injured arm, Gerald turned his attention to assist Nolan. He applied an antiseptic to Nolan's ear. Nolan grimaced in pain and cursed when Gerald wrapped his head with gauze.

"Hold still will ya?" Gerald barked.

The shock of the injury was wearing off. "Man it hurts!" Nolan cried with a curse for Troy.

"Hold on, I have some strong pain killers." He bent down and rifled through his first aid kit. He pulled out a bottle of pills and handed it to Nolan. "Here, these are the same as the ones I took."

With trembling hands Nolan washed the pills down with the water in his canteen.

"You're lucky Troy didn't blow your head off. Had he or you moved one inch to the left you wouldn't be talking to me right now."

Nolan grimaced. "I should have shot him dead when I saw him climb out of the truck."

"You're lying," Gerald snickered. "You don't fool me. The truth is you never wanted your buddy dead."

"He's not my buddy!" Nolan snapped.

"You know what your problem is, don't you? SSOSA boys are too soft in the middle. You're all a bunch of cream puffs as far as I'm concerned. You spend your energies being goodie-two-shoes by sending people like me to prison. Your company should have joined me instead. Modern day tomb raiding is a billion dollar business, boy. Get with the program, there's a lot of money to be made by selling old rocks and pottery. You guys are wasting your talents."

Nolan wasn't in the mood to talk about morals and laws, but he figured he would humor Gerald. "Well, now you see why I turned to the dark side, I want a piece of the pie."

"It's dangerous pie. Taking a bite of this pie might kill you."

"I'll take my chances," Nolan shrugged.

Gerald chuckled as he sat on a folding chair and looked at Nolan. "I will admit I had my doubts about Operation Pakal. But I'm beginning to see this might be the biggest payoff of my entire career." He looked off in the distance as if lost in thought. "If these guys really do find what they are looking for, then I'm going to be a billionaire."

"You mean 'we'."

Gerald swiped a hand over his face to ward off the persistent mosquitoes. "You don't know anything, kid."

"What are you talking about?"

"You have no idea how hard it is to be a tomb raider. You haven't put in the time sweating in archaeological digs in deep jungles or hot deserts. You've been stuck in an air-conditioned cubicle all your life playing video games and now you want a big piece of the pie?"

"Without my computer knowledge you would be nowhere. You need my talents. It's a symbiotic relationship."

"Yeah, whatever," Gerald snorted.

"Look, the point is, now that you know this thing is real, you will need me to show you how to make the machine work."

"You're holding out for more money, aren't ya?" Gerald sneered.

"I'm not holding you hostage with my knowledge. I'm *helping* you to meet your goal. Trust me. Everything I have told you has been nothing but the truth, right?"

Gerald grunted.

"If you're going to make over a billion dollars on this, I want to up the ante."

Gerald wasn't in the condition or mood to punch Nolan again for his petulant attitude. He let it pass. He figured he would let Nolan think he was his partner. Then at a convenient time he would do away with him. "Yeah, kid sure. We shall see, we shall see."

Nolan was starting to feel better, not due to the meds but because of the promise of future wealth. "What's our next move?"

Gerald rubbed his sore arm as he spoke. "As soon as your painkillers kick in, we're going to chase them down."

"Do you have any more guns?"

"Oh yeah, as a matter of fact I do." Gerald stood up and walked over to his Jeep. He pulled out two handguns and some ammo from a hidden compartment. "Let's go get them."

Chapter Thirty-Seven

"What's with all the missing trees in this area?" Rio asked as they passed a denuded section of the jungle.

"That's another problem," Chauncy answered. "The Mayan biosphere is undergoing an assault by deforestation. Along with tomb raiders, drug dealers and human encroachment, there is also wanton destruction of the jungle by loggers."

"What a pity," Rio said.

"How much time until we arrive at the temple?" Javan asked. His mind was on reaching his goal.

"See that mountain over there?" Chauncy said as they crested a small hill with an opening in the foliage. "That's La Danta."

To the untrained eye, what Chauncy was referring to looked like a very tall pointed mountain covered with the typical jungle flora.

"Wow, that's kind of anti-climactic. It looks like any other mountain," Rio commented.

"For years people thought it was just that until archaeologists started removing some of the vegetation and instituted the use of IKONOS and LIDAR technologies. As it turned out, it's the largest man-made pyramid in the world."

"Which way should we go, Dad?" Troy asked his father as he maneuvered the truck around a few curves.

Chauncy scratched his cheek as he tried to remember. "It's been so many years ago. But one thing I do recall is that we were on the west side of the pyramid. So, go west young man."

Troy turned the truck and headed west.

They finally arrived at their destination. There was a small opening at the west side of the temple base. It seemed like the area had been previously cleared by an archaeological company some time ago. But unlike the pyramids of Giza in Egypt, Troy and his

221

entourage couldn't see the entire pyramid of La Danta due to the jungle overgrowth.

Troy was the first one to get out of the truck. With rifle in hand he surveyed the area for any signs of trouble. When he was satisfied that they were alone he motioned for everyone else to exit.

"So, what's your plan?" Chauncy asked.

Troy looked up at the sky. "It'll be getting dark soon so we're going to have to spend the night here. We need to set up guard duty for the night in case Gerald and Nolan return."

"I'll take the first shift," Chauncy said.

"What about the glyph?" Javan asked Troy. "Shouldn't you ask Erick if they located it?"

Troy raised his finger. "That's a good point." He turned to his father. "Can you set up the tents? I'm going to turn the camera on and talk to Erick."

"Sure thing."

Troy turned his hat/camera on and walked a few paces away from the rest of the crew for privacy. Seconds later the camera hooked up with a satellite and then Troy heard Erick's voice on the tiny microphone that was embedded in his hat.

"Troy, can you hear me?"

"Loud and clear, boss how you doing?"

Erick's voice sounded uncharacteristically alarmed. "Troy, you're in danger. Rick Cannon is coming after you!"

It took a moment for Troy to realize Erick wasn't joking. "Say again?"

"Rick Cannon shot David down. We have evidence he deployed his parachute and we got his distress beacon."

"How do you know it was Rick?"

"David sent a message saying he was under attack by a Wind Slicer. Recall Javan told us a Wind Slicer was what he used to escape the prison. We have reason to believe Rick is using those to pursue you."

"That makes sense," Troy agreed.

"We wanted to warn you but we had no way of communicating with you."

Troy furrowed his brow. "Yeah, okay, I read you loud and clear. We need to get in the temple now. Have you located the glyph?"

"Almost," Ashni interrupted. "David sent hundreds of glyph photos. We're running a scan as we speak."

Troy ran his hand through his blond hair. He was genuinely worried. He already lost Nolan. He surely didn't want to even contemplate a death in SSOSA. "Is David okay?"

"We're not sure. All we got was a distress signal, he obviously lost his satellite phone otherwise he would have called us," Ashni answered. "Are you guys okay?"

"Overall we're okay. We're at our destination. We would have been here earlier but we got accosted by Nolan and Gerald Bollinger on the way."

"What? Nolan? Nolan Smith?"

"Yes, that Nolan Smith."

"What a jerk," Ashni hissed.

"So Nolan teamed up with Bollinger and turned traitor on us? What a shame," Erick replied.

"I thought Bollinger had been arrested," Ashni sharply responded.

"It seems he made a deal with DHS, how else would you explain his presence?" Troy surmised. "But fortunately AART saved the day. I'll have to tell you about it later. Keep me posted when you locate the key glyph, I'm going to tell the others about Rick. I suppose we're going to have to forgo some much needed sleep and get cracking. Troy out."

Troy walked over to the rest of the crew and his body language was easy to read. "We have some serious trouble."

When he explained everything to them they too became visibly concerned.

Javan was visibly upset. "I told you Rick was intelligent enough to locate us. We have to get moving!"

Rio moaned. "Now we have Rick, Bonner, Nolan and Bollinger after us."

"Forget the tents," Troy made a hand motion. "Let's get everything else out of the trailer and be ready for action."

It took half an hour to get things prepared to enter the temple. The plan was for AART to pull a specially designed mini-trailer that would haul the cables, the quantum oscillator machine and other miscellaneous items.

"It's going to be nearly impossible to locate the door glyph!" Ashni cried as she saw the data from David's computer pour in. "There are thousands of glyphs at the base of the pyramid."

Deep in thought, Erick stared at the computer terminal then typed some commands. "Complaining about it won't get the work done. I've started a search to compare the glyph with the Mayan word that Chauncy gave us." Erick started the program and leaned back in his chair and linked his hands behind his head. "It will take a while...at this point all we can do is wait. Sometimes...life is a waiting game."

Troy heard Erick's voice coming through the microphone. "Troy here."

"We found the glyph!"

"Excellent!"

"I'm going to give you the coordinates. It's not too far from where you are located."

"That's good to know," Troy answered, more relieved. "Thanks to my dad's good memory, he put us close to the spot."

"Get out your GPS tracker," Erick ordered.

"Done."

"Here are the coordinates."

Troy typed in the number on the small locator screen and started walking toward the base of the temple until he came to a spot where both numbers matched. "Here it is! AART, remove vegetation, now."

The sun was setting, causing visibility to diminish. Chauncy, Rio and Javan used their flashlights to illuminate the area where AART was working. AART was also equipped with two headlights of his own. The eyes of the insect-shaped robot shone on the area he was ordered to work on. He employed his sharp pincers to clip and pull the vegetation away.

For the first time in sixteen years, the ancient glyph was starting to be exposed as AART whittled away the vegetation. It was an awe inspiring sight, the glyph was twelve feet high and eight feet wide.

"That's the one!" Chauncy exclaimed. "Wow, it's seems like yesterday that Rene and I were admiring the glyph."

"I want the guys in New York to see this," Troy said as he tapped the camera button on.

"How heavy do you think the door is?" Rio asked.

"I say two tons or so, just as we figured," Troy responded.

"Let's hope it will move, I mean it's been over two thousand years since it has seen any action," Chauncy quipped.

The SSOSA in New York recorded the event as Troy maneuvered AART to one side of the glyph.

"Place your pincers on the right side of the stone!" Troy ordered AART. "AART, push the stone to the right!"

AART's hydraulically powered pincers pushed as the sound of his internal machinery whined.

At first the people watching thought that AART wasn't strong enough to move the stone because thousands of years of weathering had sealed the glyph to the face of the pyramid and it wasn't going to be easy to pry the stone loose. It was going to take a little time to do it.

Soon enough the giant stone started sliding. It was an eerie sight and sound. A grinding noise of stone rubbing against stone was audible as the light from the crew's flashlights and AART's headlights gave the glyph a strange, hazy look as the dust started raining down in copious amounts.

"OMG, it's opening," Ashni exclaimed.

Erick was too riveted to the video to say anything.

"Look! There's a tunnel," Rio said.

"It's true! Dr. Sova was right about the glyph," Troy said

"I don't see why he would have been wrong." Chauncy grinned.

"We must hurry," Javan said as he looked at the darkening sky. "Those Wind Slicers will be here any minute."

Troy's spirits were lifted again. The gnawing doubt he had experienced way back in New York was dissolving as he was now beginning to see the figurative light at the end of the tunnel. Troy turned to look at his father and smiled. "Dad, help me attach the mini trailer to AART's tail."

"Okay son."

"Sorry AART," Troy said. "But you're taking the lead. If we have a tunnel collapse or set off a booby trap you're going to be our sacrificial goat. AART go forward…now."

Chapter Thirty-Eight

Considering how thick the vegetation was around La Danta, the clearing Nolan and Bollinger had reached near the pyramid offered a good view from a distance, thereby preventing them from being seen by Troy and his crew. After ascertaining there were no stinging ants nearby, they lay low to the ground with the shrubbery covering them. Gerald trained his binoculars on the area where the entry door glyph was located. He made a low whistling sound.

Nolan's ear was giving him a dull throbbing pain, the painkillers weren't sufficiently working anymore, but he managed to deal with it. "What's up?"

"They had that robot move the glyph. Now they're going inside the pyramid, This is awesome!"

"Let me see."

Gerald passed him the binoculars. "Wow, that's bizarre," Nolan gasped.

"I wonder how they figured that mystery out," Gerald mused.

"Wait- I see Troy's father over there."

Gerald chuckled. "Chauncy Rollock? Well isn't that a hoot. There's the answer."

"Of course, Troy went to get assistance from his father. That other guy must be Javan Benson."

Gerald scratched his chin in contemplation. "So the pyramid does have an entrance. Even if they don't find what they are looking for, I wonder what *other* priceless things are in there."

"I don't recommend storming them right now. We should be patient and wait until they gain further access into the temple." Nolan cupped a hand over his injured ear. "I don't want a repeat of what we just went through."

"Yeah I get it. They also happen to have our two rifles, so they're no longer unarmed. Let's just sit it out for a while. Then we storm them."

Chapter Thirty-Nine

The beams of light from the flashlights bounced around in the dark tunnel showing that it was made of large stacked stones. Chauncy was having flashbacks of the time he was in another temple tunnel sixteen years prior. The difference was that the previous one sloped downhill, whereas this one was completely flat.

For some unknown reason there were no carvings, artwork or glyphs on the tunnel walls. Chauncy speculated that what awaited them was going to be grand and awe-inspiring.

AART's headlights shone at least fifty feet down the tunnel until it came to an abrupt stop. At the end of the tunnel there was a nondescript wooden double gate.

Chauncy and Troy went around AART to inspect the door. There were a few whimsical carvings, but the people in the tunnel were more concerned about getting into the main room, than to remain and admire the artwork.

Chauncy slowly pushed the double doors open, they creaked with age as they slowly gave way. Everyone sensed that they were now in a much bigger room because of the echoes of their voices.

"Bring the floodlights out, Troy," Chauncy whispered.

AART was sent into the big room first. His articulated feet made clicking sounds on what appeared to be a floor made of stone. Due to the limited visibility of the lights they had to wait until Troy had all of the floodlights out of the trailer and placed on the ground to figure out what the large area contained.

He connected the main cord to a battery and looked at the shadowy faces about him. "Okay you guys here we go. It's been centuries since any human has seen what we are about to see. I'm going to turn the lights on now."

With a flip of the switch the room became illuminated.

There were many gasps of wonderment as they slowly looked around the large room.

Javan was the first to say something. "It's true. All of it true. Behold…the machine!"

The temple room was a great thing to behold indeed. The interior walls were straight ninety-degree angles, indicating that this room was like a large box built inside the pyramid.

Chauncy pointed a flashlight above to determine the height of the ceiling. But even with all the lights on and the meager beam from his flashlight, he still couldn't see where it ended.

On the ground there were a series of freestanding glyphs about fifteen feet tall and six feet wide all placed in an extremely large Stonehenge-style circle. They looked like dominoes stuck in the temple floor since they weren't very thick. Each glyph had a series of artwork carved on it. In the middle of the large circle were the four small-scale pyramids that resembled the ones that they had built in the New York warehouse.

But instead of the hanging tear-dropped shaped throne, in the middle of the pyramids there was a stone platform. On top of the platform was an empty throne also made of stone.

Javan was so amazed at what he was seeing he almost forgot Rick was soon coming to get him. He pointed to the throne as he exclaimed. "Look, the transporter throne! I must sit on that throne to transport to another dimension."

"Well, we better get moving," Troy said as he remembered why they were in a rush.

Rio started setting up her quantum oscillation machine. "I need you guys to unravel the cables and start hooking them up to the four pyramids in the same way you did in New York."

Javan walked about the room in sheer wonder like a child in a toy store. "I would really like to know how they powered the ancient machine. It would be marvelous if we could figure it out."

"So would I," Chauncy remarked.

Javan walked about looking and touching everything. "I bet the answers are carved on the glyphs."

"I wish Rene was here. He would be able to tell us," Chauncy said as he moved the cable around the pyramids. "Blasted Rick

Cannon, if he wasn't on our tail we could spend months in here analyzing all these awesome things."

* * *

A V-shaped formation of flying Arawak Wind Slicers cruised at a good clip over the jungle in the direction of La Danta.

"ETA to our destination, Colonel?" Rick asked Bonner.

Bonner glanced at his control panel. "We should be there in thirty minutes or so."

Rick sighed as he looked down at the darkening jungle. "It's time to end this ordeal." He worked the small computer terminal in front of him. "I'm locked onto Javan's GPS signal."

"This time Javan is not going to get away from me," Bonner muttered. He looked down at his sides. His two firearms were ready for action. He clicked on the communicator for all his fellow commandos to listen. "Commandos, get ready for nighttime battle. Orders are for all terrorists to be killed on sight....we take no prisoners. Repeat, take no prisoners."

Rick had a frustrated expression on him as he gazed at his computer screen. "Something happened to Javan!"

Bonner was irritated. "Now what?"

"His signal disappeared!"

Bonner looked out at the jungle below. The lights of all the Wind Slicers were on but it was getting harder to see anything due to the encroaching darkness. "How can that be?" he growled.

"I...I don't know. But he's nowhere on my scanner."

"Maybe something is wrong with the computer."

"The computer is fine."

"We didn't come way out here to waste our precious time," Bonner growled again only this time louder. "Figure out what the problem is. I ain't going home empty-handed."

Rick furrowed his brow. "Maybe they hid him again under a pile of rocks or something like that so my scanner wouldn't pick him up."

"How did they know we were coming?"

"David Nix must have communicated it to them somehow."

Bonner banged a fist on his console. "That's why I said we should have finished the job when we were pursuing David in the first place."

"Relax. The last signal I had on him indicated Javan was in La Danta. Nobody can move in the jungle at night. At least we can still go there and hunt him down. We will find their base."

Bonner took a deep breath to control his emotions. He wanted to throttle Rick. But most of all he wanted to kill Javan. It seemed to Bonner that no matter what he did to pursue him Javan was always a step ahead of him.

He clicked the communicator on. "All commandos turn on infrared scanner. We lost primary target. Look for his camp or truck. Be careful, they aren't the only ones out there. You may be locking on a group of other archaeologists who are also working in the area. Proceed with caution and advise when you locate target."

*   *   *

Javan was still wandering around the large room with a flashlight in hand. He walked to one side of the large room. He saw a strange contraption that caught his attention.

"Chauncy, look at this," Javan said excitedly.

Chauncy was done laying out the cable while Rio was attaching them to the pyramids. He left his post to see what had intrigued Javan so much.

Upon arriving he saw the strange looking contraption. There was a stone shaft that seemed to go down into the temple floor through a visible slot that was embedded in the floor. The shaft was supported by two stationary pillars of stone. Upon closer inspection one could see the movable shaft was held up by a series of three strange-looking interlocking gears.

"It's a rotating Mayan calendar," Chauncy exclaimed. "The large gear marks the year, the medium one marks the months and the smaller one the days. See?" he pointed to the writing on the wheels.

Troy was intrigued by the conversation and he jogged over to where the two men were watching the contraption. "This is all fascinating, but we need to hurry!"

All three men turned when they heard Rio's voice. "I'm ready to start the machine. Come on, let's go."

Javan walked over to where Rio was and hugged her. "Goodbye my friend. I will surely miss you."

Rio tried to stifle a sob. "Me too. It was wonderful working with you.

Javan turned to look at the two men. "Thank you, thank you." He waved at the small camera on Troy's hat. "And thank all of you other SSOSA people."

Although unseen by the people in the pyramid, Erick and Ashni saluted him.

*   *   *

Four Small Arawak Wind Slicers and one two-seater were hovering above the great temple, their searchlights were scanning the area for Troy and his crew. The lights slowly washed over the pyramid and the surrounding area.

"Sir, we've located the black Ford truck," one of the operatives announced over the radio.

Bonner's expression lit up when he heard one of the commandos report the find. "We got 'em! He's not going to escape from me now. He has nowhere to go."

"Ask him if the truck has a large box in the bed as well as a large, enclosed trailer," Rick said.

Bonner did so and the commando replied. "That's affirmative, sir."

"I told you so," Rick said.

"Destroy the target," Bonner quickly ordered.

One of the operatives angled his aircraft down at the target in hover mode. He locked his sights on the black truck and he pressed the trigger. A missile shot out of the craft and hit the truck. A large explosion shook the area as the truck exploded in a fiery orange and red fireball lighting up the jungle.

"Prepare to land in the clearing near the demolished truck," Bonner said. "We're going in with night-vision goggles to see if they're hiding in the bushes or in nearby caves. Let's go."

* * *

Gerald and Nolan nearly jumped out of their skins as the truck in front of them blew up in a fiery red and orange glow. They both looked up into the sky to see where the rain of death had come from,.

Gerald's jaw dropped. "What the.....who are they?"

Nolan was equally astonished. "I don't know. But it looks like we have company...and competition!"

"I don't like this...we're going to get beat out of the treasure!" Gerald wailed in anger.

* * *

The people inside the temple heard a booming sound and felt a slight tremble on the floor. Ancient dust rained down upon them. They looked up in consternation.

"Rick is here!" Javan exclaimed as he walked up the stairs of the platform and sat down on the throne. "Start the machine."

Rio hurriedly pressed some levers to increase the energy level to the pyramids. The familiar humming sound that they had heard in the warehouse in New York was now replicated inside the temple.

And just like in New York, the visual disturbance was seen as Javan became a blurry image as the torsion waves emanated from the four pyramids. Suddenly everyone in the room started levitating, then they slowly gravitated toward Javan.

"It's happening again," Erick said as he watched the scene over the computer monitor.

"Turn it off," Troy yelled at Rio.

Rio tried to comply but her hands slipped off of the machine failing to grab a firm hold.

"Oh no," Ashni cried, as she saw that Rio was starting to float away from the oscillator.

234

Troy turned around and saw AART lifting in the air as well. "AART, grab that nearby glyph now."

AART did as ordered and it kept him from floating into the center of the pyramids.

The trailer and other items started rising and swirling above the room. It was a strange sight to behold.

Chauncy was near AART and he flailed his arms until he grabbed AART's tail. Now he had something secure to hang onto.

Rio had a panicked expression as she kept moving in midair toward Javan. "Somebody help me turn the machine off! If we don't, all matter within a two mile radius will be sucked into the center of the four pyramids and reduced to the size of a grain of sand!"

Troy was near the wooden double gate, he was holding on for dear life as his feet floated out from under him. He saw Rio moving away from the quantum oscillator generator and floating toward the platform. There was no way she was going to be able to return to the machine and stop it. She looked at Troy with a terrified expression. "Troy...help!"

He had to do something.

Noticing that the machine was drawing electrical power from a portable generator, he quickly figured that if he used his floating momentum to push himself toward the power cord, maybe, just maybe he would be able to yank it out of the outlet.

It was a long shot, but doing nothing meant certain death.

*   *   *

The gravitational pull of the torsion waves within a two mile radius was becoming evident outside in the jungle. Small animals and wood debris started swirling in the air and moving toward La Danta.

Since there wasn't any warning as to what was about to occur, Nolan and Gerald didn't have time to grab onto a tree so, just like the jungle animals, they too started rising in the air.

They were both in too much emotional shock to do anything helpful, they simply floated upward and forward in the direction of the pyramid.

"What's happening?" Gerald yelled as he grabbed at nothing in vain.

The Wind Slicers were also affected.

One of the operatives was trying to stabilize his aircraft as it was pulled toward the pyramid.

"Something's happening," he yelled. "I'm being pulled in and...I ...can't stop...it!"

The aircraft plummeted toward the side of the temple and exploded in a fireball.

Bonner clenched his cold cigar in his teeth as he used all his strength to pull the lever, trying to reverse the craft. "Some unseen force is pulling us toward the pyramid," he bellowed.

To his right he saw another Wind Slicer succumb to the powerful gravitational force and slam against the temple. Another fiery explosion ensued.

Rick suddenly had a revelation. "They powered up the machine and it's doing the same thing as in New York!"

"What are you talking about?" Bonner yelled back as he increased the power in the engine.

"They powered up a similar machine in New York, but it failed, everything within a two-mile radius started levitating. The only difference is that in New York the event lasted fifteen seconds, this one is lasting longer...something is going terribly wrong."

"Where's that blasted machine?"

"It has to be *inside* the temple! That's why we're being pulled toward it."

The two-seater craft started bucking against the unseen force as the engine tried to pull the craft back but the torsion waves pulled it forward. The high pitched sound of the fan turbines increased as the engine power rose. But it was to no avail, the torsion waves were stronger than the craft's engine.

"We're not going to last long!" Bonner yelled as he saw another Wind Slicer crash and burn on the temple.

236

The pilot of the last small Wind Slicer hit a learning curve after he saw what happened to his fellow commandos. He jettisoned out of the cockpit and deployed his parachute. But instead of falling straight down, powerful invisible forces pulled him at a strange angle toward the large structure. An explosion ensued when his craft hit the temple.

"We're going to bail," Bonner yelled at Rick as he saw what the commando did. "Get ready, on the count of three," Bonner started the count. "One, two, three!"

The aircraft canopy popped open, the two men shot out at a great speed while still seat-belted in their chairs. The two parachutes deployed and they too started floating toward the pyramid.

They watched as the two-seater made impact with the temple. This explosion was the largest since the two-seater carried four missiles and had double the amount of fuel as the others.

The two men fell on the sloped pyramid wall. They were amazed that they didn't roll down even though they were at an odd angle.

They heard the voice of the lone surviving commando calling for help. They walked on the temple wall toward the sound of his voice until they found him.

*　*　*

Nolan and Gerald were flying toward the temple and picking up speed with every passing second. The light coming from the fires of the truck and the destroyed Wind Slicers was enough for the two men to see what was going to happen to them. And it wasn't going to be pretty.

Nolan was thrust head first into the stone wall. He didn't have a prayer. The impact broke his neck and instantly killed him.

However, Gerald twisted just in time to avoid the headlong collision. He slammed into some shrubs that were growing on the temple wall that cushioned the impact and prevented him from being injured or killed.

*　*　*

237

Troy recalled the videos of floating astronauts he had seen in the past. He remembered how, while floating in zero gravity, they learned to push their bodies while floating. The power cord was about twenty feet in front of him on the floor. It was the same direction the torsion waves were pulling him. Now was the time to try the experiment.

He took a deep breath and pushed his floating body down onto the floor. Right before the energy pulled him back up toward the four pyramids he managed to grab the power cord with both hands.

He yanked with all his might until he pulled the cord out of the electric generator.

As soon as the gravitational pull was normalized, the men on the outside of the pyramid suddenly lost their balance and started sliding down the temple wall. The shrubbery and trees growing on the temple wall prevented them from the free fall momentum, they grabbed onto the nearest trees to keep from slipping further.

Breathing heavily, they took an account of what remained and what was lost. Of the six men who left the airport only three were alive, Rick Cannon, Theodore Bonner and Commando Jones.

"The machine stopped, something is wrong, but we need to go inside the temple before they hit a learning curve and reactivate it again," Rick hurriedly said.

Commando Jones looked down at the eerie looking slope with his night vision goggles. "It's a long way down and it's not going to be easy sir, be careful."

Bonner made a hand motion to Jones. "You lead the way. Let's go."

*   *   *

Gerald only slid a little way down the sloped wall as the normal gravity resumed. Again, the shrubbery was on his side. Nolan's body came sliding down and bumped against Gerald.

"Get off of me," Gerald cried but stopped when he realized Nolan was dead. He pushed him off and wiped the sweat from his brow with his good hand. *He's dead, oh well, that saved me a bullet.* With difficulty, Gerald searched Nolan's pockets until he found his gun and water canteen. *Now I have two guns. I guess it's time for me to take over all by myself.*

But now Gerald had another problem to deal with. He was high up on the pyramid wall. Visibility was poor. And the trek down looked ominous. There were thorny bushes and insects to deal with. No matter which way he looked at it, he was going to have to get off the sloping temple wall, staying up there was not an option. He took Nolan's holster and placed his guns side by side on his belt and finished the water in Nolan's canteen.

He gritted his teeth as he began the painful descent. He wanted to curse himself for coming to Guatemala but the idea of making millions or perhaps even billions of dollars with this fantastic machine was also the impelling force that kept him going.

He had personally felt the power of the machine throw him against the ancient temple.

Now he knew it wasn't a fantasy.

Chapter Forty

This time around it took longer to resuscitate Javan. They had dragged him off the platform and placed him on the temple floor. When his eyes finally fluttered open he looked around in horror. "It felt like a thousand elephants were on my chest...I...I couldn't breathe."

"It's going to be okay," Rio said as she tried to comfort him.

Javan stood up from the floor. He looked like an emotionally broken man. "I failed...the machine didn't work. The same thing happened again, just like New York. What on earth are we doing wrong? How can we produce the ions to get the machine working right?"

Troy too was feeling the agony of defeat...again. He rubbed his tired eyes. The mission setbacks were taking a toll on him. If the machine still couldn't work properly then this time the defeat would feel worse than it had in New York. Having come so far and spent so much time and money only to fail was going to be beyond catastrophic.

Chauncy surveyed the room. "We're out of options you guys. I don't know what to tell you. It's just a matter of time before Rick comes in here to kill us."

"Or the other two," Rio reminded them.

"Don't remind me," Chauncy nervously answered.

Javan got up and started walking around. He was determined to find the answer. "If only we had more time. I'm sure we could figure out what these glyphs say. The glyphs *must* have the answer to our dilemma."

"Troy!" Erick said over Troy's microphone. "Ask your father to read the glyph!"

Troy swung around to face his father. "Dad! What does the glyph say?"

241

"Unfortunately, my Mayan is very rusty," Chauncy lamented.

"Come on Dad, come on!" Troy prodded his father. "Surely there must be an inkling of memory from Dr. Sova's lessons that you could conjure up. Don't these glyphs remind you of something…anything? When we were at your office you remembered the number zero in Mayan, so why can't you recall something else?"

Chauncy's face registered frustration as he walked around, following Troy. "I may be able to recall one or two words but, Son, it's been sixteen years. How do you expect me to remember everything?"

"What about this glyph, do you see anything that brings back any memories?"

Chauncy approached the glyph and placed his hand on the carvings. "This one here is *K'iin* that means sun."

"Good, good! What about this word on this glyph?"

Chauncy tilted his head to one side. "Um…*ch'iich*. I think that means bird."

"Excellent! Now we're getting somewhere."

Chauncy smiled. "Yes, Dr. Sova said all of our memories are locked in our brains, we just don't know how to recall them all."

"We're running out of time folks," Javan lamented. "Come on Chauncy, think! The answer is on the glyph!"

Ashni leaned back in her chair as she spoke into the microphone interrupting their conversation. "Troy, you need to get out of there."

"Why?"

"We have to plan an escape for you guys. There's just not enough time to figure out what the problem is."

"No. There has to be a way!"

"Operation Pakal is officially over, Troy," Ashni said.

"No it isn't, we didn't come all this way to leave with our tails between our legs," Troy lashed out.

"Don't turn this into a suicide mission," Ashni pleaded. "Please, get everyone out of there!"

Erick wanted to berate Ashni for trying to scrap the mission. But he knew Ashni wasn't stupid or a defeatist, she was right, failure was imminent. But if somehow Troy or Chauncy could figure out what the Mayan glyphs contained then maybe there was still a chance. It was the last chance.

"Troy," Erick spoke up.

Troy stopped in his tracks and looked up at nothing in particular. "Yes."

Erick leaned forward. His facial features were hardened as he stared at the monitor. "Listen to me. Ask your father to concentrate hard. Rene taught your father how to hyper-activate his brain cells. Javan is right, the answer is on the glyph. Make your Dad realize it!"

Troy smiled. Erick was right. His father did have the answer. It was now a matter of do-or-die. He continued to be amazed how Erick was guiding the mission.

Troy looked around for a better clue. His eyes fell upon the strange contraption in the corner of the room they had seen before. "Dad, here we are at the Mayan gears. Surely you must know what it says, right? Concentrate. Remember what Rene taught you?"

Chauncy took in a deep breath of frustration. "Look Troy, I know what you're trying to do, but reading Mayan glyphs and understanding what they mean and trying to run this machine properly are three distinct things, okay?"

Troy walked up to his father and placed a hand on his shoulder. "Dad, don't worry about the machine, concentrate on the glyphs. Put all of your thoughts on them. Remember what Rene taught you? You used to tell me when I was a kid that he taught you how to conjure up old memories. Use that power, Dad."

As if in a trance, Chauncy slowly walked up to the Mayan wheel and kneeled down and stroked his hand over a certain glyph. Memories were starting to flow back. Chauncy was recollecting the lessons of brain cell hyper-stimulation. He remembered being in Yucatan where Dr. Sova was teaching him how to use his brain to the full while they attempted to uncover the clues to the treasure of the Mayan king. He could almost smell the musty office. He could see the old books on the bookshelves and the fragments of Mayan writings placed on the thick wooden table.

"Wait a minute… this is very strange."

Chauncy's words got everybody's attention including the SSOSA members in New York.

"What is it?" Troy asked.

"That shaft goes down into a slot, see?"

"Yes, Dad, we already know that. What's your point?"

"There is one prominent glyph on the shaft and it stands out from all the others."

Sensing his father's tone of discovery, Troy got on his knees to get a closer look at what he was talking about. "What does it say?"

"I recognize this word. It says *'Ha*, that's 'water'." Chauncy moved his hands up and down the stone shaft. "This is a gear driven mechanism, it's designed to move the shaft up or down, allowing the releasing of water through a gate somewhere in underground canals."

Father and son looked at each other with great astonished faces. They both spoke in unison. "It's just like The Missing Capstone!"

They turned toward Javan and Rio. "We know how the machine works!"

Erick slowly leaned back in his chair. A feeling of victory washed over him.

Chapter Forty-One

Troy walked around the gears as he rapidly spoke. "My dad wrote a thesis while in the university titled *The Missing Capstone*. He theorized that the pyramids in Egypt were ancient power generators. He wrote that the Egyptians harnessed electricity by using the power of physio electricity, that's a scientifically known way of extracting electricity from moving water. The famous scientist Nikola Tesla constructed a tower in the early 1900's above an aquifer to replicate what the Egyptians had done thousands of years ago. He discharged negative ions from the moving water to create free electricity!"

"Of course," Javan exclaimed. "This has to do with Tesla's study of the Wardenclyffe Tower years ago. That's the answer! These freestanding glyphs have their bases way down in the temple floor that reach these aquifers. If we move the gears the shaft will lift therefore causing the water underground to flow under the temple aquifers and create ions that travel up the glyphs and permeate the air in this room. We need *negative* ions in the atmosphere to coalesce with the torsion waves."

Exactly," Rio added. "Producing *only* torsion waves without negative ions in the air we were creating a black hole."

"We found the answer." Javan ran to the pedestal and up to the throne. "Open the water wheel and start the machine, I have to leave!"

Rio ran back to the quantum oscillator. Chauncy and Troy rushed over and grabbed the large gear. They tried to make it rotate but it was frozen in place.

"The gears are stuck," Chauncy lamented.

"Of course they are!" Erick bellowed. "They haven't been turned in over a thousand years."

Troy turned to the robot. "AART come here, now."

Rio was looking down at her generator when suddenly she felt a strong hand grab her by the throat and throw her on the floor. She gasped for air and looked up in horror to see Commando Jones in a dark assault suit pointing a handgun at her.

"Everybody freeze," Bonner yelled as he entered the room with Rick trailing behind him.

Ashni let out a muffled groan.

"I knew it!" Erick made a fist.

"I heard enough," Rick said. "I know how to run the machine. Thank you all for your hard work, but the end has come. No more running from the law."

"Hands on your heads," Bonner motioned with his gun. "You, you and you, get over here, now!"

Crestfallen, Javan slowly walked off of the throne. Troy, Chauncy, Rio and Javan were corralled into a corner with AART. They were forced to kneel on the ground while Commando Jones tied their hands behind their backs with zip ties.

Bonner was breathing hard as he rushed over to Javan and pointed one of his guns at him. "I have been waiting way too long to kill you."

"Not yet," Rick interrupted. "I want them disposed of outside so we can throw their bodies in the jungle."

"Since when does a government representative have the authority to kill us?" Troy asked.

Rick ignored Troy as he went over to the table that had the oscillation generator. On the table was AART's remote control. Rick looked at it and smiled. He threw it on the floor and crushed the device with his boot. "I saw how the robot was being voice controlled. I also figured he only recognizes SSOSA voices so I'm decommissioning him for good."

"Why don't you tell them the truth, Rick?" Javan's voice was seething with anger.

Rick twisted his lip. "Shut up, Javan."

"No, I won't shut up. Tell them you want the machine for all the wrong reasons."

"I've had it with your lies," Bonner huffed. "He told you to shut up!"

"That's what Rick would have you believe, Colonel," Javan protested. "When we were working in Washington on this secret project I found out he wanted the machine to sell on the black market. Rick's not interested in using the machine for national security for the United States. I found a correspondence in his office where rogue nations were inquiring about Operation Pakal. He was offered a billion dollars if he delivered the machine. Now you know why he had me falsely imprisoned."

"You're lying!" Bonner yelled.

"Actually it was two billion," Rick said with a sardonic smile.

Bonner turned and looked at Rick with an astonished expression. "What the...?

Rick slowly turned and pointed his gun at Bonner. "I was offered two billion dollars for the machine, Colonel Bonner. It's not every day that a man gets such an offer. What would you have done had it happened to you?"

It took a moment for Bonner to get his thoughts in order. "In the name of the United States government I put you, Rick Cannon, under arrest for treason. Drop your weapon!" He motioned to Commander Jones. "Tie him up."

Bonner felt the barrel of Jones' gun at the back of his head. "I'm afraid not, Colonel Bonner," Jones said. "Drop both guns, *now*! Put both hands up on your head."

Bonner let his guns fall and clatter on the floor. He had an astonished expression as he obeyed the order. "Commander Jones you're an operative of the Special Operation Command of the United States, do you realize what you are doing? The death penalty awaits you for treason."

"In reality, I'm not a commando, Bonner. And neither were any of the pilots in the Wind Slicers. We are all hired mercenaries."

"What? But what about the outpost in White Sands, New Mexico?"

"That was a bogus outpost," Rick answered. "None of the operatives there were enlisted men. With the exception of Kenneth Sims, they all work for me. I planned for the Wind Slicers to be shipped there. Nobody would question the Executive Secretary of the Department of Homeland Security, especially with the blessing of the President."

"Why did you bring me here?" Bonner growled as Jones tied his hands behind his back like the others.

"For two reasons: One, because I knew that once you returned to Kansas you would have found the outpost had been fabricated and you would have put a stop to the operation here in Guatemala. Two, I needed you to assist me in finding these people. Your anger and hatred for Javan served my purpose. In other words, you were my useful puppet. But I'm done with you."

Bonner threw as many swear words as possible at Rick. Unfazed he simply walked away to gaze at the machine. "This is a wonderful thing! I can build my own machine and replicate the ions to get it to work properly. I thank you all for doing the hard work. "

Erick clenched his teeth. "We have to do something people."

"But AART is down," Ashni replied. "Troy can't use voice commands."

Erick was quiet for a moment, furiously thinking. "I've got it. I remember Nolan saying he had an override system installed to control AART from his computer!" Erick started pounding away at the keyboard. The file came up on the screen. "Unfortunately it's password protected."

Ashni slumped back in her chair. "What are we going to do? We need access."

Erick shook his head. "We have to figure it out. Come on, think! What kind of password do you think he would use? What are his hobbies, his likes or pursuits?"

"He likes Star Wars," Ashni said.

Erick reached for two plastic figurines that were sitting atop the monitor. "You mean like these? BB-8 or R2-D2?"

Erick and Ashni suddenly got an epiphany and yelled in unison. "AART2D2!"

Erick pressed the appropriate keys. "We are in!"

Immediately a tutorial popped up.

"Who has time to read a tutorial?" Erick moaned.

"I know how to use AART," Ashni responded.

Erick turned to look at her.

Ashni shooed Erick from the computer. "David used to let me use his laptop to play with AART."

Erick was amazed.

"I'll have you know I'm a trained gamer."

"Of course you are," Erick grinned.

The video image on the computer screen was split in two. The left side had the video that Troy was streaming via his hat. The right side was AART'S video taken from the camera on the stinger.

"What are you going to do?" Erick asked.

Ashni was totally in deep concentration. "Just watch."

*   *   *

Rick continued walking about the room admiring the machine. "It was because of my brilliance that we have come to this juncture. The collective intelligence of Javan, Rio and the SSOSA couldn't stop me from coming to this point of success."

Commando Jones had his gun trained on the captives but he realized that they were not going to be too much of a threat with their hands tied behind their backs so he turned to talk to Rick."How are we going to duplicate this machine?"

Rick walked up the platform and touched the throne as he answered. "My customers have other scientists that can reproduce this thing. That's why I needed a working machine. I had to see if it really did work."

"We lost some operatives," Jones reminded him. "I hope that means more money for me."

"Don't worry, Jones, you'll get your fair share as well as the others at the airport. But we're not done here yet."

"Now's the time," Ashni said under her breath as she typed in the commands that controlled AART's pincers with the arrow keys of her keyboard.

Troy felt a nudge in his hands. He slowly turned to see AART and then glanced forward. He had a small imperceptible grin. He knew what the SSOSA in New York were doing.

AART was snipping his zip tie cuffs.

Ashni slowly maneuvered AART toward Bonner. Troy mouthed a silent message to Bonner as if to tell him to keep his hands behind him until the time was right.

Chauncy saw the entire operation and said a silent prayer of thanks.

Commander Jones turned his gaze back at the captives and raised his gun at them. "Let's get this over with and eliminate these people. Who first?"

Rick walked down the platform and pointed. "Let's kill Javan first. I want the SSOSA members to see their failure firsthand. Then kill Chauncy so Troy can witness his father's death, then Troy. Rio will be last. It's a pity to see such a pretty woman die."

Something caught Rick's attention. His face turned red with anger, he approached Troy and swiped the cap off his head. "What's this? It's a camera." He turned to look at Commander Jones. "Why didn't you see this before? You idiot, do you realize what they're doing? Troy is sending video to the other SSOSA members!"

Jones gritted his teeth. "It was too dark in here. Let's just get it over with now."

Bonner swiftly sprung up from his kneeling position and lunged forward. Jones saw the flurry of movement and swung around and pointed his gun at Bonner. Jones fired but missed. Bonner threw a punch at Jones' face. Surprised and unprepared Jones fell backward.

Rick quickly aimed at Bonner but Troy was already tackling Rick.

AART quickly cut Javan's and Rio's zip ties.

"Come on Javan," Rio whispered. "I need to get you on the machine."

"I can make it there myself," Javan answered, "You power the oscillator."

Rio turned to address the mechanized scorpion. "Whoever's controlling AART, have him move the gears!"

"Wait a minute," Chauncy complained. "He needs to cut my ties too."

"There's no time," Rio yelled back as she ran over to the oscillator.

Javan ran up the platform stairs and seated himself on the throne.

AART ambled over to the Mayan gears and placed a pincer on the large gear. He turned the gear making it rotate. Rushing water was heard underneath, making the temple floor tremble.

Jones flipped over and quickly stood back on his feet. He unsheathed his Bowie knife and lunged at Bonner. Bonner wasn't fast enough to avoid the fast sharp blade and received a nasty slash to his right arm.

Bonner ignored the pain as he performed a defensive karate move and knocked the knife out of Jones' hand. Jones returned some karate kicks of his own and they started sparring.

Rick was face down on the ground as Troy tried to choke him from above. Rick rammed Troy with his elbow and knocked the wind out of him.

Rick pushed Troy aside, looking up he spied his pistol a few feet away and crawled on all fours after it.

The room started filling with strange vibrations as the quantum oscillator started sending power to the pyramids. The ions started filling the room.

This time nothing was levitating.

Troy was still lying on the floor, bent over as he was trying to catch his breath.

Rick found his gun and turned around and aimed at Javan. "You're not leaving Javan!"

Rick fired, but the energy field that was surrounding Javan deflected the bullet. Rick cursed and fired again but the result was the same.

Bonner saw his perfect opportunity. He swung around and kicked Jones in the stomach. Jones went flying backward and hit one of the freestanding glyphs. He slumped down, temporarily dazed.

Bonner had a grin of satisfaction. "You didn't know I knew karate, did ya boy?"

Seeing that it was going to be impossible to shoot Javan, Rick quickly turned his attention to Bonner and aimed.

Bonner wasn't fast enough to avoid the bullet. Rick fired his gun. The bullet struck him in the ribs. He collapsed backward with a grunt.

Troy ran up and kicked the gun out of Rick's hand. Unfortunately the gun scuttled across the floor over to Jones' side.

"He killed Colonel Bonner!" Chauncy cried.

Jones, who was now coming to, grabbed the gun off the floor and pointed it at Troy.

Before Jones could fire, he heard a strange, unearthly cracking noise and quickly looked up in horror as he realized what was happening.

AART was pushing the tall glyph with both pincers. Jones threw himself on the floor and attempted to crawl away. But it was too late. The ancient relic broke in two and came crashing down on Jones.

He was instantly crushed to death.

Rick picked up an iron pole from the mini-trailer and ran over to AART and swung with all his might at AART's left pincer. The pincer broke off and hot hydraulic fluid spewed all over Rick.

Temporarily blinded by the hot fluid, Rick dropped the pole and grabbed at his face, howling in pain.

This was finally Troy's perfect opportunity. He picked up the iron pole and made contact with Rick's head.

Rick crumpled to the floor.

An uncanny orange glow emanated from the throne. It caught the attention of Rio, Chauncy and Troy. It was like something they had never seen. Orange crepuscular flashes emanated from Javan's body. This time they noticed Javan had a peaceful expression on him and not the anguish of pain they had seen twice before.

It was a strange sight indeed.

He looked like an orange-colored angel as his body became somewhat transparent in nature. He slowly rose up in midair. His body was enveloped by the eerie orange glow. The glow became so bright the observers had to cover their eyes. The room became filled with a strange noise of distorted sound from the wave energy.

252

The observers felt the disturbance in the form of nausea. They backed away from the throne as far as possible, not knowing how the bright orange rays would affect them.

Erick and Ashni were watching the live feed from AART's tail because Troy's hat was on the floor.

Seconds later Javan was gone.

"Wow, just wow!" Ashni gushed as she placed her hands on her head.

Erick pulled himself out of his chair, ignoring the pain in his knees. "The science is valid, it's real," he said, mostly to himself. "It's all real!"

Chapter Forty-Two

Rick, Bonner and Jones were on the floor either dead or unconscious. Troy was exhausted from the struggle. Chauncy and Rio were in complete astonishment.

"He did it," Rio's eyes moistened. "He finally did it."

"It was all true," Troy gasped as he picked up his hat off of the floor and placed it back on his head. "Javan is gone."

"I knew it would work," Rio said pushing her brown hair back giving Troy a serious look. "I'm glad you believed in us."

"I had my doubts," Troy smiled. "But in the end Javan was right, the machine did work. And our gut instincts were right in trusting you."

"Hey," Chauncy yelled out. "Will somebody untie me?"

Troy jumped with surprise, he had forgotten about his father. "Sorry, Dad." He stooped down to pick up a bloodied Bowie knife from the floor and cut his father's cuffs.

"How's AART?" Ashni asked via Troy's headphone.

Troy looked up at Rio. "Can you see how AART is doing?"

Rio rushed over to the robot and scanned his injury. "His arm is broken off about eighteen inches from the pincer. There was some spilled hydraulic fluid but it looks compartmentalized."

"I'm going to have AART shut down the water wheel," Ashni said.

AART used his operational pincer to do the job. The sound of rushing underground water ceased.

Troy looked up at nothing in particular as he spoke to the SSOSA members in New York. "I want to thank you all for assisting us and particularly for saving my life. I owe you a beer."

"It looks like I came in late for the party," Gerald interrupted as he stumbled into the main room.

Everybody instinctively turned to look at Gerald.

"Oh yeah, I forgot about you," Troy moaned.

"Well, here I am." Gerald didn't look good. His shirt was ripped in shreds and he was covered in blood and sweat, but the gun in his hand was enough for all to know he meant business. "Everyone move against that wall!" Gerald yelled. "Except you," he motioned to Rio. "Stay where you are."

"Where's your buddy Nolan?" Troy dryly asked.

Gerald shook his head. "He didn't make it. Your cute little machine lifted him up and slammed him against the pyramid." He quickly looked around. "Where is that little space traveler?"

"He's gone," Rio answered.

He tilted his head to one side and made hand gestures. "You mean gone, like in poof?"

"Yes, he went over to the other dimension."

"Ah, so the machine worked just fine, eh?" Gerald smiled malevolently as he motioned to Rio. "I know you have the blueprint for Operation Pakal. It's in that necklace you're wearing. Give it to me, now!"

Her lips trembled as she gripped the necklace in a protective manner. "If I give it to you, promise not to hurt me? You can do what you want with them...but don't hurt me."

"What?" Troy looked aghast.

"I won't hurt *you*. I need you to tell me more about the machine." Gerald waved the gun at the others. "As for them, I can't let them live. They are too much of a liability and I'm not in the liability business."

Rio slowly lifted the necklace off of her neck. She held it up in her hand. "Very well..."

Troy gritted his teeth. "Rio...don't."

Rio turned to Troy. "I'm sorry Troy, but the machine is more important than you."

"Are you crazy?"

"You heard what I said," she stared at the SSOSA members with quivering lips. "Operation Pakal is more important than *any* of you. Javan and I discussed it already. We must never let Operation Pakal die."

"Rio, what's the matter with you?" Troy bellowed. "What about all the things SSOSA did for you!"

"I'm sorry Troy. I appreciate all the help you gave us, but I'm going to have to show Gerald how to manage this power. I told you already, this power is greater than any man."

"You should never trust a woman with archaeological relics," Chauncy voiced his opinion.

"Actually, you should never trust a woman who is accused of being a terrorist," Rio shot back. "Because…it may be true."

"Why are you doing this?" Troy bellowed.

Rio raised an eyebrow. "There is a lot more power in this machine than I ever told you about. It's a power so great it can change the world as we know it. Getting Javan out of this dimension was just *part* of the plan. Now that he is gone, there are other things I want to do with the machine. Unlike him, I have no intention of leaving. Now that the machine works, I no longer need the services of SSOSA. Sorry Troy but like Bonner, you too were just a useful puppet. I played on your emotions to get what I wanted."

Troy gritted his teeth and closed his eyes in shame. So this was it? All of this wasted time and energy because Rio and Javan actually ended up being terrorists who had their own agenda using Operation Pakal. He felt like an idiot for falling for the deception.

Ashni looked at Erick, desperately trying to find a solution. For the first time since the operation, Erick looked truly lost. Plan A-B-C and D were done. All options had been exhausted. He slammed his fist on the desk and cursed something in German at Rio.

"Let's go, give me the necklace, woman," Gerald raged.

"You want it Gerald? Do you want to work with me and be partners?"

"I'm sure we can figure something out." Gerald stuck a greedy hand out.

She deftly threw the necklace over Gerald's head. It landed on the floor and skidded into the base of the throne.

Gerald looked at her inquisitively. "What was that all about?"

"Go get it." Rio gave Gerald an evil smile and giggled. "You have to work hard for it, like I did. Do you realize how difficult it was to convince five of the most intelligent people on earth to do my bidding? If you want the power, work for it. Prove to me you really want it."

"You foolish witch, move back, I'll deal with you later. Move it."

Rio lowered her hands and walked back and stood by the oscillation generator.

Gerald moved backward keeping his eye on the group as he bent down and picked up the necklace. Rio suddenly lunged at the generator, plunging the lever to its highest level. "Everybody hang on to something!"

The room suddenly started humming.

Like a giant magnet, Gerald was slammed against the throne. His body was stuck to it as powerful forces held him down.

Gerald screamed in agony but his voice was altered by the incoming atomic pressure that was crushing him inward. Instead of an orange glow, dark shadows bounced around his body. The invisible forces pressed his body into a fetal position. He started getting wrinkled and small like a sheet of paper that was being crushed by an invisible hand. He got smaller and smaller until he vanished into thin air.

Then he was gone.

Chapter Forty-Three

Rio quickly shut down the power of the generator.

Chauncy slowly lifted himself off the floor and walked over to the throne. "What...what happened to Gerald? Did he go to another dimension?"

"No," Rio wiped some sweat from her brow and pushed her hair away from her face. "The pressure was so intense that he was reduced and compressed into a molecular unit."

"So he's dead," Chauncy passed a hand over his hair. "Wow, that's crazy." He turned to look at Rio. "We also lost the blueprint."

"I know," Rio sadly nodded. "It was a sacrifice I had to make to save us all."

"You almost had me there." Troy got up from the floor, shook the dust off of him. "But then I realized you could have easily given the necklace to Rick Cannon also just to save your life."

Rio smiled back. "I'm glad you played along with me. You almost blew it by overreacting."

"I've been told I'm a good actor."

"You were lied to," Rio chuckled.

"I'm working on my acting skills."

"Keep working."

"That was real smart of you. You quickly realized that Gerald would be compressed because the water wheel was shut down and no ions were being produced," Troy said.

"Yes, I figured Javan almost got killed when we didn't have the rushing water under the floor, so the machine would instantly kill anyone if I pushed the power level to the max."

Troy smiled at her. "You're awesome."

"And so are you," Rio smiled back.

"Troy," Ashni interrupted. "I recommend you check to see who's still alive."

Troy repeated the message to Rio and Chauncy.

Chauncy pointed at Commando Jones' body. His feet were sticking out from under the glyph. "I would venture to say he's dead. He looks like the wicked witch in the Wizard of Oz."

"Rick is still alive," Troy said as he felt his pulse. "I must have really knocked him out."

Rio heard some groaning coming from Bonner. She left AART and bent down to see how he was doing. "Colonel Bonner, are you okay?"

Bonner sat up, he seemed disoriented. "My arm is bleeding."

"Chauncy, get me the first aid kit on the mini trailer," Rio ordered.

"I thought he killed you," Troy said as he bent down to examine him.

Bonner pointed to his vest. "I'm wearing a Kevlar vest. The bullet didn't penetrate the vest but it knocked me down something bad. My ribs are killing me though."

Chauncy delivered the medical kit to Rio and she proceeded to wrap up Bonner's injured arm and administered some pain meds.

"We're going to get you out of here," she said.

Bonner shook his head. "No you ain't. We blew up your truck and all the Wind Slicers are toast."

Troy listened to something on his headset then he addressed Bonner. "Actually Erick just told me there is a rescue operation underway."

Bonner seemed despondent. "Just leave me here to die."

"No, you're coming with us," Troy ordered. He stood up and spoke to his father. "Dad, I need your help to put Rick on the mini trailer."

"What about Commando Jones?" Rio pointedly asked. "We can't leave him here in the pyramid."

Troy nodded in agreement. "This is a sacred place. We must leave everything the way we found it." He looked at AART. "If his other pincer is okay, then maybe AART can lift the glyph a few inches off of Jones while we pull his body out."

Chauncy, Troy, Rio and AART got to the task of removing Jones' body out from under the glyph. Once that necessary job was done, they wrapped the body in a tarp and placed it on the trailer. They tied Rick's hands and feet with zip ties and placed him on the trailer, too. Rio disconnected the oscillation generator and wrapped up all the cords and placed them in their respective boxes, then placed everything on the trailer. When they were done they hooked up the trailer to AART. Bonner simply sat and watched the entire procession. He wasn't interested in helping anyone.

Troy was about to start wrapping up the light cords and turning off the bulbs, but he had to have one last look around.

Chauncy patted his son on the shoulder. "You finally made it, Troy."

Troy looked confused. "What are you talking about?"

"You're going to be famous. This is the most unique archaeological find in history! Can you imagine how this place is going to transform your life? You will now be the world famous archaeologist. You're no longer going to be living in my shadow."

Troy had a pained expression. He was exhausted from the fight and the entire ordeal he had been through. He wasn't in a celebratory mood. "I...I don't know. And come to think of it...I kind of like living incognito. I love my SSOSA identity." Troy's eyes lit up. "And I reconnected with *you* through this awesome adventure."

Chauncy smiled. "Thank you for begging me to come. Getting nearly killed wasn't fun...but being with *you* made it all worth it."

"Maybe...maybe that's all I wanted in the first place," Troy answered. "Maybe it's wasn't fame or glory. I wanted you to see my side of the world. I wanted you to experience a SSOSA adventure with me."

"And I did," Chauncy said as he hugged his son. "Troy, you're awesome!"

Ashni waved her hand over her face as her eyes moistened. "I hate these tender moments."

Troy left his father and walked over to where Bonner was sitting. He held a hand out to Bonner. "We have to go. You're not staying in here."

261

"Why not?" Bonner furrowed his brow. "What's waiting for me out there? Court martial, humiliation? I have no future."

"No Bonner, you did your duty. You did your job to the best of your ability."

"I won't have a job when I return."

"We will split some of our money with you. But we aren't leaving you here and that's an order. Stand up soldier!"

Bonner huffed, but relented as he held a hand up. "Who are you to give me orders?"

Troy didn't respond, he simply pulled him up.

With the exception of the personal flashlights and AART's headlights everything went dark.

Chapter Forty-Four

Troy was the first one to see the glare of the burning tires of his truck and trailer as they exited the pyramid tunnel. They all stood in front of the truck to see the devastation. Bonner pointed upward to show them where the Wind Slicers had crashed against the pyramid. It wasn't easy to see all the destroyed aircraft due to thick vegetation.

"What are we going to do about the glyph door?" Chauncy asked.

"Unhook the trailer and let's have AART attempt to close it." Troy pressed his hat closer to his ear to speak into the microphone. "Ashni, do you think AART is up to the task?"

"The indicators show his other functions are still running optimally," she responded. "The only problem is that you won't have the full force of two pincers. He may need some help from you guys."

"Thank you. Walk him to the right side of the glyph, have him push on my command."

After AART was disconnected from the mini trailer Ashni made him do as Troy had ordered. The robot placed his left pincer on the stone glyph. Troy motioned for all able bodied people to assist. They leaned against the glyph and Troy gave the command to Ashni.

"Okay everybody," Troy said. "On the count of three we push with all our strength. One- two- three- go!"

There was a humming sound coming from AART's interior mechanism as the robot pushed with the only pincer available. Everybody else grunted and pushed hard. The stone glyph eventually started moving back to its original position. They heard an audible clunking sound as the grooved edges of the stone reached the edge of the opening.

Everyone stood back to catch their breaths.

"Do you think you will ever return here and enter the pyramid?" Chauncy finally asked his son.

"Maybe," Troy answered as he ran a hand over his hair and placed his hat back on. He was still looking at the glyph as he spoke. "Perhaps in the future we can come back and see what we can do with the machine. For now this will be our little secret."

"I like that idea," Rio added. "Like Javan said, there is so much to learn here but we just didn't have enough time. If you return, you can spend more time examining the machine."

"What about Rick?" Chauncy asked Rio. "Do you really think he could have had rogue scientists recreate this machine?"

"I doubt it. It's more complicated than it looks."

"Things are going to change when Rick wakes up," Troy added. "Once the news gets out that he was here, working against the interests of the US, his criminal contacts will scatter."

"We hope so," Chauncy quipped.

"The truth is, Rick really needed Javan's help to build the machine," Rio explained. "This whole ordeal started because Javan *refused* to assist Rick. But now that Javan is gone, Rick will have a tough time explaining the science to would-be clients. Without the blueprint or Javan, Operation Pakal is basically dead in its tracks."

"Or you," Troy said in an ominous tone. "They can abduct you and make you talk."

Rio looked at Troy. "I know, but I'm going to go into hiding. Javan left me a lot of money. Rick won't find me."

Bonner took his cold cigar from a small pocket in his Kevlar vest and placed it in his mouth. He suddenly heard a strange sound. "Everybody shut up, somebody is coming!"

They all heard a rumbling sound in the jungle. There were visible lights of a vehicle coming through the dense vegetation. The shafts of light from the headlights created strange, moving shadows among the trees.

"That must be the rescue operation Ashni mentioned," Chauncy said.

Bonner went over to the trailer and picked up Commando Jones' night vision goggles. He looked through them and furrowed his brow as he recognized the vehicle that was coming his way. "I don't think so. That's a VCR-TT 6X6 APC."

"What does that mean?" Troy warily asked.

"It's a Guatemalan military assault tank. It's made in the USA," Bonner replied. "It looks like your rescue team is a little too late. This must be Rick's backup plan. He talked about sending a ground crew to mop up things at the end."

Rio looked nervous. "What are we going to do? We have nowhere to run."

Troy spoke into the microphone. "Ashni, have you any idea what this is about?"

There was a brief silence then she spoke. "I'm...I'm not sure Troy, but this isn't going to look good if they see Rick Cannon knocked out and tied up. You can't outrun or outgun the military and even if you did you will die in the jungle, so just raise your hands and surrender. We'll sort this out when you get back to Guatemala City."

"What about this rescue operation you talked about?" Troy angrily asked Erick.

Erick said something in the German language that sounded like a curse word to Troy. "That's the last time I will use Jake Thrasher. Sorry Troy."

The impressive-looking vehicle finally reached the clearing where the people were. It was a six-wheeled black assault tank with a series of small dark colored windows that flanked the sides of the vehicle.

Bonner imagined the tank was carrying a group of rifle-toting Guatemalan soldiers that were going to jump out in a few seconds. But nothing happened when the large vehicle came to a stop. The rumbling engine was turned off and in a few seconds the top hatch opened up.

A familiar looking person popped his head out of the hatch. "Well? What are you all doing looking at me with those idiotic faces? Let's go!"

Chauncy's eyes lit up and he ran toward the vehicle. "Jake Thrasher, you old banshee!"

Troy smiled with relief. "You old coot. You scared us half to death."

Ashni turned to look at Erick. "So this was Plan B? What was Plan C?"

Erick leaned back in his chair and nervously chuckled. "Plan C was to throttle Jake Thrasher if he did not come through."

Jake disappeared back into the vehicle and appeared again as he came through a small door on the side.

"Jake, it's been a long time since I last *saw* you!" Chauncy said as he hugged him.

The thin, seventy-seven year old man pulled back and pinched Chauncy's cheek. "I thought your trouble-making days were over, Chauncy."

"Actually it's my doing," Troy stepped in.

Jake placed his hands on his hips. "Look at you. You were twelve years old when I last saw you. You've grown into a fine, trouble-filled young man," he turned to look at Rio. "And you must be Rio Jordan." He turned to look at Bonner and his uniform. "It looks like we have a military man with us."

"I'm Colonel Theodore Bonner. Mr. Thrasher, are you aware of any Guatemalan military operatives headed this way?"

Jake nodded. "Yes, the people I rented this vehicle from told me they were coming here. We can go back to the airport through a back road. It will take longer though but we have about an hour lead on them."

"That's good to know," Troy said.

Jake motioned for them to follow him. "Come here, I have something to show you."

They followed him to the vehicle. Jake opened a door to show them the interior.

"David!" Troy exclaimed.

David was lying on one of the seats. His leg was being held immobile by a temporary splint. "Hello Troy, hello Rio and Chauncy..." David hesitated when he saw Bonner.

"At ease," Bonner replied. "Trust me, if I had done a better job you would have been dead already."

"Yes, sir," David gulped.

266

"We better get going," Jake said.

Troy turned his attention to Jake. "We've got some stuff we need transferred from our trailer to your vehicle."

Jake walked over to the mini trailer. He saw Rick Cannon, the wrapped body of Jones and the robotic scorpion. He looked around and saw what was left of the Ford truck and trailer, the still-burning tires and the glowing fires of some of the wrecked Wind Slicers up on the pyramid wall.

"Do you remember what Sgt. Schultz used to say in Hogan's Heroes?" Chauncy pointedly asked him.

Jake turned and shrugged his shoulders. "I see nothing, I hear nothing."

Chauncy patted him on the shoulder. "Exactly. Now let's go."

Troy switched his camera off and turned around to look at the pyramid one more time. Rio came up to him and placed a hand on his shoulder.

"It's time to go," she said.

Troy slowly turned and looked at her. "Yes, it is."

"Are you okay?"

Troy nodded his head. "I'm alright. It's just that...I was thinking what a great time I had with you."

Rio raised an eyebrow.

"You *and* Javan," Troy corrected himself. "You see, we SSOSA thrive on this kind of stuff."

Rio was about to reply but Jake's loud voice interrupted as he urged everyone to get moving.

"It's over, Rio," Troy said. "Operation Pakal is officially over."

Chapter Forty-Five

Two Months Later-Washington D.C.

The aging butler carried a glass of fine whiskey on the rocks, he took meticulous care in not spilling it on the fine carpet in a mansion in Washington D.C. It wasn't an easy task, since he also had to carefully maneuver around boxes of packed clothes and items that belonged to Rick Cannon. The former Executive of the Department of Homeland Security had been ousted from his post and his mansion.

Rick had requested that the furniture movers leave the study as the last room to pack. He wanted some privacy and time for personal meditation. He figured whiskey on the rocks would induce meditation.

The butler softly knocked on the door. Rick's voice was heard on the other side. "Come."

He entered and handed Rick his drink. "Thank you Carl. Are you completely packed?"

Carl nodded. "Yes sir, I am. I will be taking my leave today. It's been a pleasure working with you, sir."

"I appreciate your years of service," Rick said as he lifted a sealed envelope from the coffee table and handed it to Carl. "This is my letter of recommendation for you. I wish you success in finding future employment somewhere in this fine city. There is also a monetary gift in there for you."

Carl discreetly tucked the envelope in his jacket pocket. "Thank you sir, that is very kind of you."

There was a moment of awkward silence between the two men. Carl finally spoke. "I'm sorry you lost your position at the DHS."

Rick took a sip of his drink then waved a hand in dismissal. "It was a means to an end. This just goes to show how no good deed goes unpunished."

Carl tilted his head to one side.

Rick continued. "I gave it my all to protect the interests of my country, yet what did I get out of it? An escaped prisoner, an inept prison manager and some rogue young people who had almost put me in prison! It's a good thing the President of the United States had good sense to exonerate me."

"The news said you were not going to be held responsible for the incident in Guatemala."

"It's called diplomatic immunity, Carl, the incident didn't occur on US territory so I pulled the immunity card to save my neck. Regardless, I'm innocent! I was only protecting what rightfully belonged to our country. The things the media is saying about me are pure lies."

Carl shook his head. "Tsk, tsk, that's too bad. I hope you find employment too, sir."

"I have a generous severance package and some savings to tide me over until I find something suitable for my tastes." Rick stood up. He was done defending himself to his former butler. He extended his hand to Carl. "I wish you success, Carl. Goodbye."

Carl shook Rick's hand. "Thank you sir, goodbye."

Rick waited until Carl was out of the house. He looked out the window and saw someone driving a car pick him up. Rick had a somber expression on his face as he rubbed the knot on the back of his head where Troy had hit him with the iron pole. He turned and grabbed his whiskey glass and threw it across the room. It crashed against the wall. The amber colored liquid dripped down to the floor.

"I'm not finished with you yet, Troy!"

Chapter Forty-Six

San Diego, California

Troy once again found himself leaning on a railing standing next to Erick. This time, instead of the hectic nightlife and buildings of New York City, he was staring out at the calming swells of the Pacific Ocean and the distant skyline of San Diego. The sun setting behind him cast a gorgeous play of shadows and light across the water.

The sounds of a live soft rock band drifted on the wind from the back of Jake Thrasher's luxury yacht, *The Venture*. Troy could hear the laughter and conversations going on elsewhere, as well as the *pop* of another Champagne cork. There would be more lobster, shrimp, and all manner of side dishes waiting for him.

But right now he just wanted to enjoy the view with Erick, one little slice of quiet before rejoining the festivities. He turned his head away from the ocean and looked at his friend.

"How does it feel?" he asked the older man.

Erick smiled that superior smile of his, the one that meant he knew exactly what was being said without explanation or preamble. Sometimes, it was annoying that he could never catch Erick off-guard. Most of the time, though, it was nice to know the man's genius was on his side.

"It feels good. To tell the truth, I had missed the Mind Games. I still miss my old friends, of course. It was nice to travel the world again in my mind. I only wish I could have gone with you. How does it feel for you?"

Troy looked back at the water. It was hard to believe that it was all over. It seemed like just yesterday that they were knee-deep in jungle foliage and neck-deep in trouble. The ordeal of the last two months, spent in one government office after another, testifying before so many inquiry boards he forgot who was who, was finally over. SSOSA was now free of government intrusion. Operation Pakal was officially over, the story being that the tunnel under the pyramid had collapsed. They'd told that story to so many people so many times that he almost believed it. At least it would stall any further investigations.

"It feels great," he said with a grin. "Exonerated. Successful. We actually pulled it off."

Erick's own smile went from the superior-knowledge smile to one with genuine warmth. "It is a good feeling, is it not? A successful Mind Game. I am glad to have passed the baton to you. I admire the persistence you showed, making sure to get the job done. I am proud of you. In fact, I have something for you."

He pulled a small object out of his pocket and handed it to Troy, who then twirled it around in his hand. "This is the multi-purpose tool that Javan used to escape prison, isn't it? How'd you get it?"

"While we were on the plane from Kansas to New York he gave it to me as a souvenir to remember him by. But I want you to have it. No, no, do not object. My time on earth is limited. You have your whole life ahead of you. I want you to remember this mission."

Troy stared at the multi-purpose tool, feeling like an *actual* baton had just been passed. He placed it in his pocket, his throat feeling a little tight. "Thank you."

"You are welcome. But I believe you have been out here with an old relic long enough. You should return to your friends."

Troy sighed dramatically and stood up from the railing. "Why are you always right?"

The smile faltered, just a little. "Not always right, Troy. Always remember that you will never be always right. Get going."

"This mission is as much yours as mine. Please come with me."

Erick mirrored the dramatic sigh. "As you wish."

They both wandered back to where the rest of the party was happening. Rio, Ashni and Jake were standing near the helipad, while David sat in a chair to the side resting his leg.

"So this is where all our money went," Erick chided Jake.

"I told you I wanted my yacht remodeled," Jake said with a laugh.

"Do you actually own a helicopter?" Rio asked.

"I do. I don't fly it anymore, I don't have my pilot's license, but I can be picked up or dropped off here at any time."

"Speaking of pilots, I keep expecting Colonel Bonner to come flying by in a Wind Slicer. Has anybody seen him?"

"You won't be seeing him," Troy answered. "He's mad at the Army, he's mad at the government, he's mad at us. I think he's just plain mad at the world. He took the money we gave him, last I heard, bought a plot of land in Louisiana."

"I still can't believe that Rick Cannon got off with just a slap on the wrist," David said.

Ashni shook her head. "Politics. There's no justice in this world. If you have enough money or enough powerful friends you can get away with anything."

Rio looked around. "Where are your parents, Troy? I thought for sure they would be here."

Troy smiled at the fond memories. He'd already reunited with his parents, before Jake had managed to bring the rest of SSOSA from Washington D.C. His mother had been delighted that the rift between Chauncy and Troy was finally healing, and they'd spent two pleasant days aboard *The Venture* catching up. "They're on a harbor cruise," he answered. "My mother wasn't exactly pleased that we ran down to Guatemala without her, so Dad's making it up to her with cruises and tours."

Jake looked at his watch. "Speaking of booze cruises--"

"That's not the kind of cruise they're on!" Troy objected.

Jake smiled wickedly. "Speaking of booze, I've got a new bartender I want you guys to meet. Come on into my bar."

It was the first time that Troy had been to the cocktail lounge, and it was as immaculate as the rest of the yacht, complete with dazzling light shows and intricate water features.

A robot that looked very much like a scorpion came scuttling out from behind the bar. "What may I serve you today?"

"AART!" David cried excitedly. "I'd been worried sick, Jake. When did you upgrade his AI?"

273

"What, you think he just sat rusting in a bin somewhere for the last two months?" Jake asked, his booming laugh filling the room. "He's helped me upgrade the yacht, so I had a friend of mine finish the upgrades you started."

David leaned over, balancing precariously on his leg scooter, and pet his robot like it was a dog. "Is he paying you enough to bartend, AART?"

"Jake Thrasher's eternal gratitude is more than enough payment," the robot answered.

Everyone laughed as David glared at Jake. "Well, I might have suggested a few changes to the AI," Jake admitted. "He also has some other upgrades you can use on future missions."

They ordered drinks and got to talking about everything that had happened over the last two months. About thirty minutes into the conversation Troy noticed that Rio was missing. He excused himself and went looking for her. She was right outside the cocktail lounge, leaning on the railing and looking out at the ocean. It was a popular activity, apparently.

She heard him approach and looked at him with a smile. "What are you doing out here?"

"Checking on you. I want to show you something." He pulled out the multi-purpose tool and explained what it was.

"So this was his grand plan to escape prison," Rio said, her head tilted to the side. "How quaint. Since you're here, I have a question for you."

"Shoot."

"I saw you standing alone before Erick approached you...and I was wondering what you were thinking about."

Troy placed the tool in his pants pocket as he spoke. "I was thinking about Javan. I wonder if he made it to wherever he wanted to be. I wonder if he can see us."

Rio stood beside him and leaned on the railing. "It's hard to say. Javan and I always theorized what this other dimension was really like. If his molecules were separated when he was transported then there is a possibility that he was transformed into another type of life form."

"That's a wild thought."

"It certainly is. But one way or another, he's gone far from Rick Cannon and the government that persecuted him, and in the end that's all Javan wanted. That's what this mission was all about."

"What about La Danta? Do you think I should return?" Troy pointedly asked. "There is so much to learn there."

Rio was contemplative for a few seconds. "Yes, I think you guys should return...someday."

"I was hoping you would say that. But don't you want to come back with us?"

She shook her head. "La Danta isn't mine Troy. You guys can return anytime you want."

Troy faced Rio. "What about you? What do you want? What are your plans for the future?"

Rio shrugged. "I will never work in this country again, at least not for any government entity, that's for sure."

"I have a question for you."

"Go ahead."

"Why did you kiss me when we were in the jungle?" Troy asked.

"I admire you, Troy. You're different than any...."

"Different than your ex-husband?" Troy asked.

"No, different than any man your age I have seen. I mean...you're brave. You don't see that quality in guys much."

"You didn't answer my question, why did you kiss me on the cheek?" Troy asked again.

"Did my kiss offend you?"

"Oh no...actually I would have rather you kissed me on the lips."

"Is that so?" Rio smiled and gently approached Troy.

David interrupted the couple as he stuck his head out of the bar door. "Hey everybody, come inside, Erick has a special announcement to make."

Troy and Rio looked at each other and then at David. Troy wasn't aware of any special announcements.

"Come on!" David waved frantically at them.

When they walked into the bar Erick gathered them in a semi-circle. "Okay, I have something to say. Of course you all know that I only temporarily filled in for Nolan. But the mission is over and I'm relinquishing the position. I'm too old to be running around with the new SSOSA anyway, therefore I recommend a replacement."

They all looked at each other with inquisitive expressions.

Erick continued. "I hereby recommend Rio Jordan to take my place. All in favor raise your hand."

Everyone in the group quickly raised their hands.

Rio blushed. "Wait a minute! Are you sure…but…"

"It's okay Rio, you passed the audition," Erick said with a chuckle in his voice. "You will make a fine SSOSA member."

"Now you are gainfully employed!" Troy added with a laugh.

Before she was able to say anything else somebody in the room got the cue from Erick and the stereo started playing 'Rio' from Duran Duran:

Her name is Rio and she dances on the sand
Just like that river twisting through a dusty land
And when she shines she really shows you all she can
Oh Rio, Rio dance across the Rio Grande

As everybody started laughing. AART brought another round of drinks. Troy felt his phone vibrate in his pocket. He took it out and read a text. It was from Rio.

I would still like to collect on that kiss.

He texted her back: *Okay, let's go.*

They both looked up from their phones and smiled at each other.

Author's Notes

FACT: On August 4, 2009 in a laboratory at the University of California, Santa Barbara, scientists devised the first Quantum Oscillating Machine. In laymen's terms, they were able to cause a small metal blade (about the diameter of a human hair) to vibrate on a molecular level in such a fashion that caused the blade to 'be' in two different quantum states at the same time. This revolutionary experiment violated the laws of classical physics by creating a parallel universe. In March 2010, the journal *Science* declared the creation of the first quantum machine to be "*The Breakthrough of the Year.*"

FACT: LIDAR technology captured images of a hidden temple in El Mirador, Guatemala. The images revealed a hidden ancient Mayan city equivalent to the size of metropolitan Los Angeles. At the foot of the largest pyramid in the world, named La Danta, archaeologists discovered Mayan glyphs that represent the story of the Mayan civilization. It is believed that once these glyphs are deciphered, the veil obscuring the true meaning of the history of the Maya will be lifted, thus revealing to the world the hidden knowledge of the ancients.

FACT: In the year 1859 in his book titled *Inheritance of the Great Pyramid*, Charles Smyth discussed how the number Pi (3.14) was incorporated into the design of the Egyptian pyramid.

It makes one wonder what other mathematical and scientific clues are embedded on the ancient buildings that are waiting to be discovered.

***

Contact the author at: alexzabala2@gmail.com

Coming in 2021: *The Deadly Mind Game* by Alex Zabala

Read about the adventures of Troy's father, Chauncy:
The Chauncy Rollock Chronicles by Alex Zabala and Dyego
Alehandro

A new science-fiction thriller coming in 2020 by Dyego
Alehandro: *PsyCor*